The Devil's Elbow Project

The Devil's Elbow Project

A Detective Robert Lee James Crime
Novel—Inspired by Actual Events

RONALD J. LONG

iUniverse, Inc.
Bloomington

The Devil's Elbow Project
A Detective Robert Lee James Crime Novel—Inspired by Actual Events

Copyright © 2011 by Ronald J. Long.

All rights reserved. No part of this book may be used or reproduced by any means, graphic, electronic, or mechanical, including photocopying, recording, taping or by any information storage retrieval system without the written permission of the publisher except in the case of brief quotations embodied in critical articles and reviews.

iUniverse books may be ordered through booksellers or by contacting:

iUniverse
1663 Liberty Drive
Bloomington, IN 47403
www.iuniverse.com
1-800-Authors (1-800-288-4677)

Because of the dynamic nature of the Internet, any web addresses or links contained in this book may have changed since publication and may no longer be valid. The views expressed in this work are solely those of the author and do not necessarily reflect the views of the publisher, and the publisher hereby disclaims any responsibility for them.

Any people depicted in stock imagery provided by Thinkstock are models, and such images are being used for illustrative purposes only.
Certain stock imagery © Thinkstock.

ISBN: 978-1-4620-3138-2 (sc)
ISBN: 978-1-4620-3139-9 (ebk)

Printed in the United States of America

iUniverse rev. date: 06/17/2011

LEGAL & ACKNOWLEDGEMENTS

Some stories in this book reflect true situations experienced by this author. In these scenarios all names and locations, along with specifics about each incident, have been changed to protect those involved. Not all situations in this book are based on true events. Any similarities to specific individuals or events are merely coincidental and are not reflective of facts known to this author.

Copyright© 2011 by Ronald J. Long

All rights reserved. None of this book may be reproduced in any manner without the written consent of the author and/or publisher. Exceptions may apply when using phrases or specific lines, regarding reviews or critic articles about this book.

Tattoo art illustrated on cover—Ilse York
Cover photography—Steve Ward
Website design—Sarah Moore at "pinatasky.com"
Female model on cover—Athena Meder
Male wearing suit on cover—Mark Shea
Male in biker attire on cover—Terry Roberson
Content editors—Linda Johnson and Deborah Popp
Special thanks—Marvin, Mary Lou & Jim
Cover location—The Elbow Inn Bar & BBQ, located on Historical Route 66, Devils Elbow, Missouri. Terry and Susie Roberson—proprietors.

Author Contact Information
Ronald J. Long, P.O. Box 4291, Waynesville, Missouri 65583
1-877-793-9845, www.ronald-long.com

IN MEMORY OF

One certainty of life is that it will eventually end for us all. Making our mark in society depends on how we choose to take each step, and for some this path allows their name and memories to far exceed the longevity of the physical body. During the course of writing this book I found it ironic and sad that two men I modeled characters after, passed away following a long battle with cancer.

Thomas "Tom" Julian was my Chief of Police when I began my law enforcement career. Tom served his county and community as a U.S. Army Soldier, Chief of Police and Municipal Judge. Additionally, he donated countless hours of his free time to charity organizations, and made the term "giving" a predominant part of his life. Tom was a personal friend and mentor, who encouraged my endeavors and emphasized the ideals of law enforcement professionalism and personal integrity.

Dennis "Denny" Bays was a police lieutenant during the early years of my law enforcement career. He helped in my transformation from college student to street cop, and soon became my instructor in the topic of law enforcement street survival. Denny rapidly became a close friend and brother, who demonstrated his true strengths and selfless actions while fighting his sixteen year battle with cancer.

Memories of these modern day heroes will last for decades to come. Even though Tom and Denny no longer walk among us, each stressed their desire to continue giving to their communities by asking for our giving friends to donate to the following organizations:

- **Shop with a Cop,** Post Office Box 207, Waynesville, Missouri 65583. Please make your donation in memory of Thomas Julian.

- **The Don Nelson Memorial Scholarship,** In care of the Security Bank of Pulaski County, Post Office Drawer S, Waynesville, Missouri 65583. Please make your donation in memory of Dennis Bays.

Your gift of honoring these men is very much appreciated!

DEDICATION

Welcome to our family, and this world, little Howie!

PROLOGUE

Detective Robert James was savoring the fruits of success, after concluding the ultimate investigation of his career. Gene King, an international drug lord, was now behind bars. "The King's" demise resulted from the efforts of Detective James and fellow members of the federal Joint Drug and Lab Suppression Team (JDLST). Gene had built a criminal empire, with tentacles reaching throughout the world. Despite the fact he was now behind bars, some factions of Gene's organization would survive. Retaliation against the one responsible for his incarceration was foremost on Gene's mind, and he still commanded the resources to make this happen. Gene King had plans for Robert James, and they did not include a relaxing vacation in Missouri.

During the King investigation Detective James had experienced a new dimension of law enforcement work, one that his rookie career in southern Missouri did little to prepare him for. Human trafficking and international drug smuggling prompted the intrigue and horrors of the murders associated with them. Robert James' professional maturity was fast-tracked, allowing him to physically survive and defeat the challenges he encountered. Unlike the other aspects, the emotional scars and horrific mental images left by these cases would take years to fade, if ever.

Upon leaving Texas for a much deserved vacation, Detective James watched the state fade in the rearview mirror, as he and his infant daughter drove toward Missouri. The temporary thought that upon leaving Texas he would experience a reprieve from the wicked world of crime was a major misconception. Robert had no idea of the evils that lie just a few hours ahead of him.

Upon nearing the destination of his father's home in Springdale, Missouri, Robert was consumed with relief that his eventful journey was coming to an end. Fatigue and highway—hypnosis were making the last few miles of this late night trip a real challenge. A diet cola loaded with caffeine was what Robert thought he needed to stay awake, but the incident he was now witnessing resulted in a massive dump of adrenaline, alleviating Robert's need for caffeine. A spectacular event had just unfolded in front of his eyes, one that appeared to have been choreographed by a Hollywood movie crew. But this scene was real, way too real. Once again this young detective found himself in the middle of a complicated situation.

Robert was mesmerized as he witnessed a major crime scene being swept under the rug by Texas law enforcement officials, who were more than five-hundred miles north of their jurisdictional boundary. When Detective James attempted to exercise his federal authority to intervene and seek answers, the rarely seen, ghost-like government guardians of our country made a commanding appearance and stripped Robert of any conception of authority. These elite sentinels accomplished their task, as Robert was forced to retreat and subsequent media reports reflected a scenario that was nothing close to what actually occurred. Detective James had just witnessed the beginning of a case that would test his law enforcement skills to the maximum.

On the same day in Arlington, Texas, the JDLST had been called in to assist local authorities investigating the attempted murder of a young woman. One aspect of this case to be explored was evidence that the assault could have been drug related, which was within the unit's expertise. The female victim was one of the Texas elite and wealthy, resulting in a prominent United States Senator shadowing the investigation. Her case would therefore become a priority for this Federal task force.

The combination of these two events would soon totally consume Robert James, and would eventually draw the detective into another tangled web. A spectacular search for the truth had now begun, taking Robert James to the edge of his professional and personal life. During this endeavor, Robert discovers that for decades his father has been keeping a major secret. The unleashing of these guarded facts were troubling, but could also be a tool to help Robert solve a portion of the investigation that lies ahead.

There were many facets of this investigation when the opening of one door revealed a room filled with a dozen more leads. In this mind-boggling case, very few common denominators existed, with the exception of one: "the Devil's Elbow." Robert would soon feel that his investigation was indeed spiraling downward and that only Lucifer himself held the key to this complex mystery.

Grab a chocolate-chip cookie and a diet cola, then settle in for a long and thrilling ride as Detective James takes you to places few dare to visit. As in all of the Detective Robert Lee James crime novels, the Devil's Elbow Project will leave readers on edge, trying to sort fact from fiction, and begging for Robert's next adventure.

Chapter 1

ARLINGTON, TEXAS - THE GRAND PARK HOTEL

It was a typical night at the hotel's August Moon Bar and Grill. The name was partially deceiving, since the August Moon was notable for everything but their food and drinks. The Grand Park Hotel was located just north of Arlington's baseball stadium. Visiting professional ball teams would frequently book their rooms at the Grand Park when playing in Arlington. As expected, the hotel was posh and extravagant, catering to all needs of the ball players. Pampering and the pleasures of women seemed to be foremost on the lists when staying at this hotel. A place with professional ball players, along with their envoy of groupies, would always attract others who would pack the August Moon each game night. Having seventy-four games a year in Arlington meant the August Moon was a cash cow for the owners of the Grand Park Hotel. This was even truer this October evening due to the team playing for a division title.

One of the major attractions at the baseball games, besides the game itself, was the gathering of attractive, young women sitting or standing in the area directly behind or near the team dugouts. One could often hear the police officers working security there, talking about the gathering of these female groupies. They were more predictable and dependable than the Texas weather. During the games, these young vultures would find their prey and make every effort to assure they caught the attention of their target. This usually involved being scantily dressed and wearing seductive clothing, and making every move possible when the young players were looking in their direction. Upon returning to the dugouts, some players were able to engage in a brief conversation with these women who most likely directed them to the August Moon for some post-game activity.

This type of scenario was perfect for men who were both lovers of the sport, and the females it attracted. Therefore, the August Moon was guaranteed to be packed at least seventy-four nights a year. Besides just the sport fans, others were drawn to this type of environment. Drugs, gambling and prostitution also made their way through the doors, along with other societal improprieties. These illicit activities were often overlooked by the club's personnel, mostly because they were conducive to the customer's desires. It was not unusual for the bartender to have the contact number of a prostitute close by, or even memorized, due to the referral fees the whores would pass along to them. The August Moon was often making money for the unconventional business side of society, too. Things were no different on this Thursday evening.

A variety of people were filling the August Moon. The Dallas-Ft. Worth area nightlife usually did not peak until after the ten o'clock hour, but this Thursday night things were different. The ballgame had just let out and the bar was filling up fast, with the time being just a few minutes after eight. Men and women were seated around both the August Moon's multiple bar tops, and gathering on the large dance floor located directly in the center of the club. If one were there early and properly positioned, each person entering could be observed and evaluated as a possible target of pleasure for the evening. Nothing short of a "meat-market" was the August Moon Bar and Grill.

Two men had made their way into the club before the baseball game had concluded, which assured them a front row seat to the spectacle soon to consume the August Moon. They were seated a short distance from the bar, which normally would have required a waitress to tend to their needs, but tonight it was not necessary. Before their glasses would reach the halfway mark, the men would take turns visiting the bars themselves. Alternating between the three bar-tops, and between each man, alleviated the unwanted attention or conversation that a cocktail waitress would engage in. Anything the two could do to be vaguely seen, but not remembered, was put into practice. Each man was semi-casually dressed but anyone could easily detect they were wearing silk-labeled clothing. With Arlington being a "white-collar" community, this attire would allow them to blend in with many of the patrons that would grace the doors of the Grand Park Hotel.

As the August Moon began to fill with their customary crowds, the two appeared to be on high alert. As each woman would enter the club, a visual inspection from head to toe would ensue, unlike the customary quick appraisal most men would do to judge a woman on looks and body alone. These men were obviously on a mission but not a typical one for a nightclub. Several hours had passed before the two suddenly "alerted" on a female entering the club.

"There, my friend," were the quietly spoken words from one of these observers to the other.

A single female had just entered through the front door of the August Moon. Even though the summer heat was not far in the distant past, this woman bore a pale and fair complexion, not one that was darkened like the typical Texas woman. Obviously, this individual was not the normal sun worshiper but possibly a creature of the night. As she walked past her two observers, both men visually analyzed her from head to foot. The woman's natural flowing blonde hair and glowing eyes were impressive to both men. Her sleek, black outfit left little to the imagination. The short skirt revealed long but muscular legs. The strapless top allowed one to see the full length of her toned arms and healthy skin. The motions of her coordinated and seductive steps confirmed about the confident mental state of this individual.

Both men sat quietly and focused intently on their target, as if looking for a clue in a Sherlock Holmes mystery. The female chose a path of travel that led her directly past the table these two men sat at. Having someone starring at her was not an abnormality for this beauty, but tonight she would gravely misinterpret their desires. Feeling the visual piercing daggers while strolling by the staring men, she gave both a quick glance, followed by the quick but smooth movement of her head to a direction away from them. Even though the slight glance toward the men lasted only a second, both of these observers gathered the information they were seeking. There it was, the abnormality, two eyes of unique character. The dim lights of the bar supplied an ample vision of what they were seeking. One of her eyes was brown in color, the other, a deep-sea blue. Both pupils were elongated, similar to that of our feline friends-catlike they were. Her eyes were unique to only one in every 750,000 individuals, a rarity indeed.

A very slight smile cracked the stern face of one of these observers. A nod from his associate revealed that he also agreed. The time, location and physical description assured both that this was the female they were anticipating. The final piece of evidence would be searched for later this evening.

The men were vigilantly watching as the woman walked to one of the club's smaller bars. It was obvious that she was not there to mainline attention. A drink order was then placed and a short time later the bartender returned with a bottle of water, not what either man expected. In a bar this could symbolize one of two conclusions. First, the individual making such order was an alcoholic, or second, she was very health conscious. In this case, the second theory prevailed for each man. Their constant surveillance of their target continued.

Conversations at the August Moon were usually drowned out by the loud music as the club's D.J. continued to play current hits, and at an intensity level intended to show off the capabilities of the expensive sound system. During these songs, the lone female would stand beside the bar, shunning numerous attempts by different men who would ask for a dance, or to offer a drink. She too, appeared to be searching for the perfect specimen, or maybe not searching at all.

Either the music from Fleetwood Mac, or the raspy but sexy voice of Stevie Nicks, energized the blonde and directed her to the dance floor, alone, as the song Rhiannon began to play. Both of these male observers had been waiting and watching for a clue on how to successfully make contact with the woman, and now the time had come. As she stood, the blonde tossed her head from one side to another, in an effort to move the hair away from her face. Upon doing so, an object was observed dropping to the ground, yet undetected by the woman. Apparently, she had loosened an earring while redirecting her hair. As the blonde moved to the dance floor, one of her observers stood next to the table while the other made his way to the bar where she had been standing. As one man moved closer to the earring, the other continued vigilantly watching his target. With earring in hand, his partner needed to divert the attention of the bartender.

"What can I get you?" asked the bartender.

"Margarita on the rocks, with a splash of one of your fruity liquors."

"You got it, back in a second."

As the bartender walked away to fill the order, the second stalker moved closer to the bottle of water the blonde was drinking. After one last glance at the bar-top customers, a small amount of liquid GHB was poured into her drink. When the water responded with a few bubbles, he knew the integration with the drug would soon be finished. This portion of the mission was complete, now; it was just a matter of time for the GHB to take effect. Tonight, this date rape drug would serve a mission of a different sort—an incapacitated female but no sexual assaults would occur.

The two men returned to their table, eagerly watching the blonde as she returned to her perch at the bar. In a seemingly slow motion to her observers, the men watched as their victim began drinking from the bottle of water. It did not take long for the potion to begin working. The once energetic woman now began to mellow. The dipping of her head, along with several attempts to rub the blur from her eyes, signified it was time to approach.

From across the room, one man watched as his associate initiated a conversation with the blonde and soon opened one hand to reveal the missing earring. After reaching for both ears and discovering the missing piece of jewelry, the blonde revealed a slight smile, signifying she was pleased and now somewhat obligated to a brief conversation with him. A brief conversation was all the time needed for the effects of the drug to begin disabling her. Suddenly, one knee collapsed, at which time her newly found friend captured her in his arms, preventing a possible fall.

"Is she OK?" The bartender was concerned, knowing this patron had only water to drink.

"She is a diabetic. I am her fiancé' and we have some insulin up in our room. A quick shot and a few minutes of rest and she will be just fine. Unfortunately, this happens to us a lot. Thanks for your concern." The bartender seemed to accept the man's explanation.

Her male conqueror then draped one arm of the blonde over his shoulder, while wrapping his other arm around her waist. Upon feeling the firm, abdominal muscles of the female tighten while making attempts to stand pleased him, confirming her physical superiority. The blonde made several weakened attempts to speak to her escort but the victim was hardly able to make a sound-she was just too weak. The two made their way from the bar into the main lobby of the hotel. With the front desk clerk being distracted with customers, the man was able to carry the disabled woman across the lobby and into a waiting elevator.

Their efforts to be elusive earlier that evening had apparently paid off. The bartender did not recall that this man had been sitting next to his male associate all evening. As one associate escorted the blonde from the club, the other watched anxiously, counting the seconds so that he could also leave, undetected.

Approximately sixty seconds had passed. From his position inside the bar, the partner was able to watch his associate force the blonde into the elevator. A last effort of resistance by the drugged woman was fruitless as she was easily forced inside. She was now theirs for the taking as the elevator doors closed.

Almost in a sprint, the remaining observer in the club made his way to the lobby's elevator. Earlier that afternoon a room had been rented by him, anticipating this hotel would pay off, even if an additional night's stay were required. A cash payment and large deposit negated the need to present identification to the front desk clerk. A simple, fictitious name was given along with the cash, so nothing else was requested. If the occasion would have required it, both men possessed multiple drivers' licenses, which could have been used. Multiple, yet real driver's licenses were in their possession; all issued by State agencies. These were not needed today at the Grand Park Hotel because Room 664 had been rented by a non-existing individual.

The trailing associate conducted a short-knocking code on the door before inserting his key. One who entered Room 664 without first completing this code might be greeted by a 9MM bullet. Upon entering the room, he saw the partially clothed blonde lying on the bed, practically motionless and in a semi-conscious state. The drug had indeed been effective.

"Is it for sure her?"

Without a word being spoken, the associate who was sitting on the bed next to their young victim lightly pulled the long, blonde hair from the back of her neck, exposing a small tattoo. This final piece of evidence provided the complete identity trail they needed.

The other male then began preparing for the procedure. A leather briefcase containing four glass vials and syringes lie on the table, in wait of their patient. He then proceeded to the woman and lay next to her on the bed, as his partner continued his preparation.

"You're a perfect specimen, my little Angel, even better than we anticipated."

He then leaned over and planted a kiss on her forehead. At this time their victim began a slight struggle as the associate started the procedure. In a matter of minutes, it was over. Several vials of blood had been collected

"I have what we need, so let's finish up and clean this place."

Each man knew his duties. The one who collected the needed material began packing the vials into a small cooler containing ice. He changed his clothes and placed the slightly bloodstained ones into his suitcase. A quick, cleaning task then began on the room, making sure no traceable evidence was left behind. This took only a short time before he was at the door and ready to leave.

"Now, put her to sleep!"

With these words being spoken, the associate on the bed removed a knife from his pocket and methodically placed it to a skin crease on the blonde's neck. In a slow, uninterrupted motion, he impaled the blade about three inches and began to follow the path of the skin's crease, from one side of the neck to the other. Blood began to gush from the wound but no words would be heard from his victim. Dark, mascara laced tears were flowing from the helpless woman's eyes. She was no longer able to resist or even move—she could only lie there while life flowed from her veins.

"Goodnight, my little Angel. You should have come home when daddy told you to. Now, only a small part of you will be returning to the Devil's Elbow." The words were softly, intentionally letting the dying woman know this was her punishment for sinning against her family. Another kiss was planted on the victim's forehead as her assailant ascended from the bed.

"Get cleaned up and changed. We need to get this stuff to Missouri. I will be waiting downstairs."

The remaining associate stood beside the bed for a few minutes, as he wiped the blood from the knife and continued watching his dying victim. Her chest movements reflecting that each breath was becoming more shallow and distant. Now, her unique pupils could barely be seen as they rolled back into their sockets. Blood was covering the woman's entire torso. Their donor was just seconds from death.

It took the assassin more time than his partner to clean and change, due to the large amount of blood on him. Now, he was ready to join his associate in the parking lot. Their mission had been completed. As he began to leave the room, one last look was needed to assure the blonde was now dead. The woman lay motionless, assuring she had now met her God. The man quietly listened for the door to latch as it closed behind him. Their mission had been completed.

Both men had once again slipped by the front desk clerk undetected. The midnight shift always left the desk under-staffed.

This, along with the flood of drunk and noisy patrons leaving the August Moon club, resulted in many events going undetected in the lobby. No one noticed the two assailants who had exited the hotel.

It was just a few hours later that relief for the front desk clerks had arrived at the Grand Park Hotel. Day shift began at 6:00 AM, which was joined by the morning sun's rays beginning to illuminate the hotel lobby. The two clerks were consumed with shift closeout and counting of money, when a slight chime could be heard, signifying one of the elevators was opening. This common sound was ignored many times by the hotel staff, just as it was on this occasion.

The silence of the room was soon interrupted by a screaming guest. Seen staggering from the elevator was a tall, female. The natural color of her blonde hair was no longer detectable due to the massive staining of blood. Her hands were unsuccessfully trying to cover a long, gaping wound to her neck. The victim's pale skin color and mascara stained eyes and cheeks gave her the appearance of a walking vampire, straight from a horror movie scene. After taking a few steps, the woman collapsed.

The morning clerk soon took charge as the night shift employee stood frozen in horror.

"Call the police, now!" Orders were given to the stunned night clerk as the morning shift employee ran toward the victim. "Now, I said!"

The morning clerk took a position on the floor next to the bloody female. It was apparent the victim was trying to mumble a message to the employee kneeling beside her. By this time a few more guests had assembled around the injured woman and noticed the clerk had an ear next to the victim's mouth.

"What is she telling you?" asked one guest.

The clerk turned toward the inquiring guest as the victim's body went limp.

"The Devil's Elbow . . . . the Devil's Elbow."

Without question, the remaining life in the young victim was rapidly diminishing.

CHAPTER 2

The sun was fading to the west, seemingly directly above the point that divided the Texas-Oklahoma border. For one who has not witnessed a sunset over the flat, dust-filled skies of this area has indeed missed a page from one of God's most scenic coloring books. The peace and serenity that usually mesmerizes all who witness it, no longer captivated the attention of Detective Robert James on this evening.

Suddenly, traffic on Highway 75 slightly north of the Oklahoma border had come to a stop. Witnesses had just observed a white Ford pickup truck leave the roadway and crash into the ditch. Speeding south from the accident was a dark colored truck that continued to accelerate in an obvious attempt to flee the scene, which appeared to be that of a traffic accident. Little did anyone close to the incident realize they had just witnessed a "Hit" on a federal law enforcement officer.

As cars were coming to a halt, the lightly traveled road this evening had rapidly turned into a large parking lot, with people running from their cars to the damaged pickup truck that had come to rest approximately one hundred feet from the roadway. Smoke was still bellowing from the engine compartment as people approached. Witnesses were unable to determine if the occupants were injured and not moving, due to the thickness of the smoke which had formed an opaque blanket, blocking one's view. No one had apparently witnessed the occupant of the pickup temporarily exit the Ford, before his rapid re-entry.

"Someone call 9-1-1," were words being screamed from several of the rescuers.

Despite the pandemonium taking place outside, Robert James was only able to focus his attention on the small, baby girl that continued to sleep next to him. Despite the gunshot blast and the minor collision that followed, the child did not seem to be disturbed. A small stream of tears had begun running from Robert's eyes. This was not due to any injury or the shock from what just occurred, but from a new feeling he was suddenly experiencing. Robert had been told by his father and others that a new parent will immediately fall in love with their newly born child. Despite missing the grand birth, the feelings that were encompassing the young man had to be the same as a new father that had just observed his child being removed from the mother's womb and shown to him. The amount of time that Robert spent with his infant daughter had been minimal, but the thoughts and feelings that were engulfing him at this moment had overcome the event that just occurred. The tears were that of relief now knowing the apparent attempt to take his life left his daughter unharmed. The immediate anger that consumed him after the gunshot blast had been rapidly replaced by fear of injury to his baby. Once he realized his child was unharmed, Robert's relief was displayed by the emotional tears streaming down his face.

"Sir, Sir, are you OK? Sir, Sir . . ."

The voices from outside of his window brought Robert back to the situation at hand. He quickly wiped the tears from his eyes, cleared his throat and stepped from the vehicle.

"Everyone here is alright," Robert replied, which eased some of the excitement that was reflected in the rescuer's voice.

One of the concerned citizens continued by telling Robert that he had instructed some of the others to call 9-1-1, therefore; the police should be on their way. After surveying the pickup, there was an immediate silence now in the man's voice.

Most of the people from this part of the country are very involved with outdoor sports, especially that of hunting. It did not take a seasoned investigator to deduce what caused the damage to the front fender, windshield and tire on Robert's truck was caused from. Being a native from either Texas or Oklahoma, most of these people had a lot of knowledge regarding guns and ammunition.

"What's your name, Son?" an elderly gentleman asked.

"Robert, its Robert."

"Well, Robert, I have some bad news for you."

At this point the man pointed to the front fender of the truck, showing Robert what he already knew. Approximately ten holes, each about the size of a large B-B, were scattered about the fender. Apparently, a few had also found their mark on the windshield, which now revealed several spider-web cracks. For Robert, there was no mystery in what caused the blowout to the front tire.

"Double-ought buckshot, Son. Now, who have you pissed off lately, Mr. Robert," the elderly gentleman asked.

The man's question was temporarily unanswered as Robert's hand slid into his back pocket, grabbing his wallet. Robert then opened it to reveal his badge and ID card.

"I am a Federal agent; my full name is Robert James, Detective Robert James."

The elderly man's face became suddenly sober. He quickly realized that he had just witnessed the attempted murder of a law enforcement official.

"Then you know, Son that someone just tried to kill you!"

"Indeed I do, Sir."

And I know exactly who the bastard is that is responsible, Robert thought.

"Here is my business card, Detective James. Please feel free to call me when you catch the animals responsible for this shooting. And Robert, take care of your little girl in there. They grow up fast so enjoy her. Also, has anyone ever told you that she looks just like her father?" the elderly gentleman said with a smile. "Who knows, maybe she will grow up to be a Marine, like my daughter."

No additional words were spoken between Robert and the elderly gentleman who came to his aid. Each knew the situation was a serious one, therefore; no further words were needed.

"Semper Fi, my new friend," exclaimed Robert as the gentleman walked away. It was obvious to both that a new bond between two prior strangers had just been formed, and one that only a person belonging to a brother in combat could understand.

Robert then looked toward his truck and observed a female approaching it. It was both predictable and assumed that the woman's maternal nature would take over. For some reason, Robert sensed no danger, so he stood back and let the woman continue her mission. Robert's sleeping daughter was now in the arms of a nurturing woman, one of whom apparently had children of her own.

With the child now in hand, the woman asked, "Sir, what is her name?"

Even though Lori had failed to mention his daughter's name, Robert was able to recall the inscription on her birth certificate.

"Its Paige, my daughter's name is Paige," said the proud father.

"She is beautiful, Sir. You should be a very proud father. Now here, hold this young lady, she wants her daddy."

The glow and smile on Robert's face replaced the need for any words.

The colorful sunset was now giving in to the darkness of the slightly moonlit evening. A faint wailing from a siren could be heard in the distance. As Robert looked to the south, he noticed a speeding sedan that was displaying a single, revolving light in the windshield, rapidly approaching. It was obvious that someone had made that 9-11 call, alerting law enforcement to his situation. Robert, being accustomed to urban law enforcement, was expecting more than just one emergency vehicle to be responding to the scene. Robert assumed that a possible injury accident would require the response of numerous patrol vehicles, along with a fire truck and ambulance. Not here, not this day, and not this place. This incident had occurred in rural Oklahoma, where volunteers and first responders were the ones usually sent to the scene of an accident or incident.

As the emergency vehicle approached, Robert stood in awe. The patrol vehicle, an unmarked, ten year old sedan with no identifying markings on the side, was coming to a halt. As the car stopped, two plain-clothed deputies exited. These were no city cops and for sure not State Troopers. The two men had the appearance of cowboys who had just ridden to the scene on their horses. The driver looked like a range-worn cowhand, wearing blue jeans and a western shirt. Strapped around his waist was a thick belt, which supported only a badge and a gun. This indeed was no normal pistol; instead, it was a 44 Magnum revolver with an eight-inch barrel. If Wyatt Earp lived in the late 1900's, this could have been him. Instead, the cop was a local lawman that obviously was a fan of the Dirty Harry movies. His sidekick was nothing less that Barney Fife in western gear.

The two officers then approached Robert's vehicle.

"We are with the Sheriff's Department; whose truck is this?"

"It's mine," Robert responded.

"What the hell happened? You drunk or something?" the Wyatt Earp replica asked.

It was obvious that Robert would not be dealing with the professional law enforcement officers he was accustomed to. These men were a far cry from that.

"Well officers . . ." Robert was immediately cut off by Wyatt Earp's futuristic brother. "We are sheriff deputies, not officers, Mr. City Slicker."

"Well, Deputy." Robert was again interrupted.

"That is Deputy Crockett, Mister."

How appropriate for this clown with a badge.

At this time it was obvious to Robert that he needed to play the "law enforcement brotherhood" card with these deputies.

"I have been shot at; a murder attempt," explained Robert, while revealing his badge and Federal ID to the deputies. "Take a look at the fender and windshield."

"It just looks like some gravel flew up and hit your truck, Mr. Fed," the deputy sarcastically replied.

"I don't think so! According to my observations, along with an ex-Marine who just left here, we are guessing double-ought buck shot."

Robert then began to brief the deputies about the case he had just concluded against Gene King. A man with endless resources despite the fact he was now sitting inside of a federal correctional facility. Gene King had just been incarcerated, with millions of assets confiscated and his empire destroyed. Indeed, a man with revenge and retaliation foremost on his mind. Even after hearing about the Robert's case, these officials seemed to be unconcerned.

The deputies began to scope out the damage for a second time and then engaged in a private discussion, trying their best to be careful to where Robert would not overhear the conversation.

"Okay, Mr. Fed, so what? These may be some buckshot holes but you know it is hunting season. We have all kinds of accidents this time of year. It's Friday night and our locals drink a little of that happy juice after work, and at times fire off a few rounds. You just happened to be at the wrong place at the wrong time. This was probably just an accident."

Robert was speechless and in awe.

"We have a very low crime rate in our county, Mr. Fed, and your case will be ruled an accidental shooting by local hunters."

Just as Robert was to enter the battleground with the two ignorant lawmen, two other vehicles approached with emergency lights flashing.

Oklahoma Highway Patrol-thank God!

Robert's guess was correct. A sigh of relief was felt, as the two black-and-white State Trooper cruisers pulled up to the scene. Robert knew what had to been done here. As soon as the troopers exited their vehicles, Robert was in their face and flashing his Federal credentials.

"Federal Agent Robert James, Troopers," exclaimed Robert.

Both men immediately revealed their names and rank to Robert.

"I am Sgt. Fred Ives and this is Trooper Terry Lohmann. How can we be of assistance?"

The next few minutes Robert spent showing the Oklahoma Troopers the damage to his vehicle, along with conveying the story about his most recent case against drug lord, Gene King. It did not take long for the troopers to come to an obvious conclusion.

"Deputy Crockett, we are now taking over this case. With the obvious evidence at hand, YOU WILL rule this call an Attempted Murder of a Law Enforcement Officer, and nothing less. We will be by your office tomorrow to secure a copy of the offense report. We are also "expecting" it to reflect the facts at hand. Do we have an understanding, deputies?"

The two county deputies did not verbally respond but instead, gave Robert a look that made him grateful those eyes could not kill. A slight nod to the troopers was observed before climbing into their vehicle and speeding from the scene.

The next thirty minutes involved Robert completing a supplemental report with Oklahoma's finest. The details were of extreme interest to the troopers, who felt as if they were reading a script for a movie. Measurements and photographs were taken, along with a sweep of the scene for shotgun shells. There was no doubt that the Oklahoma Highway Patrol was leaving no stones unturned.

"Well, Detective James, we have done about all we can do here tonight," Sgt. Ives stated. "Give us a few days to complete our reports. I am sure your case will be referred to some Feds in the Dallas-Ft. Worth area, and rest assured they can expect nothing but 100% cooperation from us. God-speed, Detective James. Take care of that lovely young child and enjoy your vacation. And Detective James, haste makes waste so you have clearance from OHP to disregard that little 65 MPH sign while in our state. You are on a mission now, so get your Federal-butt to Missouri."

With a handshake and smile, Detective James acknowledged the suggestion of his newly found "brother-in-blue." While Robert was speaking with Sergeant Ives, Trooper Lohmann had changed the flat tire on his truck.

"You are good-to-go, Brother. Be careful, and Robert, maybe someday you should write a book about your case against Gene King. I can guarantee at least two book sales!" Trooper Lohmann then nodded a goodbye to Robert.

Robert realized that Paige was now awake, not making a sound as if she were listening to every word being said.

"Well, my dear, shall we go and visit grandpa now?"

As Robert placed Paige back into her car seat, he looked into the face of his young daughter.

"My dear, welcome to my world. Neither of us knows what tomorrow will bring, but we will always be here for each other. Life will be nothing less than an adventure!"

Paige looked up at her father and managed to make an undecipherable noise that only a parent and child could understand. Both father and daughter knew a bond had been formed and life's adventures would always include each other.

Robert's pickup then pulled from the ditch, as Sgt. Ives blocked the roadway with his squad car. With his truck back on pavement, Robert pressed the accelerator to the floor, smiling as the speed odometer continued to climb, leveling off at 85 MPH with the troopers still in sight.

What the heck are you doing here, Buddy? You have a baby daughter on board, you know!

Robert looked at Paige as he de-accelerated; "65 MPH and not a mile-an-hour more for my prized possession."

The young father now realized that he had a new priority in his life . . . .

CHAPTER 3

"Everyone in here, now!"

The briefing room at the Joint Drug Lab Suppression Team (JDLST) in Texas was coming to life after Special Agent (SA) Michaels barked the above orders. The Investigators in this elite unit had been around their boss long enough to recognize this tone signified something important. Within minutes, every JDLST team member had assembled in the room, anticipating the significance of this meeting. As their boss entered the room, all went silent.

"Gentlemen, it appears as if Gene King is not appreciating the all-inclusive Federal country club that Detective James sent him to. I need to brief you about some information we just received."

For the next thirty minutes, SA Michaels relayed to his investigators some information, which was just given to him by Detective Hanks, from the North Division of the Tarrant County Metro Police Department. It was common knowledge throughout the Texas law enforcement community that the JDLST team had destroyed Drug Lord Gene King's illicit empire, and sent the criminal mastermind to a Federal penitentiary for the remainder of his life. Cops also knew that a person with an organization as large as Gene King's had tentacles branching out in many directions, and snipping all of them was impossible for any law enforcement organization, even the JDLST.

Apparently, Detective Hanks has a confidential drug informant who is associated with Gene King's organization. As with all informants, this individual wanted to trade some information in an attempt to be relieved of a couple of criminal violations that were lingering overhead. What the informant had to offer Detective Hanks was nothing short of a poker player's full house. Information about "a hit" on a cop was a great negotiating tool, especially regarding the latest law enforcement media celebrity, Detective Robert James. Besides verbal networking among the law enforcement brotherhood, the media made a spectacle out of the Gene King case. A three day media blitz about real life human trafficking, drugs and murder was a definite boost for their news ratings. What more could a station want than a real-life crime drama being featured on their network!

A person who thinks that drug addicts and dealers do not watch the news need a wake-up call. As a stockbroker watching the ticker-tape, the dopers and thieves of our society keep up with the news, which can actually aid in their criminal endeavors. Maybe it is just to know which friend was busted, so they may go and burglarize their house while their crooked friends are in jail. Also, knowing the police at times use the media to boast to the public about what cases they recently solved is good stuff for the criminal world. This allows a crook to know what part of town the incident occurred, how the crime was committed and even better, live video of the detective working the case—one stop shopping for a criminal's training film.

The Gene King case was definitely headline news, so most in the north Texas area had knowledge of it, including the local crooks. When Detective Hank's informant was advising him that several members of the Bandera biker gang were talking about how "the King" had ordered them to kill Detective Robert James, the informant knew he had just struck gold. This information would be the ticket for evading his newest criminal charges. Upon being given this information by the CI, Detective Hanks knew he had to act on it. All information such as this had to be carefully evaluated, due to the source it was derived from, but this situation was a little different. First, Detective Hanks had been receiving information from this individual for several years now and was able to dissect the information, separating fact from fiction. Second, the law enforcement community knew how dangerous and wide spread King's organization was, so they could not take any chances. One of their own was a possible target, so all threats had to be taken seriously.

The information was vague, with only details regarding the biker's appearances. Detective Hank's informant was also able to obtain a partial description of the four-wheel drive pickup truck the bikers were seen driving away in, with their two cycles riding passenger in the truck's bed. This was not much information but enough for Detective Hanks to pass along to the Feds.

Following his thirty-minute dissertation, Special Agent Michaels began to whittle down the stick of chalk he held giving assignments to each team member, along with names and descriptions of possible associates of Gene King.

"Gentlemen, for the next few days this is our priority, your other cases go on hold. Chances are this is nothing but total B.S, but let's not take the risk. One of our own is on the line here. If Mr. King wishes to stretch his tentacles from prison, let's show him just how fast we can chop them off! I know Robert is not in Missouri yet but I am going to try his new cell phone to see if I can get through. Robert should be out of harm's way until he returns, but he still needs to know."

What a way for Robert to start a vacation!

"This will be an expensive call," mumbled Special Agent Michaels, while dialing Robert's cell phone number.

The call was met with a tone and message advising the caller the cell phone was either out of range or turned off. Knowing that his young detective would be driving through the Ozark Mountains, it was easily assumed that cell phone coverage would probably be non-existent for most of Robert's drive. As SA Michaels glanced at his watch, he realized how fast time had been slipping by this evening. The JDLST team members were definitely creatures of the night, but eleven o'clock was late for most of the civilian world. Despite the time, Michaels felt it necessary to place a call to Robert's father in Missouri before it got too late. Even the slightest hint of a possible "hit" on Robert necessitated the call.

Special Agent Michaels then pulled out a business card that had Robert's father's phone number written on the back, in the event an emergency situation developed while he was gone. The call was then placed to Mr. James, which much to Michaels' relief, was immediately answered.

"Mr. James, this is Special Agent Michaels; I am . . . ." Before he could finish his sentence, Robert's father interrupted with a verbal acknowledgement.

The two men started up a conversation as if two, long-lost friends had just been reunited. Their prior military service, along with a fatherly attachment to Robert, acted as a bonding agent for the two men. Special Agent Michaels soon determined that he could be blunt and forthcoming with Robert's father, and felt comfortable in passing along the information regarding the safety of his son. Upon hearing SA Michaels' words of warning, Robert's father simply acknowledged.

"Mr. James, we will take care of everything on this end, just let that boy enjoy his much deserved time off. Nothing is going to happen to my ace detective Sir; goodnight."

As Mr. James hung up the phone, his look of concern seemed to reflect what he already sensed that on this evening, an attempt on his son's life had already occurred.

CHAPTER 4

The eight-hour journey from Dallas to Springdale, Missouri was not the typical one on this date. The little delay in Southern Oklahoma added a couple of extra hours to it. Usually, Robert was an impatient man, wanting to get from point A to B as soon as possible, but not today. It did not take an ace detective to understand what had just occurred, and who the responsible party was. Robert tried his best not to let the Gene King case go to his head but he was savoring in the sweet fruits of the case. Robert was still amazed that he just concluded the biggest case of his life. When working as a detective in Springdale, having a blurb in the newspaper, or maybe even a few seconds on the evening news regarding a solved case was nothing unusual but the Gene King case was an exception. He had just arrested a criminal who was associated with the Cartel, committed numerous murders and was a one-man, organized crime ring. Also, Gene's arrest possibly saved the lives of several young women who had fallen into the web of the King organization. To add a little icing to the cake, this case was featured for three days on news networks in the Dallas-Ft. Worth, Austin and Houston areas. These were major media outlets, and "Detective Robert James" was their feature story. Robert was not an egotistical man, but he did enjoy this little reward for his labor.

The thoughts of the Gene King case were now secondary to what was going through Robert's mind, while navigating his Ford pickup truck onto the Will Rogers Turnpike in North Central Oklahoma. Next to him was a small child, his daughter, Paige

James. The feeling of being a new father seemed to overshadow the glory of the Gene King case. Reality was also beginning to set in, too. Besides the U.S. Marshals, who were obligated to secrecy, there were only two people who knew his daughter existed, he and Paige's mother, Lori Sims. Robert had never imagined himself to be a father while in his twenties, or maybe never at all. He also envisioned a long relationship before a marriage, and then several years after a wedding before a love-child would be born. Now, he was next to his daughter, conceived from a relationship between a cop and an informant. This was not what Robert had ever wanted, planned or even thought about, but reality was sitting next to him. He was now only two hundred and fifty miles from Springdale, Missouri. At the end of this voyage, Robert would be walking through the front door of his father's house with baby Paige in hand. What would he tell his dad and what would be the reaction, were two major concerns at this point. Robert had always felt his father was proud of how his son turned out, but he feared this might no longer be the case.

    Robert was deprived of a mother early in his childhood, due to cancer taking her from the family. From that point on, Mr. James has been the primary caregiver to Robert and his siblings, so on a man-to-man basis, Robert felt his father was exactly the person who could help him in this situation. Mr. James was also a logical and understanding person, so the anxieties Robert initially felt were rapidly subsiding. Robert concluded that he would take one step at a time; so concerns regarding his boss would be a thought for another day. For the time, Robert would just absorb the contentment he was feeling from having Paige next to him.

CHAPTER 5

Traffic was minimal on the interstate, as Robert was counting the semi-trucks passing him on the roadway. Normally, this would not be happening to the lead-foot cop with the "get out of a ticket badge" pinned to his wallet. So, 70 MPH and not a nickel more, would be his speed while hauling the valuable cargo seated next to him.

The young father was amazed by how quiet Paige had been the entire trip, including the little episode in southern Oklahoma when their truck had been blown off the highway.

"1:15 AM, most normal people should be in bed right now." Robert muttered as he questioned driving this late with a young baby aboard.

Interstate 44 was leading Robert toward his destination of Springdale. This night-owl detective was beginning to succumb to the hypnotic effect of a desolate interstate highway, during this mid-week night. Even the semi traffic was beginning to thin out, due to the late night hours that were greeting them.

Springdale, 23 miles, the sign reflected.

It's about time.

Robert smirked with anticipation of the little shock factor awaiting his father regarding the introduction of his daughter to Grandpa.

Something rapidly diverted Robert's attention. In his rearview mirror he could see several emergency vehicles approaching with red lights illuminating the dark skies.

The Devil's Elbow Project

"Looks like some Missouri State Police officers are on a mission!"

As the police cruisers approached Robert's truck, he realized something unusual. This was some type of escort, in which two black SUV's were being ushered by a couple of patrol cars. Immediately, Robert began to analyze the situation.

Was this a medical or VIP escort, or maybe an organ emergency transport from one hospital to another?

Robert had seen or participated in all of these scenarios while working as a patrolman in Springdale. The vehicles were approaching at speeds estimated at over 125 miles per hour. Just when the first patrol car began to pass, Robert was stunned . . .

Texas Highway Patrol, what the heck!

As the patrol cars passed, Robert's initial observations were verified. There was no mistake to what agency the patrol cars belonged. These distinguished black-and-white units with the Texas emblem on the door were without a doubt Texas State Troopers—Robert was baffled.

"Why would Texas Highway Patrol be escorting two black SUV's through Missouri, and at 2 AM? And man, are they ever hauling ass!" Robert found himself talking aloud to his baby.

There was something on the shoulder of the roadway that suddenly diverted Robert's attention. This was a sight too many times seen during the late night hours in Missouri, and on many occasions being the cause of traffic accidents. Not one, not two, but three deer. Their bodies now in a "ready" posture, not sure of what their reactions will be to the speeding, oncoming traffic.

Oh, God!

The lead Texas Highway Patrol car had just collided head-on with a large buck that thought he could escape the speeding vehicle by running across the interstate before it reached him. Male deer are known for their intelligence but in this case the buck had miscalculated a patrol car traveling at excessive speeds. The impact nearly seared the deer in half, sending remains in all directions. The speeding patrol car also fell victim to misfortune. The impact immediately sent the police cruiser into an end-over-end tumble down I-44, and then down an embankment, coming to rest in the Roubidoux River. Rising steam was now the only motion observed from the area of this vehicle.

One of the SUV's suffered the same demise when trying to evade the collision that just occurred directly in front of it. The large buck was too much for the SUV to safely maneuver around, so a secondary collision occurred. Once the speeding vehicle struck the carcass, it began a roll down the center of the interstate. Another smoke cloud began to rise due to tires skidding from the second Texas Highway Patrol car and SUV, which were following the lead cars. The pursuing vehicles were much more fortunate than the two before them—they had escaped tragedy. No human movement could be seen coming from either of the wrecked vehicles.

Robert pulled his vehicle to the center median and sat mesmerized.

Instinct kicked in, as Robert looked at his daughter sleeping calmly next to him.

I have got to help them!

Before Robert could exit his pickup truck, the second Texas State Trooper and accompanying vehicle had pulled next to the SUV that had just crashed. For some reason no one was tending to the wrecked State Trooper whose vehicle had come to rest in the Roubidoux River. All emphasis seemed to be focused on the mangled sports utility vehicle.

Robert was now in full stride running toward the accident scene. While making his way to the crash scene, Robert could see two men and one woman exiting the second sports utility vehicle and making their way toward the one that was wrecked. At the same time, two plain-clothed officers exited the Texas Highway Patrol cruisers and began walking toward Robert.

"We are Texas Rangers and you need to leave the scene immediately, Sir."

Instantly, Robert reached into his back pocket and retrieved his wallet that contained his Federal ID and badge.

"I am a Federal Agent," replied Robert, as he revealed his ID to the officers.

One of the Rangers carefully reviewed Robert credentials.

"I know who you are, Son—the Gene King case. Good work on that one but you need to get back in your vehicle and immediately leave." The sober and firm look on the Ranger's face reflected he was in no mood to discuss the matter.

"I am not leaving here, Ranger, and let me clarify things to you. I am a Federal Agent and you are a cop who is out of your jurisdiction."

Without another word being said, the Ranger whistled and caught the attention of one of the occupants from the second SUV. With a slight motion of the hand, one of the men diverted from the crash scene and began walking back toward Robert and the Texas Ranger. The Ranger and the approaching stranger engaged in a short and private conversation and then approached Robert.

"This is Federal Agent Robert James, from the JDLST in Dallas." The Ranger said in his brief introduction.

At this time, the individual approached Robert and quietly identified himself. With few words being exchanged between the men, Robert knew he was in the wrong place at the wrong time. Detective James just had an encounter with one of the United States elite and secretive warriors.

"Detective James, this never happened. You did not see anything, you did not speak with me and if a word about this is ever mentioned, your law enforcement days are over, period! Now, slide on past before the Highway Patrol arrives and shuts the road down."

"What about the Texas Trooper in the river?" asked Robert.

"He's dead."

"How the hell do you know? You have not even been down to check on him!"

"Detective James, he is dead-it's time for you to go."

As Robert returned to his truck, sirens could be heard rapidly approaching the scene. Confusion filled Robert's mind as he sat and watched, trying to digest what he had just witnessed. His hands were now grasping the steering wheel of his pickup, more in an attempt to contain himself than for relieving tension. What he was now witnessing just added to the confusion. All three of the individuals from the second SUV were approaching the one that was wrecked. Robert observed the back door being forced open, and everyone focused on a young man they were pulling from the back seat. As a person being rescued from a racecar, the semi conscious body was carried back to the second sports utility, at which time the three original occupants entered the vehicle after loading the injured man. Before leaving, Robert was approached again by the Texas Ranger he spoke with earlier.

"Son, I need to again remind you about what the Fed told you earlier. You did not see us or witness anything other than that a cop car and SUV hit a deer, you understand?"

Robert refused to verbally acknowledge the Texas Ranger but words were not necessary in this case. Robert knew, without a doubt, that he had just witnessed something extra-ordinary and that his JDLST badge was insignificant. The long, cold stare from the rugged Texas Ranger sent an unquestionable message to Robert. The SUV transporting the injured man then sped from the scene, while being escorted by the Ranger in the remaining Texas Highway patrol car.

With red emergency lights and sirens approaching, Robert soon regained his senses, at which time his basic police training began to kick in.

I have got to help that Texas Trooper before he drowns.

For some reason, Robert had ignored the SUV that was lying on its top in the middle of Interstate 44 after the solo occupant had been removed. He then looked at his baby girl and again assured himself that his daughter was still sound asleep. Once this was confirmed, Robert locked his truck's door and took off in a sprint toward the Texas police cruiser that had crashed into the river. All of a sudden the SUV behind him exploded!

The percussion from the explosion stopped Robert in his tracks. Flames were now shooting from the windows and doors of the vehicle, and a few moans were heard coming from within. Horrors from the past were now intensely consuming Robert, as memories from previous fires were disabling his rescue attempts. Prior memories of the five year old child burning to death, and the two females being shot and set on fire, were now foremost on his mind. Robert felt as if he were in slow motion, trying to make his way back to the burning vehicle. The intense heat prevented him from getting close and attempting a rescue. Before Robert could make his way much further, he could hear the percussion of a large caliber handgun exploding inside the SUV. It was obvious the occupant choose suicide over a burning hell. This demise, whoever they may be, was self-inflicted. Between the fiery explosion and gunshot, without a doubt the occupant was now dead.

Looking ahead, Robert saw another curious sight. The Texas Ranger had apparently stopped to give aid to his injured brethren in the Texas Highway Patrol car before leaving the scene. This was a relief to Robert, because he felt assured the inhabitants in the police cruiser would drown. The burning SUV was blocking his path to the submerged patrol car, so seeing the Ranger make his way toward the vehicle was encouraging.

Robert remained motionless, as if he were on the front row of a suspense movie at a theater, therefore, not being allowed to move or make a sound. His expectations for the Trooper's survival were dismal. Being a prior patrolman in Springdale, Robert knew the chances of anyone surviving a high-speed accident as this one, were extremely remote.

A few moments later, the silhouette of the Ranger could be seen walking up the riverbank and returning to his patrol car. Before entering, he glanced back toward Robert and paused, transmitting a look that words did not need to explain. The Troopers in the river were gone-dead! The Ranger confirmed this by slightly rotating his head right-to-left, verifying the worse was now reality. What occurred next took Robert by surprise, as the Ranger solemnly placed one finger against the lips, signaling that all should remain silent about the facts just seen. This law enforcement icon then returned to the patrol car and sped east; in pursuit of the SUV that was carrying the injured young man. Robert was a young cop but still seasoned enough to know about how the elite Texas Rangers operated. Like a Marine, there was no way a Texas Ranger was going to leave a fellow comrade behind, dead or alive, unless exigent circumstances prevailed.

Robert's mind was wandering in a fog. *Who, why, and what have I just witnessed?*

In front of Robert was a massive scene of crushed metal and dead bodies. Without time to evaluate and analyze what he had just witnessed, the Missouri State Police, fire units and ambulances had arrived at the scene. Robert stood motionless with his Federal ID and badge dangling from his hand-held wallet. Two Missouri State Patrolmen then approached Robert, who was standing in the middle of I-44, a short distance from the burning SUV. The flames from the fire were reflecting in Robert's badge, which made it obvious to the officers that Robert was a law enforcement officer.

"You a cop?" Asked a Missouri State Police Officer.

"Yes, Sir; a Federal Agent."

"Can you tell me what is going on here?"

"No, Sir, I can't . . . . I sure as hell can't."

Robert then handed the officer a business card and began walking back toward his truck.

"You leaving, Detective James? You can't leave us with this mess without a statement or report!"

These words were still echoing in the background as Robert climbed into his truck and looked into the face of his sleeping daughter. Shouts from the Missouri State Police officer began to fade as Robert drove his vehicle onto the grass median and past the burning Suburban. It did not matter that he was leaving behind two pissed-off cops who would have to mop up a major accident scene. Robert knew that his federal badge would allow him to escape the scene without further intervention from the Missouri officers.

The emergency lights were beginning to distance themselves in Robert's rear view mirror when another curious sight unveiled itself. Two black helicopters were closing in on the accident scene, traveling about treetop high and directly above the pavement of the interstate. Despite the horrors he had just left behind, Robert could not elude his instincts.

"This truck is a four-wheel drive, so let's see what she can do."

Robert slightly mumbled in an attempt not to awaken his sleeping daughter. His truck slowed enough to manipulate the median ditch, after which he began his return toward the accident scene. The two helicopters had just landed, one blocking the scene from the west and the other from the east. Fort Pulaski was only a few miles to the south, but the men Robert observed exiting the choppers were not in a typical military uniform. The occupants were wearing black jumpsuits and armed with sub-machine guns, with the exception of one individual that appeared to be without a weapon. He rapidly approached the Missouri State Police officers and engaged in a conversation. A short time later, the officers walked from the accident scene and returned to their cars, with their only obvious duty being that of directing traffic. It was apparent the individual in the suit pulled rank over the officers and relieved them from the duty of investigating the crash. It was obvious this scene now belonged to him.

Robert had seen enough. Once again, his vehicle jumped another median ditch and began traveling away from the mangled mess. The euphoria and excitement of the Gene King case, along with being a new father, had temporarily faded away.

Two, maybe three dead bodies.

The thoughts of the newly deceased would be like ghosts haunting Detective Robert James, until the riddle of their deaths could be solved.

Chapter 6

It was only a few hours until daylight when Robert's pickup pulled into his father's driveway in Springdale. Remembering the drill for returning home after breaking curfew as a teenager, Robert killed the headlights and slowly rolled into the drive in an attempt not to be seen or heard. This time would be different than the days of his youth. Robert was faced with several situations he would be presenting to his father. The shock of the newest female addition to the household would be certain, but Robert felt his dad would take this one in stride. Explaining the shotgun pellet holes in the truck would be an entirely different issue; one that would wait until morning. Even though both of these matters were paramount, the incident he just witnessed on Interstate 44 was still foremost on his mind. Upon parting, the Texas Ranger signaled to him to keep this incident silent. Robert questioned how this could be done since it was a major accident scene with deaths involved. And the young passenger from the SUV that was whisked away in the patrol car-who was he? Then, the helicopter followed, along with their curious passengers of unknown origin and importance.

"*Can I lay all of this on dad?*" Robert thought to himself. This eventful night was still not over.

Mr. James was an ex-Air Force pilot and Robert knew that his job description came with a Top-Secret clearance. His father was not one who spoke much about his duties and missions while in the Air Force, but it was apparent that any pilot flying during the Vietnam War had participated in many dangerous and secretive operations. Robert also knew that his father had spent some time in the cockpit of a U-2 Spy Plane during the Cold War era, but no questions were ever asked about that assignment. Mr. James had been retired from the military and flying commercially now for ten years but as with law enforcement, once a military man, always a military man. A person with many exceptional experiences but few words was indeed Mr. James.

Several minutes had now passed with Robert sitting silently in his truck with his full attention directed towards Paige. It was amazing to this new father that his infant daughter could sleep through all of the ordeals they had encountered during this night. A few times Paige had awakened but just for the amount of time necessary to be changed or fed.

God has indeed given me the perfect child.

During his youth, something Robert's father never deviated from, was making sure his children regularly attended church. A "Bible-thumper" Mr. James was not, but a believer he was. Having his kids in church was a vital part of growing and maturing, comparable to attending school, in his father's mind. Robert knew his life had been far from perfect-a moral icon he was not. Robert had thought about (on numerous occasions) how fortunate he had been avoiding possible fatherhood in the past, and his little black book loaded with women's names supported his theory. Now, the inevitable had finally occurred and God had been kind to Robert James.

The time had finally arrived to introduce Paige to his father, but Robert was nervous.

"Just a few more minutes and then, hello, Grandpa." Robert whispered to his daughter.

The silence and darkness was suddenly broken by the front porch light illuminating, along with the sight of his father standing in the doorway. Robert knew the time had come.

"Come on, my Dear." Robert then reached down and grabbed little Paige, wrapping her in a blanket before greeting the crisp, early morning air.

Mr. James looked on with curiosity as his son exited the truck, carefully handling a small package wrapped in a blanket. Not a word was said as Robert emerged from the darkness, allowing the porch light to highlight what he carried in his arms.

"Hello, Son."

"Father."

As Robert moved closer, it did not take long for Mr. James to recognize what his son was carrying in his arms.

"Looks like we have a lot to talk about," responded Mr. James in a concerned voice. As Robert paused in front of his father, a slight nod was his only response as the two continued into the house.

The story about Lori Sims and the Gene King case occupied the first hour of Robert's visit. Mr. James initially had little to interject, allowing his son to convey his story and to see what solutions he had thought of. Being a single father was no simple task, and one that Mr. James knew all too well. Upon Mrs. James' death, he was left with the sole responsibility of raising Robert and his siblings, all of whom were under the age of ten. In one aspect, Mr. James was very concerned over his son's new situation, mostly due to Robert's job and the news that Special Agent Michaels had relayed to him earlier. On the other hand, Mr. James knew his son was smart and seemed to "usually" have his priorities in a row. So, hopefully having a young daughter would be something Robert could handle.

"Does Special Agent Michaels know about Paige?" The deer in the headlights look was all that Mr. James needed to signify Robert had not yet crossed this bridge.

"We will get through this as a family, Son. Now, let me hold my new granddaughter while you unload that truck." The smile that Mr. James gave Robert while taking hold of Paige was one of acceptance and reassurance, which Robert had been hoping for.

"When you're done, Robert, I have something else we need to talk about before you hit the sack."

Robert returned to his truck wondering what was so important to keep them up even later. In a matter of minutes, the sun would be poking its head up in the east. The moon had long since disappeared and the skies were beginning to lighten over the horizon. Plus, after two major adrenalin rushes throughout the evening, accompanied by a five hundred mile drive, he was dead tired.

This better be important.

As Robert re-entered the house, he saw that his father had built Paige a small pallet on his bed, surrounded with blankets to prevent her from rolling off.

"My granddaughter is sound asleep. I have something we need to talk about, Son. It appears that someone wants you dead."

After hearing his father rehash the information given to him earlier by Special Agent Michaels, it did not take Robert but a minute to conclude that indeed a "hit" on him had occurred yesterday evening. Without responding, Robert motioned for his father to follow him outside where he led him to the pickup truck. The sun was now about to peak over the horizon, giving enough light where Mr. James could easily see the damage to Robert's vehicle.

"Looks like shotgun pellets, Robert."

"Ding, Ding; you win the prize, Dad."

"Ok, Mr. Ding-Ding, tell your old man about this."

Robert then began to share the details with his father. It was obvious that Mr. James was furious upon hearing this. Robert's dad was usually a cool cucumber, even during adversities, but this was one of the rare occasions where he actually witnessed his father in such a heated demeanor.

"This Gene King tries to have my son and baby granddaughter killed! How the hell did this happen when he is sitting his ass in a Federal prison? Never mind, I know the answer, Son. In a few hours, you need to call your boss and tell him about what happened. Now, go and spend some pillow time next to that beautiful young lady before she is wide awake, which won't be long off."

Robert sat on the couch, deeply entrenched in thought and not able to move. Two out of three issues had already been covered, plenty for one evening. Robert knew that what he witnessed earlier on Interstate 44 should be kept silent, not letting anyone know what he saw.

Being a federal agent set certain parameters one should follow, but was the death of the individuals on I-44 a possible secretive operation? Should I vent to my father about what happened?

"Since we are on a roll, I need to talk to you about something else, Dad." Robert's concerned look silently relayed to his father that this session needed to continue.

"Ok, go with it, Robert."

Mr. James sat intensely listening as Robert painted the picture of the mayhem he had just witnessed on the interstate. Robert could not help but notice that his father was attentive and intrigued, but did not seem to be totally surprised. Once he finished the rendition, Mr. James asked his son how he interpreted the situation.

Robert immediately relayed several scenarios to his father. The first being some type of black military operation that went awry, due to this occurring close to Fort Pulaski. This sounded like the most probable explanation but would not explain the Texas Rangers being involved. The second scenario gave way to a possible medical escort, but this also did not make total sense due to the apparent Special Operations team that arrived in helicopters when he was leaving.

When Robert concluded he was expecting some type of sensible or plausible answer from his father, but neither occurred.

"It's 0658 hours, Son. Get your butt to bed."

This was not the response Robert was expecting from his dad.

He knows something!

In two minutes, the morning news would be on. Robert knew that due to the enormity of the accident, along with the involved deaths, the news would be all over this story.

"Dad, let's catch the news then I will get some rest."

Mr. James then made his way to the television and turned it on, and just in time.

"Now for breaking news." The reporter began to convey.

What Robert heard next instantly caused his blood pressure to soar.

The Devil's Elbow Project

"Interstate 44, near the Roubidoux River, was closed for several hours early this morning, due to a small fuel delivery truck overturning and bursting into flames, killing the driver and passengers in another vehicle that it struck. Deer crossing the roadway were blamed for causing the accident. Hazmat teams from Fort Pulaski were called to the scene to contain the blaze and supervise cleanup efforts. Names of the deceased are not being released at this time pending the notification to the next of kin."

"BULL CRAP!" Robert could not believe what he had just heard.

"There is more to this story, Robert, now tell me everything."

Purposely, Robert had neglected to tell his father about the Texas Ranger implying to him to keep this all quiet. He did not want his father to know that he had broken the request of secrecy from his professional brethren from Texas.

"Tomorrow, we will introduce Ms. Paige to your sister and let her babysit for a while. You and I are taking a little canoe trip down the Piney River. I have something of interest to show you. Now, will you let me get some sleep?"

"Certainly will dad, goodnight."

Robert could tell from his father's last words that this day would indeed be one of interest.

As Robert made his way into the bedroom it was a relief to see that Paige was still asleep, due to his state of total exhaustion. Robert was a rookie to fatherhood and knew there were many things ahead to learn. It seemed like the small stuff outweighed the large. There were so many things; food, changing diapers, clothes and bathing, to be learned. This would come in time but what Robert knew for sure was his life would totally change. Hanging out at bars and expanding the pages in his little black book was now in the past.

And dating, what woman would want a single man with a small child?

Many thoughts of how his life would soon be adjusting to accommodate his daughter were now consuming Robert, but one thought was foremost on his mind, and to the point it was interfering with the need for sleep. Robert realized he would have to tell Special Agent Michaels about his situation. The thought of this elevated his anxiety level, due to the potential consequences. The remote thought of being removed from the JDLST and being transferred back to the Springdale Police Department was not what he had mapped out for his career. The JDLST had given Robert the opportunity to expand his law enforcement knowledge, along with sharpening and expanding his skills. Returning to Springdale under these circumstances would be embarrassing; kicked out of a Federal Task Force; Robert could not bear the thought. The last scenario was one Robert did not want to think about. The harsh reality was that he could also be fired from the Springdale Police Department; therefore, losing a professional career that he loved.

Robert had made his decision, it was time to call Special Agent Michaels and convey the news to him. This would alleviate the pain of seeing the disappointment on his boss's face, which would certainly result in a scolding. After all that he had been through over the past twelve hours, the telephone would be the simple way out of this situation.

Slowly and reluctantly, Robert dialed the telephone number of Special Agent Michaels. He held each button down to the point it sounded like an ill-fated tune being played. Even a fraction of a second was good at this point, in order to delay the inevitable. The tune had now ended and a ringing could be heard through the receiver.

"Special Agent Michaels speaking."

"Hey bossman, this is Robert."

"Rookie, you have not even been gone for twenty-four hours and already calling the office. Your two weeks off is to be a vacation, Robert, you know, relaxing and forgetting about the office! I'm glad you called, though. I guess your father informed you of the information we received regarding Gene King putting out a possible murder contract on you?"

Robert now had a diversion, as he began to tell his boss about the shooting incident in Oklahoma. Agent Michaels' voice soon changed, going from small talk to business in an instant.

"Robert, I know this may be somewhat difficult at this point but try to enjoy your vacation as much as possible. We will get the ball rolling on our end. If these guys want to screw with my cops, then we will definitely give them the attention they need . . . . Robert, what was that?"

Paige was now awake and was getting her father's attention by slightly crying, since he was totally involved in a telephone conversation and ignoring her. Opportunity was now knocking on Robert's door but he could not muster the courage to disclose the fact to the bossman that he was a new father.

"Just the television, Sir, apparently my father is up and watching the news. Please let me know if you find out who those scumbags were that shot at me. Goodbye, Sir."

As the phone went dead, Robert felt like a reprieve had just been granted. Another day of being a Fed, or just the opportunity of keeping a badge, was his. As the young cop lay down on the bed, his daughter soon reminded him that sleep would be an elusive privilege today. Over the past twelve hours, several massive adrenalin dumps had taken their toll on Robert. He could recall a portion of training in the police academy where the instructor gave an analogy of this type of situation, where one could have the strength of Samson when that intense situation came about and the adrenalin was flowing through you veins. Afterwards, a person would then feel like Sampson with a haircut, a weakened soul. Robert did not have an ounce of energy left but Paige was demanding attention and food.

Welcome to fatherhood, Pal!

Mr. James sat silently on the couch, listening with a slight smile to the newly formed father-daughter relationship coming from his son's bedroom. The thoughts of Robert entering another phase in maturity, along with past memories of raising four children alone, now consumed him. Seeing his son staggering toward the kitchen with eyes drooping, assured Mr. James that his granddaughter was already training her father well. He knew that numerous trials and tribulations were in Robert's immediate future, but for now, all was well. His son and granddaughter were under his roof, a safe haven for both.

A few hours nap was all that Robert could squeeze in after Paige's morning feeding and play time. It did not take long for Mr. James to notify the family that a significant event had occurred and they needed to come to his house, and ASAP. Robert's sister had chosen to live in Springdale after graduating from college and marrying a local, successful businessman, which allowed her to be a full-time mother and housewife. Therefore, without a doubt she would be the first to arrive and meet baby Paige. Knowing his daughter would be bursting through the front door momentarily, Mr. James rousted Robert from his mid-morning nap so he could prepare for her arrival.

As anticipated, Robert's sister was at the front door before he was able to fully awake. The introduction of Paige was joyful, and followed with a few comments regarding the sister's surprise that this had not happened to her playboy brother before now. Robert's sister had three children of her own but becoming an aunt was totally consuming her.

"Your eyes look like they are about to bleed, so get some rest Bro; Big Sis is here to rescue you, again!"

A verbal reply was not given but seeing Robert smile as he staggered toward the bedroom reflected his appreciation. For the first time since taking possession of his young daughter, Robert welcomed the alone time he was about to get. With Paige in the arms of his sister and under the roof of his father, this new father soon fell into a deep sleep.

Chapter 7

"Rise and shine, Son. You and I have some business to take care of."

Robert soon realized that he had slept for fifteen hours, a feat not experienced since his partying days at college. When he began looking for his daughter, Mr. James informed Robert that Paige would be spending the day at his sister's house, meeting her new cousins and uncle. He was also informed that his sister would be watching Paige until they finished their little outing, returning later that day.

"We are hitting the Piney River in a canoe, so dress appropriately, it will be a little chilly out there, Son."

Robert was mystified about his father's intentions. It was mid-October and not exactly the weather conducive for taking a float trip down a river. Robert had learned to trust his father, despite this being a mysterious trip. Obviously, there was something of importance lying in wait.

Mr. James was outside loading an old pickup truck that he kept around just for hunting and fishing purposes. Unlike Robert, his theory was that a pickup's sole purpose was for work and outdoor sports, and a car for luxury and pleasure. Mr. James also demanded the same superior performance from his car as from the commercial jets he flew, so a Lincoln was his car of choice. This was definitely not the vehicle for taking on outdoor excursions, so an old, four-wheel drive pickup was kept around for such occasions.

Robert then noticed the cargo his father was loading, fishing poles, binoculars and a camera.

"Fishing? Isn't it a little chilly for that, Dad?"

"Just trust me and get in."

The two men began their journey toward the Piney River, which flowed through and around Fort Pulaski. It did not require an analytical mind to detect this trip had some significance to the accident Robert had witnessed involving the Texas State Police officers. The fact that his father was taking such an interest in this incident began to intrigue Robert. Something was there for his father but Robert could not figure out what. When Robert would ask his father questions in an attempt to figure out why he was so interested in this incident, Mr. James would quickly divert the conversation to one of fatherhood and being a single parent. Yet, another clue for Robert that something was up with his father.

Their journey led them down a gravel road to a small, riverside business. The sign read, "Big Dave's Camping and Canoeing." The property consisted of a well-kept older, rock house, with a manicured lawn. Also on the property were about a dozen small cottages, each meticulously kept. This was not the usual camping ground seen in the Ozarks. Near the river, canoes were stacked on several transport trailers, signifying that winter was soon to come and the river tourist season had ended. As their truck rolled to a stop, a gentleman exited one of the cottages that was being used as an office.

"How can I help you boys?"

Mr. James replied by advising they were there to rent a canoe and float the river. The man, identified only as Big Dave, took a quick glance into the back of Mr. James' pickup and immediately informed him that bass season was now over, as he motioned toward the fishing gear. Mr. James responded by informing Big Dave that they were there for the catfish, not bass. This made the resort owner even more curious since most outdoorsmen knew that catfish usually did not bite during cold weather. Being a businessman who depends on the tourist trade, Big Dave did not reply. By looking around, this man knew how to run a business and fulfill his clients' needs. Big Dave was also able to sense when he was being lied to. He then became even more curious and started asking Mr. James a series of questions. Upon discovering the common ground of both men being retired military, along with the fact that Mr. James was a commercial pilot, Big Dave seemed pacified.

Sensing that very little fishing was actually going to take place, the offer was made to replace the canoe with a small, flat bottom riverboat that was equipped with a motor. This seemed to please Mr. James even more, knowing that significant travel time would be alleviated. After a three-hour trip was agreed upon, Mr. James handed the man forty dollars in exchange for the padlock keys for the boat's security chain.

The transfer of gear and fishing equipment from the truck to the boat took only a few minutes. Even though Robert was uncertain of their destination, the anticipation was killing him. Therefore, it did not take long for the equipment to be transferred from the truck to the canoe. As Big Dave shoved the boat from the bank, the typical words of luck and encouragement for these fishermen were not spoken. The look on Big Dave's face reflected a mixture of skepticism and curiosity toward the boat's inhabitants.

It had been years since Robert had been on the Big Piney River. The river's clear and cold water reminded both men that a careful navigation of these waters was a necessity. The Big Piney would wind its way though many of the Ozark hills, reflecting the beauty of mother nature during the fall season. Large oak and sycamore trees lined the banks, shedding their leaves into the mirror-like reflective waters. Both men disliked the fact the boat's motor had to be used to expedite the trip. Despite all that had occurred in Robert's life over the past forty-eight hours, the serenity and beauty surrounding them seemed to make most thoughts elude him momentarily. The boat began making its way north from the launch site in an expedient manner. It was apparent that Mr. James was a man on a mission, knowing exactly where he was going.

Big Dave's was located on a portion of the river located just south of the small township named Devil's Elbow. This small township was named during the early 1900's, when the Big Piney

River was being used as a logging route, supplying transport for logs through the Ozark Hills. At this point in time few roads had been built and those were impassable for semi-trucks; therefore, the Piney River was the most efficient way of transporting logs to trains waiting at nearby towns.

"Dad, I have always wondered, why the heck did they name this town Devil's Elbow?" asked Robert.

"Good question. To the best of my knowledge here is the correct answer".

Mr. James broke into a story about how the Big Piney had been far more than just a lazy, little river flowing through the Ozark hills. During the logging days around the turn of the century, the Big Piney was a very dangerous waterway for the loggers, due to the large amount of curves and shallow fords in the river. At the location where the Devil's Elbow Township is located, a bend in the river had a huge boulder in the exact middle and was the cause of many injuries and deaths for the men navigating the logs downstream. Often logs would jam, requiring men to walk on top of these floating hazards to manually force them apart. This procedure would frequently turn tragic, resulting in a multitude of injuries and deaths.

"Rumor has it, Son that at times during the night people have witnessed dark silhouette figures walking the river banks, carrying their logging poles." Mr. James snickered as he spoke these words.

"Well, Dad, I would rather deal with ghosts than some of the demons I have been putting in jail lately." A somber smile and nodding of the head reflected that Mr. James agreed with his son.

"Are you going to tell me where the heck we are going?" asked Robert.

"Just keep your eyes on the river, Robert, and look out for boulders. I don't want anyone seeing our silhouettes walking these banks someday."

It was obvious to Robert that his father was familiar with this river, due to the navigation skills he was demonstrating. The humming of the boat's motor began to decrease as Mr. James proceeded toward the riverbank.

"What's up, Dad?"

"It's time for a heart-to-heart talk, Robert. There are some things about this family's past that you need to know. I never thought we would be having this conversation but due to the circumstances at hand, it's time. I am going to tell you a story, which contains a lot of personal information but also, a lot of business. You are a federal agent with a top-secret security clearance and as you know, I possessed the same while in the military. So, let's look at this conversation as an operational briefing. This has always been "need-to-know" information, so now you need to know."

"Robert, first of all there are a few things about your parent's backgrounds that you should know. Like for instance, some things about your mother."

Mr. James now had his son's complete attention.

Robert had fond but limited memories of his mother that were accompanied by a few feelings of anger. Robert loved his mom but cancer had taken her from the family at an early age. The typical thoughts of a "Ward and June Cleaver" household possessed a majority of Robert's memories, but the way his mother chose to depart her life was still upsetting to Robert. The fact that his mom elected to remove herself from the family shortly before death seemed uncalled for. Robert felt that his mother should have spent her remaining days with the family, not in some medical facility located five-hundred miles from them; no matter how sickly she was. Her decision to have a closed casket funeral just added to his feelings of alienation by his mother.

"Robert, do I have your attention?" asked Mr. James after seeing his son's mind adrift.

"Sorry, Dad, proceed."

"Did you ever wonder how your mother and I ended up in Springdale, especially with me being an Air Force Pilot?"

"No, Sir, not really."

"I am sure the memories of your mom were limited, so let me fill you in on a few details. Your mother was an exceptionally intelligent person, with numerous college degrees. We met one year in Belgium, while I was attending a meeting at NATO. Your mom was part of a U.S. envoy to Europe; and a stopover at NATO was just a sightseeing tour for them. Knowing that NATO does not specialize in entertainment; I assumed she was part of some type of essential government group, but initially did not know which one. To cut through the boring details of courting, I only learned of her job shortly before we were married. Your mother was a physician and government scientist. Apparently, after the fall of Nazi Germany numerous books and medical manuals were seized by U.S. soldiers that detailed a lot of genetic research that Germany was conducting under Hitler's rule. Without getting technical beyond my knowledge, it appeared as if Hitler's scientists were close to perfecting genetic cloning, which was a major goal for Hitler in his pursuit to create the perfect human race. After the war, the United States government decided to secretly continue this research, mostly for the purpose of medical healing and researching fertility issues. Son, your mother was one of the research managers of a project called the Devil's Elbow Project."

Mr. James hesitated for a few moments allowing Robert to absorb his words.

"Here, in Devil's Elbow, but why?"

"Yes, here in Devil's Elbow. The project needed a secluded and remote area, and one that was close to needed resources. After nearby Fort Pulaski was built, it rapidly became a vital military installation that could supply resources and protection for a project such as this one. Devil's Elbow was far enough away from Springdale that it was unlikely for your mom to be seen by friends or neighbors. This would also allow me access to airports at both Fort Pulaski and Springdale, so I could continue flying."

"But why so secretive? It sounds like a pretty worthy project, sort of like our DNA research today."

"Robert, could you imagine the public finding out about the Devil's Elbow Project so close to the end of World War II? Don't forget the cloning aspects, too. People would not have understood or tolerated that type of research being conducted. The discovery of this project would have resulted in some serious political fallout."

"Point made. So, Dad, here we are on the Big Piney River, close to a little town called Devil's Elbow. I think I know where you are going with this."

"You would make a good detective, Robert," replied Mr. James in a light-hearted manner.

"Now, just around that bend is an older building on the riverbank, which is nestled between a small road and a bluff. This is just a scouting mission, so we need to remain as inconspicuous as possible. Now, grab a fishing pole and let's play the part. I am not for sure this place is still in business; I am just playing a hunch. Here, take this pen and write down any license plates that you see and I will do the same. Remember, we need to be EXTREMELY INCONSPICUOUS! I have a strong gut feeling this place may have something to do with the accident you witnessed on Interstate 44 the other night."

"Got it, Dad, let's go."

Once again, the whining of the boat's motor was echoing though the river valley as Robert and his father make their way up the river. As they rounded a bend in the river, Mr. James pointed to a large boulder mid-stream, with water rushing around both sides. To both men, folklore had just become reality. Without a doubt, this was the famous, demonic rock that had taken toll on so many men's lives. The famous rock; the Devil's rock, that had been the focus of so many stories, and after which the township had been named. Upon looking closely, one could see where some daring individual had been able to make their way to the rock and embed a painting of a demonic pitch-fork on it. They were indeed at the Devil's Elbow.

Coming into sight just beyond the elbow was a building resembling the one previously described by his father. It was difficult for Robert to maintain a casual demeanor after what his father had told him. Plus, this place could possibly hold some answers to the bizarre occurrence he witnessed on the interstate, making remaining cool even more difficult.

As the boat drew closer, Robert could see an older building with a basement, sitting next to the river. On the other side was a small parking lot, with a gravel road running next to it. Just beyond that was a large bluff carved into the side of a mountain.

Exactly how I remember it, thought Mr. James.

Robert then cast his fishing pole in an attempt to use this decoy to shed any suspicion in case they were being watched. Each cast he was making was directly toward the building. It took his father calling attention to this to make Robert realize what he was doing.

Now within a rocks throw of the building, Robert and his father had full view of the east side of the structure. A sign reflecting the catchy name of, "The Devil's Grill" reflected this place was now a restaurant and bar. Several motorcycles, cars and pickup trucks sat in front of the business, with the smell of Bar-B-Q and beer coming from the patio adjoining it.

"Nothing very unusual looking about this place, Dad, and this certainly does not look like some top-security lab facility."

"The main entry for the lab is through the basement, Robert. Once inside, there is a long hallway that leads to a secure lab inside a cave, which is housed in that bluff. As you probably know, Missouri is known as the Cave State and a very large one exists inside that bluff. Once the government secured this place, they sealed off the main entrance to the cave and made it look natural, like the rest of the rock. Once inside, it is a huge facility. The employees were bused in from the army base, so there weren't many cars parked around here. Not a bad concept, I have to admit."

Mr. James then pointed toward the west side of the building, which appeared to be disconnected from the restaurant. Taking on the appearance of a house and not a business, this side was different.

What the Hell!

Robert now saw what his father had just noticed. Parked next to the west side of the building were two black colored, SUV's. One of these vehicles looked exactly like the one Robert had seen at the accident scene. As the license plates came into view, it was noted that both also had Texas license plates. Robert's hand began to tremble from excitement as he started writing down the license numbers.

"These have got to be the same vehicles, Dad," whispered Robert to his father.

At this time a door leading from the basement of the west section opened and two men exited; proceeding toward one of the SUV's. Robert's heart began to beat almost aloud as he recognized one of the men as the unidentified, Federal official who arrived on scene after the accident he witnessed. This was definitely the individual who ordered him to keep the wreck confidential. The other was a stocky built man with a shaved head, wearing biker attire. A large tattoo on the right arm reflected he was once a member of the Marine Corps, and now most likely worked as a security strong-arm for what laid behind the basement door. The two men then entered the vehicle and began to back from their parking place, but suddenly came to a halt. It was apparent the tables had been turned and Robert and his father were now the ones being watched. Realizing this, Mr. James switched on the boat's motor and began slowing working his way up-stream. This action seemed to satisfy the men's curiosity in the SUV; therefore, continuing to reverse their vehicle to leave the location.

As the boat slowly crept downstream, Robert glanced back at the basement door the men had exited from. A beam of sunlight had found its way to a small door window and a reflection immediately caught Robert's eye. It only took a second for him to identify the object that was reflecting the sun's rays. A riflescope or binoculars were the two obvious sources. No matter which of the two was correct, Robert's stomach began to churn. Being at the receiving end of either was not Robert's desired choice, he preferred to be the possessor.

"Hey dad, we are being watched and believe me, you don't want to know how."

"Rifle or Binoc's, Son?" The response validated to Robert that his father was a prior warrior.

"Not for sure but let's hope it's your second choice, Dad. Who are those guys?"

"Spooks, my Son, the government's guardian angels!"

CHAPTER 8

The sun was beginning to set as Robert and his father passed the Springdale city limits sign. An enlightening but equally confusing day it had been—Robert was on information overload. A cover-up regarding a car wreck leaving police officers dead, the new information about his mother being a secret government scientist, along with the findings about the Devil's Elbow; were about all a person could handle in one day. A conversation loaded with a million questions dominated the entire seventy-mile ride home. Robert was still in awe by the information about his parents. His life-long thoughts about mom and dad being the Cleaver family type had suddenly dissolved. Instead, his parents had suddenly evolved into a cloak-and-dagger family, which made Robert question the reality of his childhood.

As the pickup was pulling into the driveway, Robert was at wits-end to enter the house. First, Paige needed some fatherly attention and second, vehicle registration checks had to be run on two Texas license plates to see who the owners were.

As the new father entered the house, he immediately caught sight of his sister holding Paige. The young baby appeared to be excited to see her father, so getting Robert's undivided attention was not a difficult task. The next few hours consisted of Robert's sister and father asking questions about Texas, the JDLST and Paige. As usual, Robert was quick to respond, but his family reminded him of the responsibilities of fatherhood and the obstacles ahead for this single parent. As Robert sat there and watched Paige fall asleep, concerns about raising a daughter

The Devil's Elbow Project

as a single, federal drug agent weighed heavy upon his heart and mind. Robert had always believed that he could hurdle most obstacles in life but in front of him lay one that would be difficult.

With Paige now asleep, the anxiety of running registration checks on the two SUV's seen at The Devil's Grill was almost unbearable. This task could easily be accomplished by calling the JDLST but if Agent Michaels discovered that he was working while on vacation, his boss's wrath would be upon him.

"Dad, can you keep an eye on Paige? I have an errand to run."

"Should I ask where are you going?"

"Springdale Police Department. I have got to find out who owns those SUV's."

"In that case I would be glad to. I have to admit that curiosity is eating at me, too. Be gone, my son!"

It had been quite some time since Robert set foot in the Springdale police station. Many great memories and friends were there, but this would not be a night for socializing. Robert needed to know about the vehicles at The Devil's Grill and wanted to know ASAP. Patience is usually not a virtue for a cop. Robert was no exception, especially regarding the mystery at hand.

Robert searched through his wallet and located his old Springdale Police Department entry card for the back door. Once it opened, the cop-shop odor and visuals of this unchanged station began immediately bringing back old memories. It was now after hours, so just a few night-shift detectives were on duty. Captain Hill and his old comrades were nowhere to be found. Robert wandered around the detective division long enough to locate his old cubical and desk. He pulled out the chair that once belonged to him. Once seated, a few territorial feelings began to emerge, wondering who inhabited his old office and if his shoes were being properly filled. Maybe a short emotion of arrogance, but one Robert felt was deserved. After savoring a few moments of nostalgia, Robert reached out and turned on his old desktop computer. After taking the usual five minutes to warm up and load, the computer was finally ready for use.

Now let me see if I can remember how to log on to you, Sweetheart.

His old log-on name and password worked. Robert would soon retrieve the information he needed.

"TCIC, here I come!" Robert mumbled as he entered into Texas Department of Public Safety information system. Robert then began to enter the information about the vehicles into the computer.

10-28 on Texas LRP-642 . . . . No return on file.

"OK . . . ."

10-28—on Texas MQB-411 . . . . No return on file.

"Damn-it, this can't be! How can there not be a registered owner for either of these vehicles!"

Robert's screams of dismay caught the attention of a night-shift detective who was having lunch in the break room. The detective rushed back to his office to find Robert pacing in anger. Robert remembered his fellow officer as one he worked patrol with several years ago. The men then engaged in a few minutes of a reuniting conversation, which was soon interrupted by a new message flashing on the computer screen.

"Man, I have never seen that before."

"Neither have I," replied Robert, as he stared at the computer screen.

The screen reflecting "no return on file" had been replaced with the following:

"TCIC User, contact Agent Ramos at the FBI, phone 800-998-9901."

Without hesitation, Robert followed the orders given on the computer screen and dialed the number.

Few words could be heard other than Robert identifying himself after the conversation began, and giving a false explanation to the reason behind the vehicle registration checks. Several "no sirs" and "yes sirs" were said by Robert, signifying this was a one-way conversation. After a few minutes, Robert hung up the telephone while a loud voice could still be heard over the receiver.

"I refuse to take a butt-chewing from some FBI prick that I don't know!"

"What did he say, Robert?" asked the inquisitive Springdale detective seated next to him.

"It's a long story, my friend, and I need to run. I will have to fill you in some other time. It was good seeing you, again. Tell the gang I stopped by and said hello."

Robert then slid out the back door of Springdale PD as inconspicuously as he entered.

Feeling his father could understand and that Paige was down for the night, Robert placed a quick call to his father, advising he was going back to Devil's Elbow. Mr. James knew that any attempts to stop his son from his mission were futile. After Mr. James conveyed his words of caution, Robert ended the conversation.

The seventy-mile trip back to Devil's Elbow went quickly. Robert was compelled to take a second look at The Devil's Grill, hoping the dark, night skies would allow him some additional cover to evaluate the facility.

Upon arriving at his destination, a new kind of atmosphere had taken over. Rock and Roll music from the 60's and 70's could be heard coming from the beer garden area. Loud voices, Harley Davidson motorcycles and the smell of cigarettes and beer filled the night air. The bar and grill was certainly a great cover-up for what was going on next door. It was assumed that no one, including the owner of The Devil's Grill, knew what was occurring right under his or her feet.

The heavy workload of the JDLST, along with the new arrival of his daughter, had drastically reversed the direction of Robert's social life. The many nights of partying and bedding females had subsided dramatically over the past twelve months, but the notion of mixing a little business with pleasure tonight was crossing Robert's mind. Once inside The Devil's Grill, it did not take long for Robert to conclude this was primarily a biker-bar. To the contrary, this was not the type of biker bar he had experienced in Texas, which consisted of Bandera outlaw gang members. Instead, the place was inhabited by a mixture of locals who enjoyed the sport of riding their two-wheeled, freedom machines. What would have at one time been an uncomfortable situation was now just the opposite. The training and introduction to biker bars by Investigator Ronnie Bays, while working the Bandera's biker gangs, allowed Robert to feel comfortable with this crowd. Also, having a badge and a 40-caliber auto pistol tucked in the waistband of his jeans certainly did not hurt the cause. One thing for certain, making the mistake of ordering a wine cooler in a biker bar would not happen tonight, or ever again. The memory of a "close encounter with death" after making such an error in a Ft. Worth biker bar was still fresh on Robert's mind. Therefore, beer or tequila would be the drink of choice tonight.

Robert found a place at the bar and watched for several minutes as the bartender serviced everyone around except for him, the new face in the bar. A room full of locals and bikers was not a place for an out-of-town city boy to cause trouble, but Robert had to find some way to get in with these people so he could ask a few questions. Several additional attempts to flag down a drink failed, so a plan had to be devised. Sitting a few seats down from Robert at the bar was one of the local bikers, who looked as if he lost his sense of humor at birth. It was also apparent this man had some respect among the locals, so Robert made his move:

"Bartender, give my buddy down there a wine cooler and I will do a shot of tequila with him."

The bar went quiet, knowing the new city boy had most likely overloaded his mouth. The biker that Robert was pointing to remained seated but pulled back his vest, purposely exposing a large knife.

"Well, city boy, I think I want two shots of tequila instead and you are buying."

"Done deal; bring my new friend two shots of tequila," replied Robert.

Robert's little icebreaker had accomplished its task. As quickly as he was viewed as an outsider, Robert had become part of the crowd. Robert knew these folks now viewed him as a man with big stones, or one with a severe mental condition; but, whichever the case his little ploy had worked. For several hours Robert worked the group, buying drinks and asking questions. Despite his inquiries, no one had the answers he wanted to hear. Robert had to be cautious with how he went about his questioning as not to bring suspicion upon himself. These people were all locals and very cliquish, and could quickly turn on him. There were no JDLST team members around or even in the same state, to run to his aid. Robert was running solo tonight in a place not his own, therefore; caution had to be exercised.

It was almost midnight when Robert concluded he was not making any headway in the bar. A walk around the outside of the building was just about as fruitless. A quick pass by the basement door revealed a covering over the window, along with the building being completely blacked out. There was no clue anywhere to be found. Robert's instinct's told him that even though the basement appeared to be vacant; at least two deadly weapons lurked just inside the door, a security agent accompanied by his weapon of choice. It was time to leave.

As Robert was walking back to his truck, he noticed a female whom he met inside the bar earlier. With a beer in one hand and a cigarette in the other, she was making herself very comfortable while leaning against Robert's vehicle.

"Where you running off to, City Boy?"

It was now past the midnight hour and a half drunk woman was leaning against the truck, awaiting his arrival. It did not take a rocket scientist to guess her intentions. After a few minutes of conversation, Robert concluded she could definitely be another number in his little black book. An invitation for a nightcap at her home was an explicit indicator she would be Robert's next entry.

"How about some breakfast first? Where can we grab a quick bite before we head off to your place?"

"There is a greasy spoon restaurant called Al's, up on I-44 near the Fort Pulaski exit. They serve all night but I can't guarantee we will survive the food to tell about it tomorrow. I will meet you there in about fifteen minutes, Mr. Robert." With a seductive smile, the female faded into the parking lot.

Robert began his voyage to the restaurant but noticed a Champs Truck Stop while in route. He was now beginning to regret the thought of having this little tramp seduce him, not knowing what she could be bringing to the table. A deadly disease called AIDS was out there and taking no prisoners, killing almost all who contracted it. This disease was prevalent among the drug world and it was no secret that biker bars have drug abusers who frequented them; therefore, Robert had begun to rethink his social life. Being the solo parent of a new child, precautions had to be taken. Dinner tonight would be at Champs Truck Stop, and alone.

Despite the after-midnight hour, Champs parking lot was lined with vehicles. Interstate traffic, truckers and cars piloted by drunks, were the lot's inhabitants. It was a sure bet the restaurant would be filed with boisterous people and cigarette smoke, both of which both were despised by Robert. Despite these unwanted diversions, his hunger pangs were much stronger than the need to evade the smoke and drunks. Robert was able to find a vacant parking spot away from the others, in hope of escaping any sideswipes or door-ding damage to his truck.

His assumptions were correct; the restaurant was filled with smoke and loud voices. Robert managed to locate a remote, corner table away from a majority of the customers. This procedure was basic police training and used by law enforcement officers throughout the U.S. If a person wanted to find a cop while in restaurant, their best guess would be the person seated in a far corner of the business. This would allow the cop to have a full view of most customers in the restaurant, along with those both entering and exiting. Most cops would utilize this training, both on and off the clock.

Immediately after Robert was seated, he began a scan of the crowd, summing them up and guessing who could be potential trouble. Along with the truckers and few travelers, the late night hours had a tendency to bring out the people that cops profile as "creatures of the night." These were individuals that wore symbolic clothing, displayed numerous tattoos and body jewelry, and associated only with similar creatures. Despite their visual oddities, this group was usually passive and non-threatening. The loud drunks posed the largest threat for problems, so Robert tried to seclude himself from them. Even though Robert displayed nothing representative of being a cop, if a potential violent situation erupted, he would be obligated to intervene. This was the last thing that Robert wanted this evening.

Despite his tactical seating position in the restaurant, Robert had to forego his practice of trying to sit where he could also see his truck in the parking lot. If someone would break into his pickup, a reward of several firearms would be theirs. Therefore, he had to forfeit having sight of his vehicle for a remote table in the restaurant. Tonight this would be a tactical error for Robert.

When entering the parking lot, Robert was too concerned about the late night drunks to notice that a vehicle was following him. A seat by the window may have revealed that he had been followed from The Devil's Grill. Unfortunately, the persistent female at the bar was not one of the occupants of the pursuing car.

One good thing about these late night greasy spoons is their fast service, purposely done in an attempt to feed this undesirable crowd as quickly as possible, so they can pay and go. Lingerers from this group were certainly not wanted.

After working several years on the midnight patrol shift, Robert had his favorite meal for restaurants such as this. Biscuits, gravy and scrambled eggs, an almost sure bet for evading food poisoning. After placing his order, Robert continued scanning the crowd. Nothing appeared to be really unusual considering this type of crowd, with the exception of a lone individual who walked in shortly after him. This man seemed to be either a loner or a cop, but by using his experience and instincts, Robert soon ruled out the police officer scenario. The man was tall, lean and muscular built, and wore the face of a person whose life had been anything but easy. A few facial scars, a boxer's ear, along with possessing several teeth that were apparently false, suggesting this man had seen his share of hand-to-hand combat—most likely, street fights. Being around a military town meant one would see many individuals such as him; but, the man's appearance was not what was bothering Robert. Instead, Robert felt that he was the one being watched, constantly on the radar of this ruff-neck. Despite his attempts to be inconspicuous, the man's stares were detected numerous times by Robert.

Probably just a loner, definitely not a cop. Robert tried to convince himself.

It did not take long to wolf down his biscuits, eggs and gravy. As Robert ate his observer quietly sat, only sipping a cup of coffee. This too, made Robert feel uneasy but this practice was not extremely out of the ordinary for a late night restaurant. As Robert bent down to take his last bite, the stranger threw a few bills on his table and walked out.

Yep, just a lonely traveler.

Five minutes after his suspicious observer left the restaurant; Robert had paid his bill and began his journey toward his pickup truck.

Go figure, Robert thought when he saw an old junker parked next to his truck.

Half the parking lot is empty but some ass has to park his piece of crap next to my new, $18,000 pickup truck. This infuriated him, but was not the first time Robert had seen this done. This was someone wishing to screw with him just because he chose to protect his vehicle from nicks and door-dings. Despite the newly acquired bullet holes, Robert still felt the need to protect his vehicle from further damage.

"Remote entry, where have you been all my life?" Robert chuckled lightly.

With his remote in hand, Robert was about to hit the entry button when something caught his attention. The odd stranger from the restaurant was standing between two vehicles, with his hand extended in Robert's direction.

"What do . . . ."

Robert was unable to end his sentence. A horrific flash blinded him, and a massive ringing in his ears was totally disabling. Robert was completely consumed by this feeling; he was passing out . . . .

"Pulaski County to Robertsville Metro Units 201 and 202; be in route to a vehicle explosion at Champs Truck Stop. Numerous reporting parties advising one man down—EMS and fire units in route."

"Unit 201 received."

"Show 202 in en route also, Pulaski County."

"Pulaski County to 201 and 202. We just received another report that the injured party is a law enforcement officer. I will have a supervisor and the State Police en route."

"10-4, Pulaski County. Show both units in route Code 3!

The wailing of sirens was the first thing heard as Robert began to recover from his state of unconsciousness. His blurred vision was becoming clearer as he noticed a small crowd hovering above him. Before Robert could ask any questions, pain rapidly consumed him, and once again things were becoming fuzzy. The ringing in his ears soon became unbearable and once again, Robert was unconscious.

The odors of burning metal and engine fluid were detected as the EMT's exited their ambulance. Being first on scene, there was no guesswork as to where the victim laid. As in most incident scenes, the crowd had surrounded the body of the unconscious victim who had been pulled away from the burning car. A quick examination of the victim revealed that scrap metal had penetrated him, along with a small amount of blood oozing from one ear—a sure sign of brain or ear-drum injury.

Numerous Metro, County and State Police units began to fill the parking lot. For an area fairly small in population, they had an abundance of law enforcement officers. This was due to the county housing a large military base within its boundaries, and having to deal with the problems that a base attracts.

Emergency medical technicians had just placed the injured man on a gurney as he started to regain consciousness.

"Son, can you tell us your name?" asked a State Trooper.

To Robert, the man's voice was unclear, mostly just an echo to him. The visual was also blurry but Robert could tell the man was a cop. Robert wanted to respond but could not.

"Son, your name? Well, I'll be . . . .". The State Trooper stopped.

"Robert James, is that you, Son?"

Things were now becoming clearer. Robert was able to distinguish by the uniform that the cop speaking to him was a Missouri State Police Officer. He could also smell smoke from a cigar, a memorable cigar, definitely the calling card of an old friend.

"Sgt. Parks, is that you? What the hell happened?"

"Let's get you to the hospital and then we will talk."

"Sarge, I need a favor." Robert said as he held up a set of keys.

"I have my duty weapon in my truck; can you secure it for me?"

"Done deal, Rookie." Sgt. Parks then took the keys from Robert.

"Now, no more talking—get your ass to the hospital."

Robert could only partially hear the words of Sgt. Parks but was relieved to see a familiar face. He also knew that his law enforcement brother would be doing more than just securing his weapon for him. A friend was indeed a good thing to have in such a situation.

The pain had intensified, alleviating the desire for a chat session with an old friend. The ringing in his right ear was excruciating and would not go away. Robert laid back down on the gurney as the EMT's rolled him to the awaiting ambulance. Before the doors closed, Robert looked back at the incident scene, which revealed a sedan that was completely demolished and afire, along with his slightly damaged pickup truck sitting next to it.

The pain was now the only thing on Robert's mind. He felt it oddly funny that he, a dope cop, was craving drugs at this point. Robert mustered the strength to make a request to the EMT's:

"I need something to kill this pain. Do you have any painkillers in here?"

His request was soon met. The sliding of a syringe into Robert's veins was painless and the much-anticipated results were soon to come. Almost immediately, a slight numbness and mental euphoria began to set in, as the pain started to elude his body. His professional enemy at this moment was his new friend. A contradiction that was not wanted but very much welcomed.

CHAPTER 9

The hustle and bustle of an emergency room had been seen many times by Robert but only once as a patient back when he was a child. By the time Robert had reached the Pulaski County Regional Hospital, he was completely conscious and had begun to survey his body for a damage assessment in the areas shrieking of pain. Several small cuts needing sutures were discovered but he could not find any serious wounds. Robert's right ear was his main complaint. The EMT's had covered it with a patch and wrapped it with gauze. Due to either the bandage or explosion, hearing was very limited in his right ear. The ensuing pain was predictive of his diagnosis—ear damage. Even though injured, Robert considered himself very lucky because things could have been a lot worse. Now was the confusing part, the details of the explosion were beginning to come back.

The stranger in the restaurant and then out in the parking lot, the explosion—sirens and cops....

It soon became evident to Robert the suspicious man he had seen in the restaurant had set off an explosive in the vehicle that was parked next to his. Collateral damage is what he had become, maybe.

Or was I the primary target?

At this point a million thoughts were racing thought Robert James' mind as the door to his room opened. Robert's thoughts and privacy were soon invaded by a nurse who had come to take him down to X-Ray.

"You took a pretty good blow, young man. You are lucky to be in the ER and not in surgery or the Burn Unit right now." Robert only acknowledged with a nod of the head.

"Once we complete your X-Rays, we have a specialist coming in to evaluate your ear. Looks like you may have a damaged ear—drum there, Mr. James."

The wait for the X-Rays gave Robert time for his mind to re-entrench itself into thoughts of the explosion. It soon became obvious that the sedative drugs he had been given were not allowing him the typical ability to flow into "cop mode" and try to figure out what exactly happened. The drugs that were good for pain were becoming mentally frustrating for the young detective.

Another round of thoughts soon set in. He was a father who possibly placed his job and sense of curiosity over the priority of parenthood. Paige had been left in Springdale with his sister, who could have easily just become a step-parent. Paige could have easily ended up a young girl with no mother and a father that was killed during an investigation. Too many times had Robert heard or read about this happening to a fellow comrade in blue. This was a fact of life that was surely unfair to an innocent child. Robert's eyes soon began to tear up.

This will not happen to you Paige, Daddy promises.

As expected, the X-Rays were an in-and-out event. Within ten minutes of the first picture, Robert was back in their emergency room.

"What's the diagnosis, nurse? I need a quick 'fix me up' so I can blow this joint." Robert was beginning to return to a semi-normal state.

"Tonight you were Joe Lucky, not Joe Superman. The doctor will give you a complete diagnosis but I will tell you there is nothing real serious that I can see. The ear would be my main concern, if I were you. You also will need a few stitches but it looks like you will be walking out of here within the next twenty-four hours. The doctor will be in shortly, so just remain patient –pardon my pun. I am leaving you another happy pill in the event your pain increases before the doc gets in here." The nurse then gave a slight smile and wink as she left the room.

Robert barely had a chance to take a breath before the door slightly opened, revealing two uniformed officers.

"Can we come in?"

This was a voice that Robert could never forget. His old buddy, Sgt. Parks, was at the door with another officer.

"Of course, Sarge, come on. Just hose down that cigar before you walk through my door."

"Obviously the blast jarred something loose between the ears, Rookie. I am still Mr. Sarge-Sir, to you!" It was apparent the two men were please to be reunited.

Following Sgt. Parks into Robert's room was another officer, soon identified as Robertsville Chief of Police, Tom Dennis. Both men were very rigid in appearance. There was no doubt by any who came in contact with them that these men were seasoned professionals. Professional by nature, both supported an appearance that few could challenge and none would conquer. This was more than a signature of the job; this was a requirement for commanding other officers and controlling the vices and crimes surrounding a typical military installation.

"Okay, Gentleman, can someone give me an explanation to what just happened?" Robert asked.

"You want to take this one, Tom?" Sgt. Parks then stepped back and signaled to Chief Dennis.

"Simply put, a vehicle parked next to yours exploded and burned. Right now we have no idea who the car belonged to. The license plates were missing, which is not unusual for someone to remove before stealing a car or using it to commit a crime. Regarding the reason for this one, at this stage of the game we cannot be one hundred percent sure but have two theories. The first being that you were just at the wrong place at the wrong time. Since you grew up close to here, it should be no big surprise that it is like the Wild West around this military base. Drugs and prostitution, along with pimp and turf wars, are still prevalent. We do our best to take care of these but total eradication is impossible. Recently, we have been having some turf wars between some organized crime groups out of Kansas City and Chicago. One of the local crime lords has a "strong-arm" import from Eastern European who is one of Hell's hounds.

Right now this man is on the books as a suspect in over twenty homicides alone, and neither of us have the time to list all of the other crimes he has been involved in. Next time we meet I will have a lineup prepared to see if this guy is your man. The second thought is that someone is pissed at Robert James and decided to send a warning shot before the fatal blow."

"Well, I can think of a few of those right now."

"Care to give details?" asked Chief Dennis.

"Soon, Chief Dennis, very soon."

"Chief, let's get out of here and let Robert catch some shut eye. I am sure he would like a little relaxation after an exciting night in your town." A sense of humor was a trait that Sgt. Parks never left behind.

After bidding their farewells, the lawmen exited the room. The spring-loaded door slowly closed behind them giving Robert a room once again filled with silence. The patient then glanced down at the sedative the nurse left behind and focused on the small stature of something that was so powerful. A short battled ensued, weighing the pros and cons of sucking down another dose of something Robert considered being an enemy on the streets. He then decided that tonight, the small pill would be his answer for making the pain go away. Tomorrow, he would tackle the pain in a more practical way.

For them, those addicts, this is how it all starts for some. Tonight Robert had yet received another lesson in life.

Ten to fifteen minutes had possibly passed since Robert had taken his last sedative. It was difficult to estimate exactly how much time had really gone by, due to the loss of actual reality caused by the drug. Once again, the door to Robert's room had opened, with the long awaited physician appearing. The doctor seemed to be in a hurry, possibly coming from and returning to an operating room. Being dressed in scrubs, cap and mask was typical attire coming from the Operating Room but not so much for visiting a patient in the ER. The doctor said nothing more than a simple hello as he approached Robert. In an expeditious manner the doctor reached into his pocket and pulled out a syringe, and rapidly imbedded the needle into Robert's IV line. Robert soon became sluggish and sedate, and had little time to ask the physician any questions before he was given the injection.

"What the heck was that, Doc, another sedative?

In an unexpected response, the doctor walked next to Robert's bed and leaned over, placing his lips next to the detectives' ear.

"You are not wanted here, Detective James, you are . . . NOT . . . WANTED . . . . HERE! Enjoy your trip back to Texas, Cowboy!"

Robert's eyes were becoming heavy once again. All efforts to react, stand or talk were rapidly becoming futile. After losing all faculties, he began to drift off until reaching the point of total sedation.

"Nurse, here is Robert James' chart. As you know, he is a federal agent so the government wants to give the best to their own, so he is being immediately transported back to Dallas. There is a medical evacuation jet waiting at Fort Pulaski's airport. Prepare him for transport, STAT. I gave the young lad a sedative so he is off in slumber land right now."

"Yes, Doctor."

Not a question was asked by the nurse as she barked the doctor's orders to the support staff in the ER. Being close to an Army base, military doctors rotated in and out at an accelerated pace; therefore, personnel rarely questioned a new face. The preparations then began as they readied their patient for the awaiting ambulance. Within minutes, Robert had been loaded into the ambulance and was in route to Fort Pulaski's airport.

Upon arriving, the ambulance was given immediate clearance to enter the tarmac and proceed to a small, government Med-Evac jet. On this evening, Robert James' fear of flying would not be an issue for him. Being totally sedated, not even the humming of the jet engines or the turbulence at thirty-five thousand feet would be noticed by the young detective.

CHAPTER 10

At the JDLST regional office in Dallas, Special Agent Michaels had just arrived. After grabbing his routine cup of coffee, the boss sat reviewing intelligence reports that had been received the previous evening from team members regarding Det. James' case. His team was more than just a group of employees working together; they are a close-knit brotherhood of cops. Therefore, when anyone would mess with one, the entire group would take it personally. Vigilance and persistence were two descriptive words for their efforts.

It's like letting loose a pack of starving wolves in a grocery store, there is no stopping them. Special Agent Michaels smiled as he held the thick stack of reports his men had generated.

As with many men and women in leadership positions, Special Agent Michaels was a creature of habit. The 8:00 news was just minutes away. Armed with a fresh cup of coffee, a cereal bar and the TV remote, he flipped on his television and turned on the Channel 25 news. The first story of the day caught his attention.

> *We have breaking news just in from Arlington. A young woman has survived a brutal attack at the Grand Park Hotel early this morning. We only have limited details at this time, but the battered woman was discovered early this morning after she was able to leave the room she was assaulted in to make her way to help. The victim was taken to Dalworth*

Regional Hospital where she is listed in critical condition. The only additional information the police are giving us at this time is the woman had one massive wound to her neck, and suffers from an immense loss of blood. Our reporters on scene have interviewed numerous individuals who witnessed this horrible incident. According to several of those we spoke to, the woman was near death and kept muttering the words, the Devil's Elbow. Obviously, this poor lady knew she was knocking on death's door. Anonymous sources are identifying the female victim as Angela Tyler, the twenty-five year old daughter of Houston oil tycoon, Samuel Tyler. Tune in to our local news at noon, at which time we will update you on this breaking story.

Special Agent Michaels had heard his first and final news story of the morning. Being a father himself of a female college student, this story was very bothersome. Even though most of his investigators would not yet be out of bed, he felt this was important enough to wake up Blake Waterman. Blake had cultivated many connections with local law enforcement agencies, with Arlington being one of them. This was a case that no federal jurisdiction had yet been established but Special Agent Michaels still wanted to offer the unit's assistance in the matter. He was also familiar with millionaire Sam Tyler, after meeting him at several political and charity fundraisers throughout Texas and Oklahoma. Mr. Tyler was very supportive of law enforcement efforts, especially regarding narcotics trafficking. Houston was listed as a major hub for illegal drugs, arriving by boat and plane, in addition to border smuggling endeavors. To Sam Tyler, this was a black-eye on the city he loved, so he was a generous supporter to all avenues that could alleviate the problem.

Sam and he were also on a first-name basis, and had often engaged in bragging sessions about their children. Another item both men had in common was that each had only one child, a daughter. The difference was the busy schedule of SA Michaels and his wife which kept them from wanting additional children.

This was immensely different from Sam Tyler and his wife, who wanted a large family but fertility issues prevented them from doing so. On many occasions Sam would refer to Angela as their miracle baby. Even though he had never met Angela, Special Agent Michaels felt like he knew her, and was compelled to help.

The call was then placed to Investigator Blake Waterman, at which time orders were given to report ASAP. Blake knew these orders were rarely given, so no questions were asked; he would report immediately. As soon as the call to Waterman ended, SA Michaels' phone rang—Sam Tyler was the caller.

As expected, the call was long and very emotional. Special Agent Michaels felt fortunate that he was alone in the office that morning. Tears rarely flowed from his eyes but today was an exception. To hear the heartbreak of a friend, a pillar of the community and state, was heartbreaking. The girls similar ages, joined by many parental stories over the years, caused him to make this case a priority for his unit, federal jurisdiction or not. One item Agent Michaels could not remove from his mind was how elusive Sam had been on several occasions when asked about Angela being a "miracle baby." No details were ever given, despite the numerous inquiries on the topic. The only answer Sam would ever give was that Angela was a gift from God. Being a religious man himself, Agent Michaels felt that all babies were gifts from God but Sam Tyler's gift appeared to be more complicated than others. Over time it became obvious that Angela was a gift Sam was not willing to discuss details about.

Special Agent Michaels was now restless. A man, a friend and a situation that could happen to any parent, was close at hand.

Some way, somehow, I will find a federal jurisdiction connection to this case.

Minutes later, the JDLST office was growing distant in Special Agent Michaels' rearview mirror. He was becoming somewhat angry at the thoughts racing through his head. His ace detective was five hundred miles away, enjoying some much-deserved time off. To cancel Detective James' vacation would go against the grain of his theory on management.

You work the horse too hard and you are going to cripple it—a motto he promised himself never to forget while in management.

Robert was indeed a workhorse that needed his much deserved vacation, but this might just be an exception. Sam Tyler was a friend who was in need of any and all law enforcement resources to bring justice to his daughter's assailant. Sam and Angela deserved the best from their friend.

Manipulating these new cell phones was a hard task for Special Agent Michaels, especially when driving down the highway in rush-hour traffic. Soon after entering the highway, the agent's Mercury veered swiftly off the roadway, onto the shoulder of the busy road. The burning of his brake pads was surely smelled by several of the vehicles that had been following him. Agent Michaels grabbed for the bag containing the phone, pulled it out and began dialing the number of the vacationing detective. The voice on the receiving end was not the one he wanted to hear.

"You have reached the cell phone of Detective Robert James. Please leave a number and I will call you back as soon as possible."

Where are you, Son? Agent Michaels could not muster the courage to leave a message for Robert, as he pushed the off button. Little did he know that Robert had already returned to Texas.

CHAPTER 11

Like awakening from a mid-afternoon slumber, Robert was confused as he slowly scanned the sterile hospital room he was lying in. Unlike the one in Missouri, things were now different. No machines, no loud voices and the void of numerous doctors and nurses scurrying from one patient to another. This room had curtains, which were open, allowing a bright sun to warm the room. Robert was very relaxed and comfortable, to the point of having to command his arms and legs to move to reassure himself that he was not paralyzed. He began focusing on an alarm clock sitting next to the bed—4:32 PM.

This moment reminded Robert of a childhood injury where he was thrown from a horse that had been spooked by a copperhead snake. The horse was known to be a gentle mare that could accommodate and care for any youngster riding her. Things changed when the horse was startled by the snake, while taking Robert for a ride down a county road. When the copperhead lashed out at the mare, she broke into a hard run, with Robert desperately holding on to the reigns in a combative attempt to remain on. Some cattle-guards crossed the roadway in front of the rapidly approaching, runaway mare. A miss calculation on her part caused a hoof to become entangled in one of the crossing metal bars; therefore, interrupting the mare's attempt to jump over the obstacle. This failed attempt sent Robert crashing downward, coming to rest head first on the metal bars. Time then stood still, while he lay unconscious and bleeding by the road. Due to Robert's many journeys away from home for hours at a time during childhood, his absence did not alert Mrs. James that her son had been injured.

Robert could still remember the feeling when he first regained consciousness from this accident. His mother's face was the first he noticed as she stood over him next to a bright light, while the doctor attended to his head wound. Even though this memory was a painful one, the vivid memory of his mother caused Robert to lie still, savoring the moment as if she were still standing next to him. For this short moment, Mrs. James was real and alive. Robert tried to elude reality but the thoughts of his mother began to fade as his mind and body began focusing on reality.

Where the hell am I?

Robert's jelly-like body was beginning to return to normal as he forced himself to sit up in bed. Upon looking around, Robert noticed he was in a private room. A small closet faced him from the opposite wall, and a door slightly ajar gave him a peak into its contents. His clothes were neatly hanging, with one pair of cowboy boots sitting under them. Robert then managed to stagger to the closet, feeling as if he were still hung-over from a night in Margaritaville. Upon opening the door, he began taking inventory of the contents as fast as his lethargic arms could move. Finding his federal shield and ID, gave some relief to the detective. A more desperate second search revealed a 40-caliber pistol hidden in one boot, with two clips full of ammo stuffed in the other.

"Thank God, now I am at least partially whole again. Welcome back, Detective Robert James."

Robert was somewhat relieved to hear his own voice, which assured himself that all faculties were working and his hearing was returning to normal. It was all beginning to come back to him now. The hospital in Missouri, the unknown doctor who sedated him, many questions needed to be answered.

"First of all, Detective James, you need to figure out where the hell you are!"

The aching in his ear was somewhat painful while talking but Robert needed this to assure himself that body and mind were fully functioning. He shed the hospital gown and quickly dressed into his clothes that someone had placed in the closet. Once again, Robert examined the wallet containing his badge and credentials before sliding it into his back pocket. As a baby handling their security blanket, the detective methodically examined his 40-caliber pistol, making sure it was in good working order. The slide was ejected from the grip and Robert began counting to make sure all fifteen bullets were still loaded. The extra clips then received the same attention. Once the inspection was complete, the pistol was tucked into the waistband of his jeans, as the extra clips made their way into his jacket pocket.

Before exiting the room, Robert began scanning it, looking for a clue to where he was. The telephone was spotted and determined to be a possible answer regarding his location. Robert grabbed the phone and forcefully pressed the zero-button.

"Yes, operator, I am embarrassed to have to ask this question but I cannot recall the full name of this hospital. Can you please help me?"

"I certainly can, Mr. James. You are in Room #314 of the Dalworth Regional Hospital in Arlington."

"Thanks for your help, Madam."

"Arlington, ARLINGTON!" Robert was stunned. How could this have happened?

I am back in Texas, five hundred miles away from where I was last night, and I have no idea how I got here....

A million thoughts now invaded his mind.

Who did this, why did it happened, and, Paige. I have to get the hell out of here!

Robert rushed to the closed door but soon came to a standstill, wondering what, or who, may be awaiting him outside. Thinking strategically, Robert tapped on the door, hoping to cause anyone that may be waiting on the outside to respond. Nothing happened; there was absolutely no response back. He then cracked the door slightly; remaining to the side in the event of an adversary being on the outside to hinder his escape, but there was nothing. No nurse, doctor or secret government agent—absolutely nothing. He began scanning the hallways before leaving the room, looking for the best escape route from this nightmare. Another thought came to his mind. As Robert reached into his pocket, another look of bewilderment would have been easily detected by any bystander. A set of keys was in his pocket, with a folded piece of paper accompanying them. Anxiously, Robert removed both. The keys were indeed the ones to his pickup and home. As Robert unfolded the paper, he noted some typewritten words on the paper; "Your truck is in the parking lot, courtesy of Uncle Sam." This picture was now getting clearer for him. The message gave an intentional clue to who was behind his sedated trip back to Texas. Robert was now able to remember the words spoken by the ER doctor at the county hospital about his unwelcomed presence.

You're right, Dad. These guys are government Spooks. I have got to get out of here and call the boss.

Two elevators lie just beyond a nurses' station down the hallway. Robert looked for an alternative way to leave but saw none. He slowly exited his room, looking around as inconspicuously as possible to see what dangers the hallways might contain. At this point Robert felt he could not trust anyone he did not know. The only occupants of the hallway were a few patients and four nurses at their station next to the elevator. From his room to the elevators was only a distance of approximately a hundred feet, but to Robert, this felt like a dead man walking in a prison. The walk toward the elevators seemed to take forever. This was like a flashback of an acid (LSD) trip he took after accidentally absorbing some of the drug while testing it. During the horrific drug-induced trip, Robert felt like he was fifty feet tall, with legs and arms filled with concrete. The walk down a similar hall at the JDLST office seemed to go in slow motion and take forever, while he was hallucinating from the LSD. The walk down this hospital hallway seemed like déjà vu, slow motion and taking forever.

The nurses at the fourth floor, station six, seemed to ignore Robert as he strolled past them. It was almost as if they were trying hard to not look as he passed, or maybe had been instructed not to do so. Robert could feel his heart pounding and adrenalin rushing, just as if he were in the process of committing a crime himself. He refused to look back after passing the nurses' station, but anticipated at least one verbal confrontation. Once again, there was nothing, just as if he were invisible. It was obvious these nurses had strict orders to abide by.

Robert felt himself slowly exhaling as the elevator doors closed but his anxiety quickly returned after the elevator only went down one floor and then stopped. An older lady, probably a visitor, entered and once again his heart rate began to decelerate. As the doors were beginning to close, Robert forced himself to peek into the hallways to see who occupied them.

"Excuse me, Ma'am." Robert said to the woman as he reached over and began slamming his closed fist against the "open door" button. The women stood back in an almost defensive position as the excited stranger forced his way out of the elevator.

With the elevator door open, Robert observed a group of uniformed police officers, along with a few detectives, crowded around a room at the end of the hallway. Standing to one side was a familiar face—Investigator Blake Waterman.

"Sir, you need to stand back, this is a restricted area!"

Several uniformed officers maneuvered to block the approaching man. Robert then removed the wallet containing his badge and Federal ID from his back pocket and shoved it just inches from the officer's faces.

"Stand down, Boys, I'm a Fed."

Investigator Waterman was initially ignoring the approaching man but the loud commands and familiar voice that responded caught his attention.

"It's Okay, officers; this guy is with my unit." Blake responded as he caught sight of Robert.

"What the heck are you doing here, Robert? Are you not supposed to be hanging out with your hillbilly buddies back in Missouri? May the good Lord be with you if the boss man finds out you are here."

"It is a very, very long story; one that I do not yet have answers to myself, Blake."

Investigator Waterman then put his arm around his comrade's shoulders, stood close and whispered to his fellow officer.

"Have you been hitting the tequila there, Buddy?"

"I wish it was that simple but I will have to fill you in later. So, what the heck in going on here, Blake?"

"There is a young lady inside the room. Her name is Angela Tyler, and she is the daughter of Texas millionaire, Sam Tyler. Long story short, last night she went to a local bar in North Arlington and met up with the Grim Reaper. Apparently, some guy slipped her a Mickie and took her up to one of the rooms at the Grand Park Hotel. For some reason, Doctor Doom took a knife to this poor girl's throat and tried to de-tonsil her. It is a miracle, nothing less than a miracle, that she lived. I have NEVER seen a wound of this magnitude where the victim survived. And get this; she was able to gather the strength to make her way to the hotel's lobby for help. I bet the people who found her felt like they were watching a horror movie. Anyway, so far Ms. Tyler is defeating the odds. The doctors actually think she will survive but are expecting some brain damage; to what extent is unknown. It's a shame, Robert; this gal is a real looker, cover girl material. She has some funky tattoo on the back of her neck but still, she's pretty hot. Like the old saying goes, when you see a beautiful woman you can bet that there is at least one man in this world that hates her guts! Unfortunately, Ms. Tyler found him last night."

"Once again, Blake, what are you doing here?"

"Well, seems as if our boss knows the victim's father. To what extent I am not sure, but apparently close enough that he sent me down here to find a way to muscle into the investigation. I am not going to question this one because the animal that did this needs to be found, and ASAP.

"I agree, Blake. Are there any leads or suspects at this time?"

"No suspects, Rookie, but she was able to mumble a few words before going totaling unconscious in the hotel lobby. How she was able to speak is beyond me, but each witness said they heard the same words. Ms. Tyler kept repeating, "The Devil's Elbow," before going out."

With these words, Robert became motionless.

"Hey, Robert, you OK? . . . Robert . . . ."

"Yea, yea, just thinking. The tattoo on her neck, tell me about it."

"It is actually fairly small and on the back of her neck, just under the hairline. I am not sure why someone would want a tattoo in a place where no one can see it. To me, it is not the average run of the mill tattoo. I think it is symbolic of something, but of what I don't know. I just don't get it; the girl rambling about The Devil's Elbow has a tattoo of a demonic pitch fork on the back of her neck."

"Blake, point me out to the detective running this show. I need to talk to him."

"What about?"

"I will fill you in later, Blake, just point him out."

Investigator Waterman then directed Robert to a suited cop who was among a group of detectives near the victim's doorway.

"You in charge here?" asked Robert as he approached the detective that Investigator Waterman pointed out to him.

"My name is Robert James, a federal agent with the JDLST. I can't go into details with you right now but there is a federal interest in this case. I am going to pull up a chair in Ms. Tyler's room and personally babysit her until she becomes conscious."

It is common knowledge among the law enforcement community that federal and local cops fail to see eye-to-eye, on occasion. Some local cops view the Feds as a bunch of glory hounds, in that they let the local cops do most of the work and then step in and take over the case once most of the work has been completed. This would not be the case with Angela Tyler's case. The local detectives welcomed the federal assistance, mostly because of the elite status of the victim's father, which would require a quick resolution and incarceration of the suspect.

"Ok, Super-Fed," the detective replied. "We know all about you, heard it on the news . . . . What the hell, she is unconscious anyway; so there is not much we can do right now. CALL US if she happens to wake up while you are in there. We are going to hit the pavement and solve this case while you are in there napping."

Robert just smiled and nodded as the lead detective and his partners began working their way down the hallway. He could not blame the detectives for their attitude toward him. It was nothing personal, just the rift between the locals and feds that has existed since the days of J. Edgar Hoover. Robert could easily recall the days when he had the same attitude, especially while working the double-homicide back in Springdale a few years ago. In that case, the feds were nothing but a hindrance to his investigation, throwing up roadblocks and hiding leads and evidence. This was not always the case between the locals and feds but more often than not it was. Once becoming a federal officer, Robert promised himself to remember his roots and the hard working local cops who put their lives on the line daily. He just happened to be one of them.

Investigator Waterman overheard the conversation between Robert and the detective. It did not take a seasoned investigator to figure out that his co-worker was onto something.

As Robert entered the room, his eyes became affixed to a long, thin figure that was cradled by a white sheet. The yards of gauze that were bandaged around her neck, accompanied by her pale skin, would give the average person the impression that the body was lifeless. The many monitors with lights flickering and the constant beeps being emitted made it evident that the person attached to the machines was indeed alive. Despite the staff's attempts to cleanse her body, the patient's blonde hair was dulled from the blood stains that saturated it just hours ago. Despite the grimness of her appearance, Robert could tell that Angela was just as Blake Waterman had described—a real looker. Her facial features were stern, with each being symmetrical and balanced. Angela's arms were about the only part of her that was not covered or bandaged, but they told any observer she was toned and fit. Despite her injury, Angela appeared to be the perfect specimen, both in her physique and looks. Robert could not help but stare at this beautiful, wounded creature.

Curiosity was about to kill the cat, as Robert stood silently, hoping that Angela would move her body from one side to another, just enough to make her tattoo visible. A few moments passed and he could no longer stand the wait. Robert began inching his way closer to the bed, focused only on the intended target of Angela Tyler's neck. If what Blake had told him was true, the small tattoo should be visible above the bandages, which were wrapped around her wound. Just a small nudge of Angela's head would allow him to inspect her hidden secret.

"May I help you?"

Robert was somewhat startled by the sudden invasion of a woman's voice. Upon seeking its source, he noticed a woman, mid fifties, sitting in a chair obscured in a corner of the room. As Robert spotted the women, he could tell she was not one of the attending medical staff.

"Yes, Ma'am, I am a federal officer, Detective Robert James. You must be Mrs. Tyler."

"Good guess, Mr. James, did the running mascara and sunken eyes of this mother give it away?"

"Just the striking resemblance to your daughter," replied Robert.

Despite this comment, Robert was telling anything but the truth. Mrs. Tyler's features were far removed from those of her daughter. The mother's dark hair and eyes, oval face and petite body were nothing close to that of her daughter's features. Her civilian clothes, along with the hollow look on a face that obviously had been weeping for hours, was the giveaway. In his line of work Robert had seen this many times when facing relatives of victims from horrific crimes or death.

"You are more than kind, Mr. James. You are a new face to the sea of detectives I have been speaking with over the past twelve hours. So, what can the Fed's do to help us find this animal? Are these detectives I have been meeting not capable of doing their jobs? Forgive my bluntness, Mr. James, I am a person who does not beat around the bush and I want answers. My husband should be arriving soon and just a word of warning; Angela is his little angel. My husband's life revolves around his daughter so if you think my bluntness is awkward, just wait until he arrives. Don't get me wrong, we appreciate all that is being done but Mr. Tyler carries a big stick and knows just about every politician in the South. If you are not the best, Mr. James, then I would recommend that you dig in your agencies talent chest and find the best, because my husband will demand it."

Robert stood momentarily as Mrs. Tyler's words were absorbed and evaluated before responding.

"Mrs. Tyler, I am from a federal narcotics unit that specializes in major drug trafficking and organized crime. I know my presence may be somewhat confusing but there is a purpose for me being here, which unfortunately I can't share with you at this time. If it may be a comfort to you, I have worked on numerous homicide cases too, not just drugs. I don't want to sound egotistical but please understand that I am on a very elite special enforcement team and I guess being here speaks for my qualifications. Mrs. Tyler, I do have one question for you. When your daughter was discovered in the hotel lobby she was semi-conscious. Just before passing out, Angela began repeating the words, "The Devil's Elbow", over and over. Do you have any idea what she meant by these words?

With this question, the grieving mother became silent and her facial expression rapidly changed. Through his law enforcement training and years of experience, Robert knew he had hit on something.

"I have no idea, Mr. James. It is funny what the mind can do when someone is near death. I have to confess, spirituality was not one of my daughter's finest features. Angela was an only child and we tried our best to instill religion on her but as many teens, she was somewhat rebellious in that category. We had a fire and brimstone Southern-Baptist preacher, who spoke heavy on the price of sin. Maybe my daughter's lack of Christianity suddenly became a priority in the moments she was dying. Obviously, that is what happened with Angela. Her fear of possibly meeting Satan himself must have been overwhelming—poor baby."

"Now, my daughter seems to be in good hands for the moment. A hallway occupied with a sea of cops, and a federal agent by her bedside leaves Angela in a good place. Mr. James, if you don't mind being my daughter's guardian for a while, I want to run downstairs, grab a quick bite to eat and freshen up a little. Mr. Tyler was out of state on business when this happened but should be here shortly. His jet landed twenty minutes ago in Addison and he is en route to the hospital right now. I was told he has a law enforcement escort, so it should not be long before Mr. Tyler arrives. Thanks for all you will be doing to help my daughter. I will be back shortly."

Robert watched as the worn woman forced herself from the chair and moved slowly to her nearby purse. A closer look revealed to Robert he was looking at money, big money. The clothes, shoes and purse were only a few clues, which supplemented the numerous trips to the cosmetic surgeon her face reflected. There was no doubt that Mrs. Tyler was on a first name basis with her plastic surgeon.

The slow motion of this woman also revealed to Robert that she had not moved from her chair in hours. This was the one and only child for the Tyler's. Despite the concern and dedication to Angela that her mother displayed, Robert knew Angela was going to be a "daddy's girl," so he would have to be on his best game when Mr. Tyler arrived. As Mrs. Tyler made her way out the door, Investigator Waterman stuck his head in.

"I'm out of here, Rookie. Just one bit of advice, you need to tell the boss you are back in town before he finds out himself and kicks your skinny little ass." Blake smiled as he disappeared from the door.

Robert could hear his fellow investigator tell Mrs. Tyler that he would be glad to escort her downstairs, and she readily accepted.

God, he is such a brown-noser, Robert thought, but was somewhat comforted knowing Mrs. Tyler was in good hands.

Robert pulled a chair up to the hospital bed and once again began focusing on the sleeping victim. Only a few seconds passed before a nurse came into the room to check on the patient. She briefly acknowledge Angela's bedside official, knowing this would be a constant scenario until the patient was able to leave. As quickly as she came, the nurse left after telling the investigator that all vitals still looked good.

He was now alone, and Robert's curiosity was overwhelming him. The tattoo had to be inspected. Slowly, almost methodically as if a leopard preying on an animal, Robert moved his hand toward Angela's head. His touch finally contacted the side of her head. In a gentle movement, Robert slightly turned the victim's head away from him a few inches. Robert was careful, very careful, knowing Angela's neck was saturated with stitches. Only a slight move was needed to give him access to the back of the victim's neck. Her head was now to the right, with only the blood-hardened hair covering the mysterious tattoo. Upon brushing Angela's hair aside, the marking was now visible. It was almost exactly as Blake Waterman had described it, just an inch below her hairline was a small tattoo of the Devil's pitchfork. There were no words attached like some tattoos, just a small pitchfork that was no more than three inches long and the same in width. Blake had described the symbol "almost" to a T, but apparently he had not looked closely enough. There were also two small lines that invaded the prongs of the devil's mark, beginning at the top middle prong and fanning out to both sides, like an upside-down V. Robert was not an expert in the art of tattooing but the marking did not appear to be fresh. Angela's tattoo appeared to be old, which was confusing to him.

Now, why would some wealthy Texans tattoo their daughter at an early age?

Robert knew answers would not come easy in this case. First, Angela's attending physicians would have to nurse her back to health. Also, with a deep cut to the throat, she may no longer have a voice. Then the crime itself, one so heinous, would be complicated to solve. Was Angela Tyler involved in something that caused her harm, or was this a random act? Last, but not least, The Devil's Elbow. At this point none of the investigators had any idea that a place named The Devil's Elbow actually existed, besides Robert. For now, he indeed was holding a trump card.

Suddenly Robert was startled by a thought; 'Paige, my dad, Missouri! How the heck am I going to explain this?'

A quick scan of the room revealed a telephone close to Ms. Tyler's bed. After briefly contemplating the use of it, Robert figured the necessity to contact his father exceeded potential consequences. Without a second thought, he began dialing. Even though he was an adult, Robert's fear of talking to his dad at this moment was totally consuming. He felt like a teenager that had just wrecked his father's sports car after sneaking it out at 3:00 in the morning.

The phone rang only once before Mr. James answered. If one were listening to the conversation and watching Robert, they would immediately notice the tension leaving the young man as he listened to his father's words. Mr. James relayed to his son that he was notified by Robert's old friend, Chad Cooper, of his situation and location. Apparently, Chad did not give Mr. James an explanation to why his son was suddenly removed from Missouri but Mr. James felt it might have something to do with what Robert had witnessed on the Interstate a few nights ago. Having a top-secret clearance while in the Air Force, Mr. James did not question Chad's information. He knew that Cooper was a CIA operative, who lived by the sword of his profession. To tell a source or give too much information to Mr. James could mean Cooper's job, or even worse. The intelligence community was very close knit and the "breaking of the code" could be a career ender for Chad. The fact that Robert was a federal official, and his father a former Air Force pilot with a top-secret clearance, meant nothing to this society of "super spooks." Dishonoring the brotherhood and death were two synonymous terms. Mr. James was just appreciative for the information Chad had given.

Mr. James advised Robert that arrangements had been made with his sister to watch over Paige for a few weeks, due to all that was happening. A strong emotion was causing Robert's eyes to tear up, knowing he was not going to see his little girl for awhile. Robert wanted his daughter to have the best home life possible. He knew from experience that growing up without one parent is difficult, but temporarily Paige would be without both. In the little time that Robert had been with his little angel, a strong love and bond had developed for her, a feeling he had never experienced before. Without a doubt little Paige was quickly changing his life, and the once shallow priorities of adding numbers to his little black dating book were now meaningless. Yes, he was finally discovering a different type of maturity. Fatherhood had fallen into Robert's lap and surprisingly it was very fulfilling. It was agreed between Robert and his dad, that Paige being in Springdale was the best place for her, until he had resolution and answers to this situation at hand. Safety was a priority for little Paige and being with his sister and under his father's watchful eye was comforting for this new father.

"And dad, tell little Paige that her father misses her and will be home soon."

"Will do, Son. Now, be careful and get this thing resolved so you can get your butt home. And one last thing, Chad Cooper left you a little surprise in your truck. Yes, Robert, he was the one who drove your pickup to Arlington. Isn't it nice having friends in high places?"

"Go figure, Chad strikes again . . . And dad, I will be careful—Goodnight."

Robert sat silently in his chair, with the phone still in his lap. A thousand thoughts had been rushing through Robert's head but now just one occupied it, his daughter. Robert felt detached but somewhat sorry for Paige because she was in a situation he never wanted for his own child. For him, growing up without a mother sucked and now his little girl was without either parent. Despite being very young, Robert knew that she still could sense that neither parent was around. The room was becoming blurry from the water pooling in the new father's eyes.

"So, you have a little daughter, Mr. Detective?" A weak voice invaded the silence of the room.

As Robert looked up, the head he slightly pushed away earlier had moved back toward him. He was now staring into a set of beautiful eyes. They were odd shaped, like those of a cat, but mesmerizing.

Angela Tyler was now awake, and talking . . . .

CHAPTER 12

The few words spoken by the beautiful victim left Detective Robert James stunned, frozen in time like a wild animal caught in the lights of an oncoming car. It was apparent that she had been listening to the telephone conversation between Robert and his father. The exact time the victim woke from her induced slumber was unknown but apparently in enough time to conclude that her bedside guardian was a law enforcement official, who was also a father to a small child. For a few moments the victim and detective did not attempt any words. Robert, being caught off guard by Angela's comments, was speechless. The victim remained quiet, waiting for a response back. As time was passing, detailed images of both were engrained in each other's minds as they just sat staring at each other.

"How about an official introduction, Detective?" Ms. Tyler spoke these words slowly, being careful not to further her injuries. Angela's voice was expectantly raspy and soft, but each word was easily identifiable.

"Detective . . . ."

Robert finally snapped to, realizing he had been entrenched in thought after her sudden words caught him by surprise. The few seconds it took to recover were somewhat embarrassing.

"My name is Robert, Detective Robert James, Ma'am; I am a federal law enforcement officer."

Before Angela would reply, the room was invaded with a small regiment of medical staff. Doctors and nurses rapidly entered and all approached their patient as if she were an oddity of nature. The monitors attached to Ms. Tyler had signaled a sudden change in vitals, which could have indicated either an improvement in her condition or a feared turn for the worse. All were pleased, but somewhat surprised as they observed their patient lying on her side with eyes affixed to Detective James.

"Detective, you need to leave the room. We need some time to examine Ms. Tyler." A doctor barked his orders to Robert.

With these words, Angela reached her arm toward Robert as if in an attempt to convince herself that he was real and not just a part of another broken dream or illusion.

"Detective, please leave a card on the table and thanks for being here for me."

Robert did not speak a word. The intense eye contact with Ms. Tyler let her know this was not the last she would see of this young detective. With a nod of confirmation, Robert placed a card at the location directed by Angela and started toward the door, at which time a volley of loud voices could be heard from the exterior of the room. Orders were being barked at the uniformed officers who were stationed outside the room. With force, the door swung open and three men entered. It did not take long for Robert to figure out who the first individual was. Obviously, this visitor was a businessman on a mission. After entering the room, he proceeded toward Angela in an aggressive but compassionate manner. One nurse jumped into the path of the approaching stranger but was physically pushed aside. After her attempt, none of the remaining medical staff tried to hinder the approach of this man. It did not take long to conclude this man was the victim's father. Samuel Tyler had arrived.

With all attention on Mr. Tyler and his daughter, Robert had failed to look at the other men who had accompanied Sam to his daughter's room. As Robert began walking toward the door, he kept his eyes focused on the reunion between father and daughter. Unexpectedly, a hand touched his shoulder.

"Robert . . . ."

The surprises kept coming for Robert, who had failed to take Investigator Waterman's advice earlier and notify Special Agent Michaels that he was back in town. Now, it was too late because he was standing face-to-face with the bossman. Robert's face immediately went flush, something he now shared with Ms. Tyler.

"Robert, I would like you to meet a friend of the Tyler family. This is Senator Trey Buckley, and Senator, this is Detective Robert James. Robert is one of the investigators in my JDLST.

As the two men shook hands, Robert completed his greeting with a few carefully chosen words and then asked to be excused. He was compelled to make his way out of the room as soon as possible. Hanging out in a room with doctors, an emotionally charged father and a United States senator made Robert feel uncomfortable. Not to mention the presence of his boss whom he had failed to notify about his return to Texas, along with the unbelievable details about it. Therefore, a quick exit was now his priority. Robert's journey seemed to be in slow motion, counting each step with ears keen to any that might be following. To his dismay and without a need to look, Robert could tell he was not alone. Yes, Special Agent Michaels was in pursuit. Robert could hear the door being closed as the pursuer exited Mr. Tyler's room.

"Would you like to tell me what the hell you are doing here? To the best of my knowledge, my rookie detective is in Missouri enjoying a two-week long vacation with his daughter and family. The next thing I know, he is sitting in a hospital room next to Angela Tyler's bed. Help me out here, Robert, and I would like the condensed version."

Any version of the past foggy and mysterious twenty-four hours was not totally possible but Robert tried his best. The visit to the bar, the car bomb, the hospital and then, back to Texas. Many details were left out but the general facts were passed along to Agent Michaels, who stood stunned by the story.

"If I did not know you, Robert, I would think I had just heard the biggest BS story of the year. I do have some thoughts going through my mind that we will discuss later. I need to get back inside and try to get a handle on what is going on. In case you have yet to figure it out, Sam Tyler is an old friend of mine. We go back a long time so I am going to do whatever I can to aid in this investigation. The locals are probably not going to be too happy with us invading their territory, so I need to find a federal door that we can open on this case, and fast. If you want to hang around on this one, I could surely use your help. Now, I need to get back in there and see what I can pick up from the doctors and Angela before the locals return."

"I am here for this one, boss. Before I leave, I do have one question. Senator Trey Buckley, what is he doing here?"

"Well, Robert, apparently the senator and Angela spent a lot of time together when they were young. Sam told me that Angela and the senator attended a private school together for years and became very close during that time period. As you probably know, Adam is the son of the renowned former Texas Governor, Kenneth Buckley. The senator told me on the way here that he thought of Angela as his younger sister. When the call about Angela went out to Sam, he was attending a fundraiser with the senator back east. Robert, it appears that a few minutes ago you shook the hand of a presidential hopeful. Yes, Senator Buckley will be on the presidential ballet next fall."

"Impressive, very impressive." Robert replied to Special Agent Michaels. "Now, I am out of here. Just give me a call later with my marching orders, Boss. I want to catch this creep before we have another victim like Angela Tyler."

Robert watched as Special Agent Michaels made his way back through the group of uniformed officers and disappeared into Angela Tyler's room. As he began his journey down the hallway, Robert began to refocus on his own situation. He was almost in overload mode, now. His life could not have become more complex in the past few days than what it had. He had been shot at, witnessed a mysterious and horrific accident, introduced his family to Paige, learned of his mother being involved in a top-secret, government research project, been hospitalized from a parking lot car-bomb, been drugged and involuntarily returned to Texas and now; the Angela Tyler case—TOTAL OVERLOAD.

Finding his way out of the hospital was also a challenge. Not often does one enter a medical facility in the manner Robert did. New scenery, new hallways and an exit path never traveled before, were before him. Then, once in the parking lot he faced the additional challenge of locating his truck. A smile suddenly replaced the look of confusion on Robert's face.

Now, what little surprise did you leave in the truck for your ol' buddy here, Chad Cooper?

It did not take long for Robert to locate his pickup truck. It soon became obvious that Chad had driven it to Texas. Chad Cooper was an anal-retentive individual. The thought of driving a dirty vehicle further than across a parking lot must have been unbearable for him. There she was, parked at the back of the lot to avoid any door-dings, and she was spotless. Yes, Chad Cooper had left his trademark. Robert then removed the keys from his pocket and slid them into the lock. For some reason there was just a little doubt this was actually his vehicle, despite the familiar number on the license plate. Lately, his life had been an enormous mystery; so, Robert was in a defensive mode and expecting the unexpected.

The pickup door opened and Robert noticed a small box on the seat. "For my old buddy, K-Ball," were the words written on a small, index card. Chad had known that after a day like Robert had, he would be extremely suspicious of any package sitting in his vehicle. Seeing the words "K-Ball" on the box would be a signal to Robert that all was well. K-ball was significant to him, a word that Chad and a few others on the high school baseball team had nicknamed him. In school, Robert was a pitcher on the baseball team and had made the knuckle ball a signature pitch. Seeing this, it was obvious that only one of his high school pals could have placed the box in the truck.

Upon opening the package, a smile encompassed Robert's face as he looked into a box full of chocolate chip cookies. It was no secret with his working comrades that he had an addiction to these cookies but the note inside the box told the story.

"Three dozen cookies, a debt long overdue. Enjoy, my friend."

Reading this note put Robert's mind at total ease. The "K-ball" reference, along with the note, reminded Robert of Chad's theft of three dozen cookies sent by his sister via Chad a few years ago; reassuring him the cookies were there to enjoy. A safe package sent by one of our country's super-spooks was definitely a contradiction of terms, but would not be questioned by Robert. The passenger floorboard revealed another unfamiliar item, a cooler. Figuring it to be another gift from Chad, Robert quickly discovered the contents to be that of an iced-down, case of Diet Cola. Chocolate-chip cookies and diet cola, a perfect combination.

Ah, just what the doctor ordered!

Robert then put his truck in motion while partaking of his two dietary addictions. As he pulled from the parking lot, he noticed the sign directing him toward East Interstate 30. Eighteen miles to the north lies his apartment, one that could not appear soon enough. Tonight would be an early one, an evening to unwind and relax in preparation for the huge task that lie ahead.

Tomorrow would be the beginning of the enormous undertaking; trying to figure out the numerous and complex crime riddles that had invaded his life. This indeed would be the biggest test his law enforcement skills had ever encountered.

The question; is Detective Robert James capable of handling such a task? The question soon eluded Robert's mind as the intoxicating pleasures of his culinary delights made the realities of life seep away . . . .

CHAPTER 13

Weeks had passed since Robert had spent much time at his desk in the Joint Drug Lab Suppression Team office. The Gene King case had kept him working everywhere but there. Many work miles had been covered during that time, taking him from Texas, to Missouri and Florida. As he looked at the title of his group, Robert wondered how such a long title could be so confining. Of course, their main focus was to locate and eradicate drug labs, their financiers and operators, but the work of the JDLST unit went far beyond the scope of their title. Adding organized crime, murder, human trafficking, among other major crimes, would be just as fitting.

Quite a ride it had been for this small town cop from Missouri but now it was time to buckle down. Robert thought that after the King case things might settle down, hoping for a possible routine but this would not be the situation. Three major cases lie ahead; Angela Tyler's attempted murder, his own shooting case in Oklahoma, and the strange and confusing situation he encountered in Missouri a few days prior. Trying to prioritize them would be futile but without a doubt the shooting in Oklahoma with his daughter in the vehicle would top the list. The thought that some piece of crap had the audacity to shoot at his vehicle, possibly bringing harm to little Paige, was inexcusable.

To begin a workday before 8:00 AM was an abnormality for Robert, unless the day was to be spent in a courtroom. With all of the work to be done, he almost felt like he deserved a schoolboy tardy slip for getting there late. It was also no surprise to Robert that upon arriving, Special Agent Michaels was already at his desk, with one pot of coffee almost gone. Robert had wondered if the boss man had seen or heard him enter, due to his normal addiction to the morning television news which accompanies the coffee. There were numerous things that he did not want to be confronted with or interrogated about by his boss, but Robert knew he would not be so lucky as to elude them. Maybe he would be fortunate enough for this to occur at another place or time and not on the first day back at his desk, with so much to do. These thoughts rapidly disappeared as a news story caught Robert's attention:

> "Now, for an update on that horrific incident at the Arlington Grand Park Hotel, involving Angela Tyler. It appears the victim has been upgraded from critical to serious condition, as she struggles to recover from her violent attack a few nights ago at the hotel. Law enforcement authorities have not released any motive or suspect information yet about the case. Reports have confirmed that Senator Trey Buckley arrived this morning with Ms. Tyler's father, the renowned Samuel Tyler, which surely will aid in the expedition of bringing this violent offender to justice. According to our sources, Senator Buckley and Ms. Tyler have been friends since childhood. We will continue our efforts to closely monitor this situation."

"Detective Robert James." These words rapidly diverted Robert's attention from the newscast. "Now, Son, are you well rested from that 'long' vacation you are returning from?" The psychological war games that Special Agent Michaels was so good at had started, as he began his verbal interaction with his young detective.

The typical words of "in my office," which Robert expected to hear, were not conveyed by his boss. Instead, Special Agent Michaels pulled up a chair in the rookie's office, sitting silent, just looking at his young detective.

"Well, Detective James, anything you want or need to tell the old boss man here?"

Robert was unsure about which exact topic his boss wished to discuss. Did he know the truth about him breaking the Cardinal sin by having a relationship with his ex-informant Lori, who is the mother of his child? Or maybe was it time for a tongue-lashing for getting involved in an off-duty incident that caused a couple of brief hospital stays over the past two days? Maybe today was his lucky day and the boss just wanted to discuss the Angela Tyler case. Without a doubt, Robert did not want the truth to be known about Paige, but there was no way he would be able to lie to SA Michaels. In many ways his boss reminded Robert of his father. Special Agent Michaels was an understanding person but also a man of integrity. Under no circumstances would he tolerate one of his own lying to him. It would certainly be an end to Robert's career if a lie was to cover up a violation of policy. If asked, the truth about having a relationship with his informant would be told, but only if necessary. After a few long seconds of thought, along with the continued stares from his boss, Robert broke the silence.

"Ok, bossman, I should have taken my two weeks off and enjoyed them. Not to make excuses or justify what I did, but I really doubt if too many law enforcement officers could have shunned their curiosity if they witnessed what I did a few nights ago on Interstate 44. Boss, it was like something out of a 'who done it' movie and there I was right in the middle of it. The ensuing news reports were telling anything but the truth, so obviously I had witnessed something that was very significant, but non-existent, which made me even more curious. Then, upon telling all of this to my father, I learned about my mother managing a top-secret government research project just a few miles down from where this incident occurred. The icing on the cake came when I ended up in a hospital back in Texas, possibly because I was doing a little snooping around. Can you see Boss how this could play on a cop's mind? I am in overload mode right now."

"Ok, Robert, just chill out. I can't blame you for being curious DESPITE my orders to go back to Missouri and relax for a few weeks. It seems like your adventures have been keeping me busy these days, too. Not only am I tasked with trying to find out who attempted to assassinate my young detective, I also have an old friend whose daughter met one of the devil's offspring a few nights ago and I intend to help track this animal down. I have to admit, Robert, this thing in Missouri you witnessed the other night has also peaked my curiosity. It is obvious that your curiosity got you in some big trouble last night. As you know, I am no stranger to the intelligence community, myself. For whomever these people are in Missouri; to have gone to the extent of doing what they have done to you, definitely tells me you stumbled across something big. You have no idea how lucky you are, Robert. Most people who witness something like this do not get warning shots, they just disappear. It is fortunate for you these characters knew you were a federal agent; thus, your death or disappearance would have initiated an investigation. Otherwise, we might not be having this conversation right now. I have been trying to evaluate all of this, which caused me a very sleepless night. No, Robert, I did not come in early this morning; I just arrived very late last night. Now, I have a few ideas so let's get this ball a rolling."

For the next thirty minutes, Special Agent Michaels outlined the avenues he wished to pursue regarding the tasks at hand. He would be assigning Robert to work with Investigator Adam Ainsworth. The boss did not want Robert to have much involvement in the Oklahoma shooting incident, due to the possibility of a conflict of interest, since mistakes in the investigation could be driven by Robert's emotions. Robert and Adam Ainsworth would be working with the local law enforcement authorities on the Angela Tyler case.

This was not exactly what Robert wanted to hear. First, Blake Waterman had been working on the Tyler case and had a very good rapport with the local cops. Blake is an excellent investigator and this type of case was right down his alley. Second, if there was a misfit in the unit, Adam Ainsworth would be the one. Adam was an egotistical loner. It was no secret that a majority of his work shift consisted of Adam spending time at the gym and then hanging out in local stripper clubs "gathering intelligence." The fact that vice and corruption ran rampant in this type of club was no secret. Over the past few years, the Dallas-Ft. Worth area had seen an influx of men's strip clubs, some being upscale. Million dollar business deals, ten dollar beers and five-star restaurants were contained within their walls. Despite the upscale look, the century old improprieties of comparable establishments remained. Prostitution, drugs and sex slavery could be found at most. For some reason, Adam was drawn to these clubs. The bossman allowed him to continue this endeavor due to the amount of intelligence Adam extracted from the dancers working there. Intelligence was Adam's main forte'; as he certainly did not produce like the others in the unit regarding drug purchases and criminal cases being filed.

"Adam Ainsworth, Boss?" Special Agent Michaels noted a look of confusion or dismay on his young detective's face.

"Yes, Robert, Adam Ainsworth. Since coming to this unit Adam has been producing some good intelligence but the rest of his numbers are lacking. I don't want him to become focused on intelligence alone, and not out there busting some ass like the rest of you guys. Let's get him out there Robert and, per-se, throw him in the tiger's den. Adam has potential and it's time to see it, and you are just the man for the job. Plus, I am not too fond of him living in those stripper clubs. I don't want any of my investigators impregnating some dancer; it just would not look good. As the old saying goes, "you lie with the dogs and you will eventually get bitten by fleas." I don't want my guys having this type of trouble, Robert. He should be in here shortly, so once Adam arrives, you guys need to get over to Arlington P.D. and meet with their detectives. I want Angela Tyler's assailant in jail before the blood can dry on his knife. Here is the initial report from Arlington and I want you to memorize every word on it. "

"Will do, Boss."

As SA Michaels exited the room, the "impregnating" word stood out like a bright neon sign. Robert could not help but wonder if his boss was opening a door to discuss little Paige, and the unknown mother. The boss was like this, at times the fatherly type who wanted to hear a confession before forcing the information from the child. If his boss was throwing out some bait, Robert refused to bite. If it would be his choice, this topic would wait for the exact right time before Robert would discuss it with Special Agent Michaels.

Robert soon became entrenched with the police report detailing Angela Tyler's violent assault. Working assaults and homicides was definitely not his intention when he chose a law enforcement career but for some reason, fate had taken him down this path. The fact that Ms. Tyler could survive an attack such as this was remarkable. Her throat had been cut from jaw-bone to jaw-bone, leaving not an inch untouched. The wound was also deep enough for a certain death; but apparently what the devil had planned for Ms. Tyler, God had vetoed and chose for her to live. According to doctor's report, what had saved the victim's life was a mere positioning of her body. When Angela was assaulted, she was lying flat on her back, exposing her throat in a backward tilt. An ensuing slight movement, either a last effort by Angela to move or possibly the assailant removing himself from the bed, caused a forward motion in the neck. This motion compressed the wound, causing it to almost completely seal shut. Even the most trained killer would have concluded Angela Tyler had met her maker, so he left the room believing she was dead. Indeed, Angela Tyler is a lucky woman.

The report was lengthy, as expected. Special Agent Michaels did not need to instruct Robert to memorize each word because this report would be of interest to anyone. Despite the description of the crime, Robert had other interests in mind. Investigator Waterman had mentioned the last words that Ms. Tyler had whispered before becoming unconscious at the hotel. Now Robert was at the anticipated point in the report:

> "Witnesses observed the victim exiting the elevator and making her way toward the front desk. At a point approximately twenty feet from the clerk's counter, Ms. Tyler collapsed. Witness #1 and Witness #2 quickly went to her aid. Upon reaching her, each noticed a large, gaping wound crossing Ms. Tyler's entire throat. She was in a semi-conscious state, obviously due to the loss of a

large amount of blood. Both witnesses attempted to question Ms. Tyler, despite her massive wound. In her weakened state, the victim was able to whisper two words repeatedly before passing out. These words were, "The Devil's Elbow, The Devil's Elbow." As of this report date, no leads have been developed from the information."

These words seemed to paralyze Robert. Obviously, at this point, the involved investigators were clueless to the meaning of Angela's words. The Devil's Elbow was more than real to Robert but this information would remain his secret, for now anyway. The history behind the Devil's Elbow would be surreal to many, even a seasoned investigator. Special Agent Michaels would understand but he would be about the only one at this point. So, The Devil's Elbow would belong only to Ms. Tyler and himself, for the moment. These words were like a shot of adrenalin to Robert, causing his mind to race a million miles an hour.

How in the heck can Angela Tyler be associated with The Devil's Elbow?

At this point, Robert was totally consumed by the victim. He felt they had some connection now. When Angela first opened her cat-like eyes and looked into his, Robert could immediately feel a unique connection with this woman. She was strong-willed, beautiful and certainly one of a kind. Now, they both possibly had a common connection, the Devil's Elbow.

"Wake up, rookie, your mentor has arrived." Without a doubt, Adam Ainsworth was in the house.

"My dream was more pleasant, Adam," replied Robert in a semi-joking manner. "This is a good case, my friend. Are you ready to go out and do some real police work?"

Most of the remaining day was spent by Robert and Adam reading reports, briefing with the boss and developing a strategy. The morning was interrupted by one call from Investigator Blake Waterman, who had developed some information about Robert's situation in Oklahoma. Apparently, while Robert was in Missouri, his informant, Rusty, had called looking for him. Blake took the call and met with Rusty at his request. Rusty established creditability with Investigator Waterman by telling Blake that he was Lori Sims' brother. Blake knew about Lori being the key informant in the Gene King drug case, but thankfully he was unaware about Lori having a child; let alone that Robert was the father. Needless to say, when talking about Lori, Robert felt like he was walking on a thin wire over a fire pit.

Investigator Waterman relayed the information Rusty gave regarding a methamphetamine cook who worked for Gene King. About all they knew about this cook was that he was tall, thin, white male, who had the nickname of Snakeskin Billy. He basically lives in a men's stripper club in Ft. Worth, called Fantasy Dreams, and drives a red Corvette. This club was one of the newer, upscale clubs that some wealthy individual or corporation sank millions into building it. It was simple to figure that Snakeskin Billy was apparently very successful in his illicit endeavors. A night at Fantasy Dreams was an expensive one for those who entered their doors.

"Robert, this guy must know the cops are on to him. There have been two occasions where the police department had officers in pursuit but this rascal eluded them. Trust me, we will keep after Billy until we can de-scale him. No one takes a pot shot at our Robert James and gets away with it! And one last bit of icing for the cake, that idiot failed to appear on a Possession of Methamphetamine charge two years ago; so, there is an outstanding warrant out for his arrest."

Investigator Waterman ended the conversation with a vow to keep silent about the information just given to his buddy. Blake knew that Special Agent Michaels was not allowing Robert to be privy to the investigation into his Oklahoma shooting case, due to personal conflicts that could ensue. Both of these men had grown close in their trust and friendship since Robert came to the JDLST. Compromising a work buddy would definitely not be the situation with Robert.

Investigator Ainsworth's pager interrupted the silence in Robert's office. As Adam looked at the numbers reflected in the device, without a word he exited Robert's office and headed toward his. Robert overheard a conversation Adam was having over the telephone, and it was obvious by his tone that he was talking to a female. Flirtatious, to say the least. Robert concluded this was just another of Adam's flock members. His newly assigned work partner was chiseled in physique, with a face resembling to a male model. On several occasions the unit would find a happy hour at a local establishment, in search of cold beer and amorous women. In one way, Adam was a good one to take with you to a happy hour, due to the number of females he would attract by just walking through the door. The downside of being with Adam was as soon as the women would see him, all others accompanying him did not exist. Yes, a lady killer he was. After a few minutes, Robert could tell the conversation had concluded.

"Come on Robert, let's blow this joint. I have a CI that I need to meet." Most cops referred to confidential informants as CI's, thus shedding long words and formalities.

As the two men entered the parking garage, Adam pointed toward his car, indicating he would be driving. As expected, Adam drove a vehicle symbolic of his personality; a Porsche 911 that had been seized from a local drug dealer. This was a common tactic for drug units, seizing property, vehicles and money from individuals involved in the drug world. A fresh coat of paint and new wheels would easily remove personal identifiers of the last owner.

As they made their way from the lot and onto Highway 121, Adam began to brief Robert about the phone call from the CI. Adam would be meeting with this individual at the Grand Park Hotel in Arlington. Adam then revealed to Robert the CI was a dancer at one of the local stripper clubs in Ft. Worth, and she had some information to pass along. This news excited Robert, due to it being the location where Angela Tyler was assaulted. It always helps an investigator to observe the crime scene when working a case. Robert did not ask what information the CI had to relay. He would be present and hearing it first-hand. Robert knew Adam would reveal more after the meeting.

Working confidential informants was a unique and delicate assignment. Most CI's were from the drug world and working off a criminal case or arrest warrant, or needing the money that cops traded for information. On occasion, there would be a case where a CI was a law-abiding citizen and would have information to pass along, but this was a rarity. Most confidential informants had a motive for snitching, and most were self-serving.

When working undercover, identity and obscurity were necessary to maintain one's cover and most of all, for safety's sake. This would be addressed upon arriving at the hotel. During their ride over, conversation consisted mostly of Adam relaying details of the numerous dates he had been on lately and describing the kinky sex he had with most. For some reason, Adam was not shy enough to leave out details of several nights he was not able to properly perform, due to "coming down" from his steroid usage. While on the juice, Adam said he would perform like a racehorse. When off, well, he was off. Looking at Adam's two hundred and fifteen pound body that supported a thirty-two inch waist, there was no guessing that Adam was a roid-boy. In months past this conversation would have been two-sided, with Robert exercising his bragging rights, too. Now, things were different. Being the father of a young daughter was definitely making an impact on his life. Robert now had different motives for his off duty time, with little Paige being his priority.

As the Porsche edged its way onto Highway 121, Adam pushed down the accelerator as if he was engaging in a hot pursuit with a bank robber. Adam drove like he lived his life, hard and fast.

"What's the hurry, Joe Studly?"

"You will see when we get there, Robert. This gal is sizzling hot and haste makes waste, my friend."

It was obvious to Robert that Adam's CI had more to offer than just information. Being a female dancer in one of the Dallas—Ft. Worth Metroplex's hottest clubs, there was little doubt the CI would be attractive with a body to match. Despite these factors, Robert silently hoped that Adam had his head screwed on right, with priorities in order. Robert wanted to tell his fast-lane friend about the choice he had made one night with a CI—one that changed his life forever. In the short time he had known Adam he knew that a spontaneous decision resulting in a pregnant CI and a child would be much different if it happened to Adam. Without being arrogant, Robert knew a fatherly figure was something that Adam was not capable of at this point in his life.

During the drive to Arlington, Adam seemed to dominate the conversation with female talk and not the expected cop-talk that was expected, and needed at this point. Coming into view on the horizon was their destination, the Grand Park Hotel. The information Robert had been awaiting regarding Adam's informant never came, so Robert needed to ask.

"Adam, fill me in on what we are doing here. I know she is a CI, but who is this gal and what kind of case is she helping you with?

"Just sit back and relax, Robbie, and watch the master at work. All work and no play is unhealthy for a person. With this gal, I get the best of both worlds."

Before Robert could respond, Adam's demeanor went from boisterous to verbally violent. Just one block away from the hotel, a signal light had turned red. Apparently, the vehicle in front of Adam did not take off quick enough. Robert watched with amazement as Adam rolled his window down and extended his head and arms out the window. Adam then extended his left arm and began shaking his hand violently with only his middle finger extended:

"The whole pole is not going to turn green, you jackass!" Adam shouted at the driver, who appeared to be an elderly individual in his seventies.

"What the hell are you doing?" asked Robert as he reached over and pulled Adam back into the vehicle.

"I'm on a mission and that old fool needs to pay attention!"

"You're a cop, Adam. Act like one, dude. We need to get along with the locals, which means not having them talking about a crazy federal drug cop during their next briefing."

"They will get over it. Besides, we are the feds and THEY AREN'T!" Adam almost reflected a sadistical rage in his reddened face when screaming these words.

There was no need to argue the point with Adam. The side effects of excessive steroid usage were evident; Adam was definitely on the juice. Robert sat silently as the Porsche pulled into the parking lot of the Arlington Grande Park Hotel.

Robert followed his working partner as they entered the lobby of the hotel. Robert took only a few steps inside before he stopped, standing a few feet from the front desk. The floor was composed of white, marble sheets of decking. One spot was somewhat tainted, as if something dark had been spilled there. This would not be a concern to the patrons of the hotel, or probably not even noticed by them, but to Detective Robert James, it was significant. This must have been the location where the blood covered Angela Tyler had collapsed. Even though marble is a rock-like substance, it is still slightly porous and blood would be almost impossible to completely remove, once absorbed. Without a doubt, this marked the spot where Angela Tyler laid.

"You coming, Robert?" Adam asked as he waited at the entrance to the elevator.

Reluctantly, Robert moved toward his new work partner. Now, the Angela Tyler case had consumed his thoughts, and not the task of meeting Adam's CI. He then forced himself to accompany Adam into the elevator. The ride went quickly and surprised Robert when they reached the top floor.

"We're on the 22nd Floor, Adam. I may be a country boy, but I know these rooms do not come cheap."

"Only the Penthouse for this CI, Buddy. Only the best for the best. You will understand when you see my little gal."

Both men made their way down the hallway toward the very end. The further they went, the further the distance between the room entry doors. Just from the hallway one could tell these rooms were double, or triple the size of the ones contained on the lower floors. A grand hallway would most certainly reflect a grand room.

As they arrived at the end of the hallway, Adam reached out to the door on the right and knocked. Only a few seconds passed before the door opened, revealing nothing less than a woman with a model's appearance. Her clothing left few to guess what her profession was. She was a beautiful woman, with long black hair, huge brown eyes and a body that most likely graced the doors of a gym almost daily. Her lips were slightly swollen, reflective of a recent dose of collagen. There was also no doubt that her breasts were augmented, as with many others in her profession. An expense of the job that took only a few weeks to pay for. Definitely a worthy investment for a woman who exhibits and sells her body for a living.

As Adam entered, the vanity and inconsideration of both became evident, as they embraced for a long kiss, not caring who was present to watch.

"Robert, I want you to meet Dallas, and Dallas, this is Robert."

Only a few words passed between the two before Dallas was devoting her entire attention back on Adam. She grabbed her man by the hand and led him to her bedside, which was in a separate room. Robert looked around at the penthouse room, which was larger than his entire apartment. He then observed a sign mounted on the back of the door, which reflected the cost of the room could not exceed $950 a night. Robert had once been told by a hotel clerk that these mandatory signs usually reflected a maximum price the room could rent for nightly, which was approximately 25% above the actual nightly cost. In summary, Dallas was paying out a week's worth of his salary for the room on a daily basis.

Since the doors remained open, Robert could see several carts full of food parked next to the bed. The food trays contained hoards of fruits, vegetables and seafood, along with several bottles of wine. This was indeed a feast fit for a queen, and one that only a queen could afford. As Dallas sat, she tugged on Adam, sitting him next to her on the bed. The two had the appearance of a couple that had just been reunited after being separated for months. Despite their flagrant display of affection for each other, Robert watched with curiosity, wondering why Adam was behaving in such a manner. He was on the job but behaving like a college boy without any responsibilities or inhibitions. Adam and Robert had worked on other projects together with the others from the JDLST unit, but this was a first for them as a team. Robert stared with wonder.

The bedside display soon became too much for Robert to watch, as Dallas began mauling her catch. On this evening, one could not tell that Adam Ainsworth was an on-duty law enforcement officer. The amazing part of this was that Adam did not seem to care. Maybe his thoughts were that he had no fear of Robert telling the boss about this encounter, or maybe Adam just didn't give a crap. Whichever the case being, Robert was not feeling very comfortable about his work partner right now.

As the foreplay between the stripper and Adam continued, Robert could not stomach much more. They both were on the job, with tons of work in front of them. There was no time for play, especially while they were on the clock. Robert was usually a pretty good judge of character but Investigator Adam Ainsworth was throwing him some curve balls right now. There Adam was, right in front of his new work partner and about to have sex with a confidential informant.

"Hey Adam, I am headed down to the lobby. Just hit me on the pager when you are ready to go. I will meet you back up here."

"10-4 pal. There is a nice bar in the lobby. Go have a few cocktails and maybe you can find you some companionship. There are plenty of rooms in this hotel, pal, to pass the time away if you find a little hottie."

"Hey Robert, there is a spare key on the counter. Go ahead and take it in case we can't make it to the door later." Dallas was making it known that she had evening plans for Adam.

Robert was disappointed in Adam's conduct but he was not going to let his partner's bad behavior stand in the way of work. There was just too much to be done.

If Adam wants to play, well, it's his life but I'm out of here.

Robert grabbed the key and fled the hotel room. The second-rate scene in the penthouse began to disappear as soon as the door shut. The hotel's bar was indeed one of his stops but not for the reason Adam had conveyed. The August Moon bar was the spot where the Angela Tyler case began. The police report reflected the August Moon was a weekly stop for Angela Tyler. The bar was attached to one of the most elegant and expensive hotels in the Dallas-Ft. Worth area, which usually played host to an upper class, middle aged crowd. For years past this had been a safe place for Angela to have a cocktail and dance, until evil entered the doors and changed her life forever.

A criminal investigation such as Ms. Tyler's assault began in a routine manner for Detective James. At first, the work started in the office. All reports would be reviewed and evaluated, along with background checks being run on all players involved. Then, a plan of attacked would be drawn up. After the initial office work was done, it would be essential for the investigator to visit the crime scene. Once there, a good detective would begin looking for clues, evidence and witnesses. Most important, the cop would be searching for that "gut-feeling", an indescribable instinct that would drive the investigator in directions he or she could not explain on paper. In court, the gut feeling was not admissible but was many times responsible for directing the cop in the path of solving the case. One thing Robert was taught as a rookie and could never forget was in order to be a successful investigator a cop had to put themselves in the mind-set of the criminal they were working. In other words, if you are working a burglary, try to think like a burglar, etc. Robert soon learned the voice you needed to listen to the most in police work was the voice of your instincts.

The August Moon bar was far from full this evening; but still, there were enough patrons that a person of either sex could easily find some companionship. Robert could definitely tell that he was no exception upon entering the bar. As Robert made his way to one of the side bars, he noticed a small group of businesswomen sitting several tables away, close to the side entrance to the bar. They were making it obvious that Robert was a target. Over the past decade, things were rapidly changing regarding infidelity. Now, married women were cheating on their husbands as much as men were on their wives. A businesswoman that was traveling ranked #1 on the national list of unfaithful spouses. With the Arlington Grande Park Hotel being such an exclusive place, it was usually occupied by professionals in town on business. These travelers also ranked among the worst regarding cheating on their spouses.

Once becoming a new father, one of the vows that Robert made to himself was to put away his little black book and turn a new page in his life when it came to dating and women. Fast, overnight relationships originating in bar rooms were no longer on his list. Besides, he was not an Adam Ainsworth. While on the job, Robert was on the job. Playtime would have to come at a different time and place, not here and now.

Feeling somewhat uneasy about being a target of these women, Robert tried to find a more secluded table, or place at the bar, so contact with them would be minimal. Upon moving, he discovered the table where the women were seated was a visual vantage point to any chair or table in the bar. The old gut feeling was beginning to engage, as he wondered about the location where the perpetrators sat a few nights ago, when Angela Tyler was at the August Moon. For sure, the table where the women were seated was a definite possibility. This was an area away from the main flow of the bar but a strategic visual point for all locations.

Robert sat watching the crowd for almost an hour, as if wishing for a clue or some evidence to fall into his lap. Thoughts of Investigator Ainsworth's little endeavor upstairs in the stripper's room were now far removed from his mind. For some reason, Angela Tyler's case was priority. Being shot at in Oklahoma was a case that his JDLST unit was capable of handling. The words, "the Devil's Elbow," were embedded in Robert's brain. Maybe, just maybe, these words would help solve several of the mysteries in Robert's life right now.

While Robert's mind was adrift, the bar began to fill rapidly. No longer were there many unfilled tables and bar stools. It was as if a herd of cattle had just been released from their pen.

"Hey bartender, where the heck did everyone come from?" As with many cops in this situation, Robert needed an answer to this little mystery.

"You must be from out of town. The ballpark is right across the highway and the game just let out. This place fills up fast after the game is over. We have a lot of fans, and groupies, who come in. There are a lot of ball players who also come here to relax and find some evening entertainment, if you catch my drift. They are a big crowd drawer for us. This place is pretty popular, you know. Several times a week we have a local television channel that comes in to do some clips for a late night, local entertainment show. We really hate it when the season is over. So, what can I get you?"

"Let's go for diet cola, tonight.... I have a question for you. A few nights ago was the TV crew in here filming?"

"Why, you're old lady cheating on you, Buddy?"

Robert did not verbally reply. His wallet was in hand in preparation for his drink to arrive so he could pay. Now, Robert had a new task for it. Upon unfolding it, the wallet revealed his federal shield and ID.

"I'm a federal officer."

"You must be working on the case where that babe got her throat cut. Look, I have already spoken with some detectives but could not really give them much."

"Please, just answer my question," instructed Robert.

"Yes, Sir, they were."

"Details, please, I need to know who they are."

"Channel 17, DFW Entertainment. They are a local cable channel that specializes in local entertainment. They hit a lot of city bars for a late night show they run on weekends. Once here, the crew stays until things get late and crazy. The nuttier the women are in here, the higher their ratings are. Hopefully, they can help you out."

"Thanks, you have been more than helpful."

Robert laid a ten-dollar bill down as he worked his way past the table of his earlier observers and into the main lobby of the hotel. A quick look at his watch revealed that Adam had been in the room with his CI for almost two hours now. Robert then glanced at his beeper to see if he had missed a page from his partner but as expected, there was nothing.

I don't give a crap what you are doing now, Mr. Adam, but playtime is over.

The elevator soon stopped at the top floor and Robert made his way toward the hallway's end. Upon reaching the last door, he slid the key in and slung back the door. Robert had expected to see Adam and his little mate entangled under the sheets but he was wrong. Dallas and Adam had made their way from the bedroom to the main room in her suite. They both sat on a couch, with a coffee table in front. Robert was somewhat surprised as he saw Adam counting a large amount of cash on the table. Not just a few hundred bucks that most topless dancers earn a night, but thousands. The entire table was covered with bills.

Without an immediate explanation to Robert, Adam stuffed a gym bag with a majority of the money.

"You ready, Partner?"

Only a nod was given by Robert. He was somewhat confused by what he just witnessed and was not for sure how to respond to Adam. He just stood by as Dallas and Adam gave each other a short embrace goodbye.

"Pretty hot mama, eh Buddy?"

"Yea, you bet, Adam."

"Sorry about the delay, but I had to tame that little Philly!"

"You must have been pretty good at it. Looks like she pays well for your services."

"Oh, the money. Dallas and I have been friends with benefits for several years now. I seem to remember telling you a while back that I recently went through a divorce. Well, that little endeavor stung the ol' pocketbook, along with screwing up my credit. I am personally in need of a new set of wheels but my credit is too poor to get financing. So, my little lady back there volunteered to help me out. She makes some good cash dancing at Fantasy Dreams."

"Well, tell me, Studly, how much does a gal like her make a night?"

"Well, Robert, let's just say that a thousand dollar night is a very slow work day for her."

"You have got to be kidding?"

Adam did not reply, instead he just pointed to the cash-bag. Robert just shook his head as they both exited the hotel and made their way to the Porsche.

"Hey, Robert. I know you think I was just screwing around and taking care of personal business up there but I was doing a little work, too. Sometimes a man just has to sacrifice his body for the team. Anyway, Dallas told me about some dude that is a regular at Fantasy Dreams. He is new in town and pumping a lot of methamphetamine into our town. I want to run over and check that cat out. Any objections?"

"Nope, let's ride, Lone Ranger, let's ride...."

Few words were said as Adam cranked up the stereo as his Porsche entered westbound I-30, headed toward Ft. Worth.

Robert could not but help wonder what Investigator Adam Ainsworth was all about. An undetected look at the roid-boy driving his Porsche and his duffle bag of cash reflected Robert's doubts about his new partner. The JDLST unit had a reputation for being the cream of the crop, but the jury was definitely still out on which crop Investigator Ainsworth was from.

As the sports car sped toward Ft. Worth, Robert closed his eyes and focused on the music, in an attempt to erase his suspicious thoughts about his new partner.

CHAPTER 14

The skyline of downtown Ft. Worth laid just to the west as Investigator Ainsworth directed his Porsche up Interstate 35, toward the north part of the city. An industrial section of north Ft. Worth was the home to several new gentlemen's clubs, including Fantasy Dreams. Federal and State zoning regulations left few new territories in the city for these strip clubs. The vast expansion of the city encompassed areas comprised mostly of residential, schools and churches that were clustered in close proximity. This type of development excluded the possibility of strip clubs, since zoning regulations require them to be one thousand yards from family oriented areas. This industrial area in north Ft. Worth was void of these family areas; therefore, numerous men's clubs invaded this locale. As Adam navigated his vehicle through this maze of industry and gentlemen's clubs, it was obvious he had made this journey many times before. His vehicle seemed to be on autopilot.

As Adam pulled into the parking lot of Fantasy Dreams, Robert received a number on his pager, one which was not familiar to him.

"Hey, Adam, do you have your cell phone with you?" Robert's question broke the long-standing silence.

"Yep, certainly."

"I need to make a quick call. You mind?"

"Certainly not, Robert. I will be inside the club, so we'll meet you there when you're done."

The old gut feeling was eating away at Robert for some reason. The number on his pager was one he had never seen before but for some reason he was compelled to immediately return it. He dialed the numbers of 817-555-4625 and waited for the cell phone to find a tower. A couple of rings then ensued, when a female with a soft, raspy voice answered.

"Hello."

"Yes, this is Robert. I just received a page from this number."

"Detective James, this in Angela Tyler . . . . Detective, are you still there?"

A knot immediately developed in Robert's throat, almost choking any subsequent words. The voice of Angela Tyler both surprised and stunned him.

"Yes, Ms. Tyler, I am here. How may I be of assistance to you?"

"Detective, as you can understand I am limited to my words right now but I was wondering if you could stop by the hospital tomorrow. I would like to discuss my case with you. Would around 3:00 PM be okay?"

"Certainly, Ms. Tyler. I will see you then."

As he hung up the phone, once again Robert was feeling a little shot of adrenalin flowing through his veins. For some reason, his pulse was thumping in his neck as he anticipated meeting the mysterious and beautiful victim of such a horrific crime. The thoughts of his unethical partner seemed to no longer matter.

Once inside Fantasy Dreams, Robert was amazed by such a Vegas type atmosphere contained in this north Ft. Worth club. The exquisite and expensive décor and exotic women made this place reek of money. The clientele were not what one might expect; they were not mostly blue-collar workers. Men with thick wallets and never ending corporate expense accounts inhabited this den-of-sin.

After the initial awe subsided and Robert had done his quick scan of the crowd, a search for Adam began. It did not take long for Robert to find his buddy. It only required taking a close look at a covey of strippers hovering over one of the clients. Right in the middle of the group was his work partner.

"I can tell this is your first time here, partner." Robert said sarcastically.

"Well, ol' Robbie boy, this is a tough job but someone has to do it. Have a seat and let's see if our meth boy that Dallas was telling me about, shows."

Robert then made himself comfortable, preparing himself for a long wait for the new player to show up. Fantasy Dreams was a large club containing many small rooms for patrons to enjoy a private dance from a stripper of their choice. Once this meth dealer arrived, keeping tabs on him would certainly be challenging. There were two things that captivated the attention of these dancers. First was money, with a close second being drugs. With some, the reverse order was true. Whichever the case was, a surplus of either could finance an after-hour's rendezvous.

Despite the club being a place Robert would not be hanging out at during his free time, he could not deny the visual enjoyment of the beautiful women working there. It was obvious how easily a weak-willed man could be absorbed with this atmosphere and go home with an empty wallet. Not only were these strippers attractive, but their talents for using psychology on their patrons was cunning. Their promises for future dates, accompanied by personal hard luck stories, seemed to make money flow their way. Only few who walked through the doors would recognize these tactics were lies and protect their finances. Watching the women work this crowd of suckers, made it easy to believe how Dallas could make thousands a week.

While Adam was distracted by the semi-clothed women, Robert was thinking about his meeting with Angela Tyler tomorrow, as he continued scanning the room. A meth dealer in a room filled with suits should be an easy target to find. Despite the fact that some methamphetamine dealers made fortunes on their destructive potions, few ever considered investing much of it on a professional wardrobe. Blue jeans and an inexpensive shirt, accompanied by long, un-groomed hair, were symbolic of most. Tonight though, Robert had spotted an exception.

As with his partner, Robert noticed a group of women constantly entertaining a man who partially fit the description of a meth cook or dealer. The man remained seated at a corner table, as if he wanted to remain unnoticed to most patrons in the club. Despite his obscure location, the dancers seemed to have no problem locating him. Once money or drugs are detected, it almost becomes a catfight between the dancers to see whom the lucky one, or few, will be his for the evening. This individual was slim and seemingly tall, bearing long hair and a ruddy complexion.

After watching his target for some time, Robert noticed the man standing from the table and making his way in the direction of the men's room. It was a place that no person in a bar can elude for a long period. Robert carefully scoped out his target as the man made his way toward the restroom. One thing suddenly caught his eye. After moving to Texas, Robert became somewhat familiar with cowboy boots and the many skins they could be made of. Initially, Robert thought his target was wearing a pair of snakeskin boots, but something did not look right. It almost appeared as if the footwear was actually tennis shoes, and not boots. In addition, he was also wearing a belt made of the same material.

"Hey Adam, check out the dude walking to the men's room, the one who is wearing the snakeskin shoes and belt. Have you ever seen him before?" Robert knew the answer to his own question but it was time to test his new partner.

"Yea, I have. He's a no-body, Robert. Let's not waste our time and effort on him."

"Ok, but who is Mr. Nobody? I'm curious." Robert did not wish to share his suspicions with Adam.

"I am not for sure of his real name but he goes by Snakeskin Billy. Maybe those shoes and belt will help you remember his name."

This had to be him, the Snakeskin Billy that Investigator Waterman told him about earlier. The chances of two societal oddities such as this were slim, real slim. A guy like him does not pass un-noticed, which was verified by the heads turning as Snakeskin Billy passed the table of local business executives. The lack of concern by Adam also struck a sour note with Robert. Investigators in the JDLST are trained and possess skills that allow them to find the crooks in the crowd and focus on them. Trying to figure out "who and what" is an unconscious game that a seasoned cop initiates whenever they notice someone like Billy. Robert questioned the reasoning why Adam did not notice the doper who was sporting the snakeskin sneakers and belt. Just the fact that the man looked like a meth cook or dealer should have alerted Adam, not to mention the attire. Then, once the man was brought to Adam's attention, he seemed to want to immediately avoid the topic.

Robert tried his best to justify Adam's inattention to Snakeskin Billy. Being a lady's man, maybe Adam was too absorbed with the dancers who immediately surrounded him upon entering the club. Based on what he had already seen from his new partner, there was little doubt that Adam's priorities were women. It was rapidly becoming obvious to Robert that teaming up with Adam was more burdensome than working solo. There was no wonder why none of the other investigators wanted to work with Investigator Ainsworth. When teaming with another cop, each had to trust the other and know that no matter what type of situation was encountered, your partner "had your back." During their short tenure as working partners, the only back Adam had demonstrated he could cover was that of a half naked female. With or without Adam covering him, Robert had a job to do and Snakeskin Billy was his new target.

It only took Billy a short time to take care of personal business in the restroom before he was back at his obscure table with dancers swarming like flies. Despite the multitude of businessmen with their wallets filled with Gold and Platinum cards, Snakeskin Billy was a main attraction for many of these dancers. Drugs and money, or money and drugs; both were equally important to these women.

Time passed unnoticed for Robert, as his attention focused constantly on his new target. It seemed as if Billy was corralled by these women who were protecting some sort of prized possession. Despite the obvious appearance of a drug dealer, Billy was of elevated interest to Detective Robert James. According to an old informant, Rusty Sims, this meth dealer had a connection to drug Lord, Gene King. If Rusty's information was close to the truth, this man could have in some way participated in the ambush that almost harmed his daughter. This was an inexcusable sin for which all who were involved had a price to pay. Robert had been instructed by Special Agent Michaels to leave the situation alone; to let the other team members and local law enforcement handle it. For something of this magnitude, things were not going fast enough for him. As Investigator Waterman had just told him earlier, Snakeskin Billy had eluded police officers on several occasions over the past few days, while driving a red Corvette.

Now, Billy was sitting just a few dozen feet from Robert's table, when it appeared as if something of importance had suddenly caught his attention. Adam Ainsworth apparently felt the call of nature and was proceeding toward the men's room, when Snakeskin Billy observed him. Billy shot from his seat and was quickly walking toward Adam, without a doubt a man on a mission. Prior to being on the JDLST unit, Adam was a local cop who worked the Ft. Worth area.

This could be bad news.

Soon after his hand confirmed the presence of his loaded pistol, Robert began making his way quickly toward the two men so he could cover his law enforcement partner. His journey soon came to a halt when he saw the two were seemingly old friends, greeting each other with a smile and hand shake. This was definitely not the greeting of a hostile criminal who was seeking revenge on a cop responsible for his boss's prison stay. This was the greeting of two old friends that were happy to be in each other's company once again. After a brief conversation, Billy followed Adam into the men's room. At this point Robert did not feel as if Billy was a threat to his partner, so returning to his table seemed to be the best choice for the time. Adam more than likely was also packing a pistol and knew who Billy was, so he would not have continued toward the restroom after making contact if there had been a threat.

Robert returned to his table, watching impatiently for the men to emerge from the room. A few minutes passed and a subtle sign of relief was upon him. Exiting the men's room was Adam, with Billy just a few seconds behind him. Instead of returning to his table, Adam walked over to the bar to order another round of drinks. Robert then watched as Snakeskin Billy returned to his brood of strippers. For some reason, Billy seemed to have a change of disposition upon returning to the girls. After a few words, several of the dancers left his table and began working the floor. What Robert had expected, but dreaded, was now upon him.

"Hey there, Mister, need some company, or maybe a lap dance?"

Robert immediately recognized the woman as one of the strippers that had been previously entertaining Snakeskin Billy. Working the floor was normal for these women, which was the avenue that usually yielded the most tips. Dancing on stage was required of each dancer by management, but this avenue of work resulted in the tipping of smaller bills. The personal lap-dance was where the big money was.

The female's assertiveness went beyond her words. With these women, body language went far beyond what their words usually could. Each dancer had her own method of inflicting her body upon her potential prey, and in a manner that most men could not refuse. Trying not to be rude and still remain inconspicuous, Robert maneuvered the female to the side, so that she would no longer block the view of Snakeskin Billy. As the vixen was moved aside, Robert no longer had Billy in his sights. Snakeskin Billy's entourage was gone, and he had just vanished.

Now in a panic mode, Robert quickly scanned the building looking for Investigator Ainsworth. He figured the easiest way to locate Adam was by searching the room for a group of dancers hovering around their prize. Therefore, it did not take but a few seconds to find his law enforcement partner.

"THE KEYS, GIVE ME THE KEYS!" Robert ordered Adam in a shouting, whisper.

"Where are you going, Robert?"

"Just keep your beeper on and I will call you from the cell phone in a few minutes. Just carry on with your undercover work here, Buddy." Robert then grabbed the keys from Adam's hand before he had an opportunity to question him any further.

As Robert burst through Fantasy Dream's front door, the sight and sounds of a red Corvette speeding from the parking lot was proof evident that Snakeskin Billy was on the run. Somehow, he had been tipped off and Robert had a good idea whom the culprit was.

"You're not getting away this time, you Bastard!" Robert shouted to himself.

The Porsche's five-speed transmission made it somewhat difficult to drive and talk, but Robert knew this situation necessitated the assistance of some patrol vehicles. Despite the capable speeds of the Porsche, marked patrol cars and possible aerial support would be needed, for safety reasons.

Both vehicles were winding their way through the industrial area at high speeds. Robert knew the Corvette would be able to outperform most patrol vehicles but the Porsche would be an equal match. Snakeskin Billy was a paranoid meth-head, who had already noticed he was being followed. After setting a pace with the Corvette, Robert was able to free one hand in an effort to search for his hand-held police radio.

"Federal Unit 664 to Tarrant County." The excitable voice left no guessing from a dispatcher that Robert was involved in a critical or emergency situation.

"Federal Unit 664, this is Tarrant County. Go ahead with your traffic."

"Tarrant County, I am in pursuit of a red Corvette that is being driven by a felony fugitive. We are northbound on Blue Mound Road approaching Interstate 820. I need some patrol units and a possible chopper, if yours is available."

"10-4, Unit 664. I will have several traffic and district units in route to assist. Please keep us updated on your location."

Just as suspected, Billy had directed his Corvette onto westbound I-820. This was a wide, moderately used road that would allow him to reach speeds that most patrol cars were incapable of. Robert then began winding each gear of his European chariot to speeds he had never traveled before. 140, 150, 165 miles per hour, and still climbing. At these speeds, Robert was too scared to take his hands from the steering wheel to give a location update. Upon approaching an upcoming overpass, he felt some relief seeing two patrol units sitting on the shoulder of the road, awaiting their approach. The patrol vehicles were several of the sheriff's new Camaro's, which sported Corvette engines under their hoods. These cars were capable of being contenders in this contest of speed. Yes, the race against this jackrabbit was on.

"Federal Unit 664, this is Major Long with the sheriff's office. Do you copy?"

Reluctantly, Robert maneuvered slowly and carefully in order to confirm the Major's transmission via his radio.

"10-4 Major Long, go ahead with your traffic."

"The sheriff's office now has two ground units on your suspect, with Air Unit 102 closing in on the pursuit. You can break off your involvement at this time."

Robert was astounded by what he had just heard. This Major was trying to get him to drop out of the pursuit since they now had units involved. Snakeskin Billy was too hot of a suspect to back off. Besides the felony warrants, this crook may have been involved in shooting at little Paige. It did not take much hesitation for Robert to respond back.

"Negative, Major Long. This is a hot pursuit of a fugitive. This unit will continue."

The reply back to Robert was almost instantaneous, as if the sheriff's ranking officer was expecting it.

"Federal Unit 664, I am giving you a direct order to shut it down. You are not in an emergency vehicle and your continued involvement could create a hazardous situation. SHUT IT DOWN, 664!"

Robert knew the Major was right. His vehicle was void of any lights or sirens. He was driving a vehicle that did not comply with the state laws that outlined an emergency vehicle. If for some reason he was involved in an accident, a civil suit and possibly even a criminal case against him could ensue.

"Federal Unit 664 to Tarrant County, I am no longer active in the pursuit."

"10-4, Federal 664, we have you marked out."

The high-pitched humming from the Porsche's gears began to subside as Robert watched Billy's red Corvette and the pursuing patrol vehicles round a corner and fade from sight. The first exit from the freeway revealed a convenience store. A cold drink was certainly in order. He could sit there and monitor the pursuit until he heard the location of Snakeskin Billy's apprehension.

As Robert coasted his machine into the parking lot, a loud noise caught his attention. Flying directly overhead was Air Unit 102, which was a Bell Jet Ranger chopper. Despite being somewhat afraid of flying, Robert was pretty familiar with aircraft and knew the capabilities of the helicopter. Despite the fact it could fly in a crow's path, the ground units had a faster top end than the law enforcement copter he just observed. Plus, by now the bird was several miles behind the pursuit that was exceeding the 160 MPH mark. Robert was to remain optimistic, knowing there is no way to predict the direction of a vehicle pursuit.

Before Robert could exit his car, he overheard a disappointing report from the patrol units. They had lost sight of Billy.

"Damn, damn, DAMN . . . . That bastard has done it again!"

The screaming from the Porsche was overheard by two patrons who distanced themselves as they approached the store. Avoiding the madman in the sports car was their priority.

The JDLST detective had little concern for the chatter over the radio between the patrol cars and their commanding officer. They were to meet at a location several miles south of his location to debrief with Major Long. Robert heard the Major call for him several times before he could muster the control to respond—he was pissed off.

I was right on Billy's bumper and got called off. I had that guy; he was all mine!

Controlling his anger would be necessary before meeting with the pursing patrol units. This was mandatory after all pursuits, and most certainly the sheriff's office would need the justification for the pursuit to list in their reports. Robert had been in their shoes many times in similar situations. Despite the chase being initiated by him, the sheriff's office also had reporting requirements that needed to be met.

The de-briefing between the JDLST detective, Major Long and the pursuing deputies lasted about thirty minutes, which was much longer than Robert initially figured to be with them. His temper had cooled and his attitude rapidly de-escalated as he listened to details of the chase from the patrolmen. The high speeds and reckless driving that was demonstrated by the driver made it necessary for the pursuing deputies to reduce their speeds once the suspect exited the interstate and entered a business and residential area. The risk of innocent lives, especially children, was not worth the immediate apprehension of a fugitive, as told to all by the Major. He continued by apologizing for the helicopter not making it to the area in time, but the speeds the suspect was driving made it difficult for even a helicopter to catch up.

Once the deputies completed their de-briefing, Major Long dismissed them to return to their districts. Robert and the Major had some additional time to discuss why he was called off the chase. Without being told, Robert knew and agreed with the decision the commanding officer had made. Despite being a federal officer, Robert knew that in this situation the Major was right; therefore, submitting to his orders to discontinue was the right decision. He then modestly apologized to Major Long for the brief defiance, which followed with a short discussion about Robert's law enforcement roots, along with his assignment.

"Now I know who you are, Detective James. If I am correct, you are the officer that took down that doper, Gene King. Did this chase have anything to do with him?"

Robert responded with a few modest words to the Major, and continued by giving a few details about Snakeskin Billy's arrest warrant, along with being wanted for questioning in his own shooting in Oklahoma.

"Quite a story there, Mr. James. We will put out an all points bulletin for Billy and try to bag that turkey for you. If the broadcast is successful, then I will instruct my supervisors to call you immediately. These dopers usually don't go too far away from their nest, so sooner or later, we will bag him. And Robert, drive careful, okay, Son?"

The light humor from the Major was a good ending for an initially intense situation, causing Robert's face to erupt into a moderate smile as he entered the Porsche. As he turned the ignition, a warning bell went off. Robert had not thought much about the fuel situation but if he had continued much further in the pursuit, both he and the Porsche would have been sitting on the highway's shoulder waiting for a tow truck to arrive. At least Robert knew he was close to one convenience store—that is if the workers don't call the cops when they see the "mad man" returning.

As he pulled into the parking lot, Robert could not believe what his eyes were seeing. A red Corvette, with the same custom work that Snakeskin Billy's had. The car was parked on the side of the store, close by two pay phones, and Snakeskin Billy was sitting inside. Apparently, Billy did not see Robert pull in, so he steered the Porsche next to a three-quarter ton pickup truck and parked on the blind side of it. Thoughts of how to handle this situation were racing through Robert's head. Knowing that Billy was a bad boy, chances are he would be armed with a gun. This was not Robert's main concern, due to being in situations like this many times in the past, and being very well trained in hazardous take-downs. The element of surprise would be a key factor here. Robert knew that if he could just get close to the car, Billy was all his.

Luck seemed to be with the detective. By the time Robert had crept around the back of the convenience store, Billy had exited his car and was talking on the pay phone. Outdoor pay phones were primarily used for drug deals these days, but Robert was betting against it this time. Most likely Billy was calling someone to explain the situation and maybe get a place to hide out for a few days. Without a doubt, Billy knew he was hotter than hell with law enforcement right now.

Snakeskin Billy stood facing the parking lot and not paying a bit of attention to the back of the store, which was the direction Robert was approaching from. Dusk had just fallen, aiding in facial obscurity that could work in his favor when approaching Billy. Just when the detective was within twenty-feet of his target, bad luck once again struck—Robert's pager went off, giving away his stealthy approach. For some odd reason, Billy did not even look at the pager bearer who was approaching. It was common knowledge that most people using these phones would be returning a page from someone, which must have been the assumption of Billy. Without pondering his strategy, Robert went to the pay phone next to Billy and dropped a quarter in. With his back toward the wanted fugitive, the detective began a conversation with his personal home message recorder after dialing the phone.

Having a conversation with his own voice recorder was a challenging task for anyone, including Robert. With his back turned toward Billy, there was little chance the fugitive would recognize the cop he had only seen once before. Pausing between his lines in his fake conversation, Robert was able to eavesdrop on Billy and confirmed his suspicions were correct. Snakeskin Billy was trying to line up a hideout for a few days, but with who was not known. Robert was able to conclude that Billy was speaking with a female but her name was never mentioned. Possibly, one of the strippers back at Fantasy Dreams but he was not for sure. As Robert listened, he could tell Billy's conversation was about to end.

The time to act was just seconds away. Robert's heart began to pound in a fast paced rhythm caused by a massive adrenalin dump. The detective began to position his body to where Billy would be seen but still not allowing the criminal a full view of him. Time seemed to stand still as Billy hung up the receiver and began his journey back to the Corvette. The fugitive then opened the door and started sliding his body into the car seat. For Billy, at this moment time began to stand still, too. The fugitive was frozen in his car seat, with a 40-caliber pistol attached to his cheek.

"Move you Bastard and I promise you will die! I am a federal officer, Billy. I'm Detective James, as in Robert James!"

Robert had wondered how his encounter with Snakeskin Billy would begin, and more importantly, end. A million thoughts about how to handle their encounter had been rushing through Robert's head but nothing seemed to be the exact fit. It was finally concluded he would just let his instincts take over. Billy was initially speechless, sitting in the crosshairs of an enraged detective pressing a large caliber pistol against his face with one hand, with the other around his neck. The criminal knew he could do nothing at this point but comply.

"Please, do not pull that trigger, Mr. James, please, I am begging you!"

Fury and fire were still running through Robert's veins, as he increased the pressure of the pistol against Billy's cheek. The entire situation in Oklahoma of him and Paige being blown off the highway by Billy or one of his buddies kept flashing through his mind. Both men knew that if this encounter ended with a bullet in Billy's head, not a grand jury in the land would indict the detective. The big, bad, Snakeskin Billy was no longer elusive and here he sits at the mercy of a badge-toting vigilante. Billy could sense the detective was mentally in another place, and not in the proper mindset of a cop. This criminal knew at any moment his life might go dark forever.

"Detective James, I am begging you, please put down your gun. I know what you want and I will tell you everything!"

Those words, combined with an odd odor, began to bring Robert back to a semi-normal state of mind. Upon looking at the submissive and cowardly expression on Billy's face, Robert knew his prey had become completely obedient. Looped around the cop's belt was a set of handcuffs that he had grabbed before exiting the Porsche. With extreme caution, Robert sternly began barking orders to the criminal that his pistol's sights were still affixed to.

"Put on your seatbelt, Billy, and do it now!"

Confused but compliant, Billy quickly secured the seatbelt around himself.

"Now, Billy, place both hands on top of the steering wheel and do it now, Billy!"

The words of Detective James would go unchallenged. At this point Billy was finally able to take a breath, knowing the detective was in the process of making the right decision. The first cuff was secured around the left wrist. Robert then interlaced the cuff chain through the steering wheel and attached the second one to his captive's right wrist. A quick and thorough search for a pistol revealed two things. Under the driver's seat was a Smith and Wesson 9MM semi-auto pistol. The second observation revealed the source for the odor Robert had smelled. After feeling the cold steel of Robert's pistol against his cheek, Snakeskin Billy urinated on himself. Apparently, Billy was not all that tough after all. At this point Robert knew this elusive fugitive was all his and ripe for the picking.

Now it dawned on Robert where he was. Fearful of curious customers, or maybe even one who was carrying their own weapon, he slowly turned around. Much to his surprise there was no one around. The confrontation between him and Billy had gone undetected.

Snakeskin Billy had been broken and Robert knew there would be no better time to interrogate his captive than this moment. He quickly made his way to the passenger side of the Corvette, opened the door and climbed into the seat of his new interrogation room. Snakeskin Billy's confession would now begin. Robert knew the smell of victory would soon accompany that of Billy's body odor.

This would be one of the easiest confessions Detective James had ever extracted from a suspect. After entering the car, Robert only spoke a few words before Billy consumed the following thirty minutes with details about the Oklahoma incident. According to the suspect, he had been contacted by his boss and given the orders to execute Detective Robert James. Billy was supplied with details of Robert's vehicle, along with the location of his residence in Dallas. The information Billy was supplied with informed him that Robert would be leaving for a vacation in Missouri within a few days of receiving the assignment. Billy swore to Robert that he was not involved in the actual shooting, but coordinating the hit was his sole responsibility. The names of the shooter and driver, along with their personal information, were given up. His confession also included the location of the involved suspects and weapon used in the shooting. Everything Robert wanted was now at hand, with the exception of who gave the order. One thing Robert was good at was reading an individual during an interview or interrogation. Robert's gut instinct was telling him that under no circumstances would Billy be giving up the name that contracted him. When the suspect was asked if Gene King was the one who ordered the hit, Billy just sat in silence. He knew that snitching off Gene King would mean certain death; despite the fact the King was in a federal prison. To Robert, silence was a definitive answer to his question but not one he could take to court. He also knew if Billy rolled over on Gene King, the drug lord would sign a death warrant for the rat. Detective James sat contently as Billy finally went silent.

"One last question, Billy. Tell me about your conversation between you and that other guy in the men's room earlier."

"You mean that make believe Federal Agent, Adam Ainsworth? Let me warn you about that stripper-loving cop. I don't trust him, my friends don't trust him and neither should you!"

"Why?"

"Just give it some time, Detective James, and you will see—just give it some time." Billy had now completed his confession and then slumped his head in silence.

Robert then reached down and removed the Corvettes' keys from the passenger floorboard where they had fallen.

"Be right back, Billy. Don't go away."

As Robert jogged back to the Porsche to retrieve his radio, the thought of the enormity of what just happened made him shudder. Anger and rage had completely possessed him like a demon, forcing away the law enforcement officer that he was. Robert quickly made a promise to himself that he would never reveal to anyone that he truly had considered killing Snakeskin Billy this evening.

"Federal Unit 664 to Tarrant County Major Long." Robert egotistically said into his police radio.

"Go ahead Federal 664, Major Long here."

"Send a couple of squad cars and a tow truck to the Lake Worth Quik Stop, at I-820 and White Settlement Road. Snakeskin Billy needs a taxi ride downtown."

In seemed like only a matter of seconds had passed before Robert heard the approaching sirens and saw several county deputies speeding into the parking lot. The transfer of the soiled prisoner to the deputies assured Robert that he could now relax.

One of the three crime riddles facing Robert had been solved and it was now time to head home.

A little evil smile crossed Robert's face as he reached for Adam's cell phone and dialed his partner's pager number. The wait for Adam to return the call made Robert snicker aloud several times. Within a few minutes, the car phone was ringing.

"Where the hell are you, Robert? You left me stranded, and where is my Porsche?"

"Sorry ol' pal, but I took your advice and like you, found a woman. I hooked up with one of the dancers and it looks like I won't be able to make it back to the club tonight. I promise I will take care of your shiny Porsche and will have it back at the office bright and early tomorrow."

"YOU JACK A . . . . !" Robert did not let his screaming new partner finish his words before pulling the plug on the call. A message had just been conveyed to Adam Ainsworth.

"Now take me to Dallas, you sexy European Beast! I think I could get used to driving you, little Ms. Porsche."

The jailing of Snakeskin Billy and putting his questionable new work partner in his place gave way to a perfect ending to Robert's day.

CHAPTER 15

One of the small pleasures Robert enjoyed about being on the JDLST unit was the flexibility in hours. Each Monday, Special Agent Michaels made it mandatory for all team members to be in the office by 11:00 AM for a weekly briefing; but otherwise, each was on their own time schedule. The boss was seasoned enough to know it was not feasible for a cop working illegal drug and organized crime cases to be punching a time clock. Also, most of the men working in the unit were dedicated to their jobs to the point the boss man did not doubt that each was on the streets putting in more than their time. Indeed, if these investigators were punching a time clock, the cost for overtime pay would be an expensive tab for the taxpayers. The cops on the JDSLT unit were exceptional in their dedication to law enforcement, most of them anyway.

Prior to going home last night, Robert made a stop by the office so he could drop off Adam's set of wheels. There was no doubt that Adam was pissed at him but a lesson had to be taught to this loose-cannoned working partner. Without a word being spoken, Adam received a very definitive lesson that his actions at the hotel and Fantasy Dreams were not approved of. A taxicab fare back to the office was a mild form of punishment for his bad behavior. The door to the JDLST office was controlled by an electronic keypad and spare keys to all unit vehicles were kept in a common location, so Robert was not concerned about Adam being able to retrieve his precious Porsche, once he made it back to the office.

Upon waking this morning, Robert had decided to make a late working day of it. After breakfast, a call back to his father in Springdale was his first priority. This new father was missing his daughter, along with the guilt feeling of somewhat abandoning little Paige. Most of the ten-minute long conversation consisted of stories about the little girl and how she loved spending time with her grandfather and auntie. Robert expected nothing less from his father, due to the track record with his family for the past thirty years. Being a single father is no easy chore with one child; but is minor by comparison to having three to tend to as his father did. Before concluding, Robert had to inquire if there had been any more news reports about the accident on Interstate 44 he had witnessed. It was no surprise when Mr. James informed his son that it had been a mute issue around town.

A 3:00 PM appointment soon dominated Robert's thoughts as he began preparing himself for work. All of his actions from showering to brushing his teeth were more time consuming due to the mental diversion of the Angela Tyler case. A quick call to the Crimes against Person's Unit at Arlington PD confirmed that no one had yet been able to interview the victim about her case. Ms. Tyler's physicians had instructed the detectives that once she was ready and able to speak with officers, they would inform them of such. Up to this point, all law enforcement authorities had been kept at bay.

The drive to Arlington went faster than usual, possibly due to the mid-afternoon traffic being the lightest than during any other time throughout the day. Driving through this crowded metropolitan area of millions was usually a time consuming and frustrating event. At times, a ten-mile drive could take a person as long as one hour to complete. Today this was not the case, allowing Robert to arrive at Dalworth Regional Hospital almost thirty minutes ahead of schedule. With his appointment being with a female, especially one who was a hospital patient, popping in ahead of schedule would not be welcomed.

It had only been a few days since Robert had mysteriously ended up as a patient at the hospital himself. However, being back in town and with many other issues on his plate, his own dilemma had been put on the back burner, but not forgotten.

The incident in Missouri was too complex to solve without one dedicating their entire attention to it; and time for this was not possible now, more pressing matters were at hand.

A gift shop caught his attention and the idea of a small token for this victim seemed to be a good choice for gaining her acceptance. The gift items on the shelves seemed to concentrate mostly on flowers, candy and cards; but none of these would be appropriate for the moment. This little token had to be strategically chosen, something not personal but showing Ms. Tyler she was in his thoughts. Off to the side was a magazine rack that was loaded with material. This would be his choice, a small gesture of something showing consideration, but also a tool to put Ms. Tyler's mind back in gear. A few choices were made and as Robert paid, a glance at his watch reflected their meeting was only five minutes away.

As it did a few days ago, it did not take a facility map, or even a room number to find Angela Tyler's hospital room. The armed police officers and their blue uniforms blatantly marked the spot. Several of them began to alert when this unidentified man dressed in civilian clothes was approaching the room. The motion of Robert's hand toward his badge pocket set in motion a chain effect; Robert observed two of the officers maneuvering their hands toward their weapons.

"At ease, officers, I am a federal investigator." These words were accompanied by Robert showing the uniformed guards his law enforcement credentials.

"Just one second, Sir. I need to make sure you are on the list." The words were spoken by a female officer, wearing the "butter bars" on her lapel, symbolizing she was a lieutenant in rank, and the superior officer at the scene.

The visitor's list was a short one and it only took a few seconds for Robert's passage into the room to be approved.

"You're good to go, Detective James, but just let me announce your arrival to Ms. Tyler."

The lieutenant was only in the room for a short time before she re-appeared, and then allowed Robert into Ms. Tyler's room.

The door was left partially ajar by the lieutenant, allowing Robert a partial view of the room that included only the bed, which was apparently void of the victim. Much to his surprise Angela was sitting in a chair next to the window, staring outside as she was longing to be present there.

"You would think, Detective James, that with the price I am paying for this place at least they would give me a little better view. Come on over and pull up a chair, Mr. James."

Robert was caught by surprise with the intensity and clarity Angela Tyler was able to speak. Just days ago she was almost dead, with her throat cut severely and a grim prognosis. Today, Ms. Tyler sat speaking clearly and firmly. When she turned and faced him, the pale look of the living dead was no longer reflected on her face. Instead, the victim was colorful and glowing, obviously happy to be alive. Her hair was now clean, long and flowing in a manner reminding Robert of a Lady Madonna painting he had once seen. The beginning of a large smile was quickly subdued by the pain such movement must have caused. A clean, white bandage encompassing Angela's neck seemed to be almost chic and stylish for her look and personality.

"Will do, Ms. Tyler," was Robert's immediate response.

"Detective, if my mother was here, the title of Ms. Tyler might be fitting but she is not, so Angela is sufficient."

This little icebreaker was enough for Robert to know what type of person he was dealing with. Despite the fact that Angela Tyler was the only heir to the Sam Tyler fortune, one of the states most financially elite, she did not wish to be treated as such. Ms. Tyler was a victim and the law enforcement official she had chosen to help her was now present, so Angela's world seemed to be content, for the moment.

As Robert pulled his chair next to Ms. Tyler, he was somewhat mesmerized by her eyes. Like a cat's they were, with one being elongated and the other normal. Another thing Robert had never noticed before was this beauty possessed one brown eye and the other was blue in color. This was truly a genetic defect but one that added to the mystique of Angela Tyler.

"Well, Angela, obviously you know that I have been assigned to work on your case. I am curious though; I am the first cop who you have spoken with. So, why me?"

"Detective James, the fact that I am even here is a miracle and I guess God decided to keep me around for a while, for whatever reason. I cannot even begin to describe the thoughts and feelings that go though one's mind when knocking on death's door. Some are too horrific to even talk about, while others were actually warm and calming. I remember almost everything, from the assault itself to my ensuing struggle to exit the room and look for help. From the time I forced myself from the bed to when help finally arrived in the lobby, it seemed to take an entire lifetime, but in slow motion. I was scared, weak and cold. My mind was involved in a struggle between wanting to lie down and die, versus fighting to live. It was nothing like I had ever imagined because when I was on the brink of death, the sensation was actually a warm and calming feeling. For some reason, the instinct to survive dominated me to the point of giving me the strength to go on."

The story was totally captivating. Robert had seen death many times with his job, but he had never heard a near death experience being conveyed to him like this.

"Am I rambling too much, Detective?" asked Angela.

"No, please go on."

"Then it was lights out and the next thing I knew, I heard a voice talking about a small child, next to my hospital bed. I was able to pry open my eyes and there you sat. At first it was a struggle to figure out if you were part of reality, a mental illusion, or maybe even the first person I was meeting in heaven. For several moments I just laid there, looking at you while my mind sorted through each thought. Reality set in when I overheard something about you being a detective. Between those words and the pain that was shooting though my neck, I knew I was alive. So Detective, I hope you know I feel that for some reason you were the one chosen to be here, per se, my guardian cop. First impressions mean a lot to me and the compassion you show your child means a lot. A compassionate person who is a federal agent puts you on my A-list, Detective James. In the event you did not notice, I have yet to meet any of the other detectives working on my case. I have appointed you my "point man" for this investigation, so I hope you do not let me down, Detective."

"No Ma'am, I won't."

"There you go with that formal stuff again, Robert. Please, I am Angela Tyler, not Miss or Madam, OK?"

"Certainly," responded Robert, "Angela it is."

A knock on the door interrupted Ms. Tyler's conversation with her detective. Angela then motioned for the visitor to enter; it was Senator Trey Buckley.

"Detective James, I find myself somewhat tiring fast and would not mind spending a few minutes with Trey, so could I please talk you into another visit around this time tomorrow? We have a lot to talk about."

Robert acknowledged Ms. Tyler's request, stood from his seat and made note of the magazines he was leaving behind for her leisure time.

"Thanks, Detective James, and I will see you tomorrow."

As he began to make his way toward the senator and reached out for a handshake, Senator Buckley requested a meeting outside of the victim's room. The two men then exited and made their way past the guards to a secluded part of the hallway.

"Detective James, in speaking for the Tyler family and myself, I want you to know how much we appreciate your involvement in this case. I know you are assigned to the JDLST unit but your boss has advised us you are one of his best men, and that you also have worked some very complex murder cases throughout your career. I also seem to recall hearing about you recently on the news regarding that Gene King case. Therefore, we all feel that the right man is on the case. Also, for some reason Angela has already taken a liking to you, which I am assuming will work in favor of this case. If there is ANYTHING that I can do to help, just let me know. I am usually one who does not open the favor envelope until something of a high priority comes along, but here we are. I have some pull in Washington, so anything regarding money, travel or manpower; just give me a call and you have it. And Detective James, Angela is one of my closest, childhood friends that I love like a sister. She was brutally violated—I want these animals behind bars! Now, I better get in there before she falls asleep and once again, thank you."

"Your words of confidence and support are appreciated, Senator. Have a good day, Sir."

Despite having few words with Senator Buckley, Robert liked this guy and without a doubt, he was close to Angela Tyler and would do whatever necessary to see her perpetrators brought to justice. Besides, having a United States Senator in one's corner was definitely a good thing.

CHAPTER 16

Two men were escorted into a small office located in one corner of the underground government facility in Devil's Elbow. The two had just arrived from a journey to Texas. They were greeted at the door by a suited, security officer, who escorted the men to their destination. Despite being dark and damp, the room was filled with lavish furniture and state of the art electronics—definitely an executive's office. Standing behind the desk was a face known to both of them.

"Do you have the samples?"

"Yes, sir, we do." One of the men replied, as he handed a small briefcase to the requestor.

The briefcase contained a small box, which when opened, revealed two lab tubes that were filled with blood.

"At least someone did something right. Now, are we sure these are from Angela Tyler? You know, the girl that is STILL ALIVE!"

Both of the men paused, seemingly embarrassed that professionals such as themselves did not successfully complete their mission, and knowing they had pissed off the executive standing in front of them.

"You know who I am? Let me answer that, YOU SURE AS HELL DO! Not only is your error an embarrassment to our group, but it is also a danger to my professional aspirations. You both are failures!"

Two muffled explosions were then heard, just after both of the men's heads hyper-extended backward. The effects of a bullet to the back of the skull—one shot, one kill. Thus, the punishment for not completing their assignment. The man who initially was their security escort, ending up being their executioner.

The executive behind the desk seemed pleased.

"Mop this place up, and get rid of these clowns."

"Yes, Sir," replied the executioner.

The trigger-man took one last look at the men who had been shot, for assurance they were both dead.

With one last gester of disapproval, the executive turned his back to the deceased, took out a cigar and bent down to light the herbal log on a candle. The candle did its job, and more. The cigar was afire, and the candle's flame shed just enough light to reveal not one, but two makings of the pitchfork tattoo on the base of his neck. The executive was also a member of the Devil's club.

CHAPTER 17

Obviously it was now time to face the music; Robert thought as his pager went off, reflecting the call back number of Investigator Adam Ainsworth. He knew the taking of Adam's Porsche would cost him an ass chewing the following day but it was definitely worth any retribution Adam could dish out.

"What's up Adam?" Robert asked as he returned the page.

Astonishingly, Adam did not convey one word about the night before. As Robert had wished, his partner must have figured he was being punished for his bad behavior and justly so.

"You need to get in here, Robert. The boss has some good information for us about the Angela Tyler case."

Robert confirmed he was in route to the JDLST office but did not want to tell Adam where he was or give any information about the meeting with Angela Tyler. For some reason, Robert felt he needed to protect her from all other cops at this time, and especially a partner he personally did not trust.

Upon entering the office, Special Agent Michaels was standing outside his own office, motioning for Robert to join him and Adam. The night before had been an eventful one for Robert, in that he apprehended possibly one of the main players in his Oklahoma shooting. As with other cases in the past, he was expecting his boss to be generous in congratulatory remarks regarding the apprehension and arrest of Snakeskin Billy. Today, such remarks were nonexistent.

"Robert, earlier this morning the police department called regarding Angela Tyler's case. Apparently, they have come across a possible lead, which points to some retired cop-gone-bad, who lives over in Ft. Worth. They have identified him as Harvey Blackburn, going by the alias of Blackie. The last time Blackie was arrested the sheriff's office recorded him having numerous tattoos, one portrayed a devil—just above his elbow. It's not much of a lead, but it is a lead. Since Blackie lives in Ft. Worth, the police department asked if we would do a follow-up on the lead. Any questions, gentlemen?"

"No sir, Boss. Actually, I have an informant who hangs with the Ft. Worth crowd. I will give him a call to see if he knows this guy." Robert responded.

After affirming the information to Special Agent Michaels, both Robert and Adam stood from their seats and started toward the door.

"Robert, I need to discuss another matter with you. Adam, he will join you shortly." Special Agent Michaels assumed a stern demeanor as he dismissed Investigator Ainsworth.

"One more thing, Robert. Just FYI, the rest of the unit is writing warrants and is out rounding up associates of Snakeskin Billy, who were involved in your shooting in Oklahoma. First of all, I want to say that I am relieved these creeps will soon be in custody. Second, Detective James, I AM PISSED! Obviously, you disregarded my instructions to remove yourself from the Oklahoma shooting investigation. This unit has numerous investigators who are capable of handling this situation without you. You have played this game long enough to understand that personal involvement can jeopardize an entire case, not to mention your welfare. There is also some rumor floating around about how Snakeskin Billy was "convinced" to confess his sins. I really don't want to know the truth but if rumors are reflective of such methods, this would be a prime example of how emotions can interfere with law enforcement work. This is the second time you have disregarding my instructions but make no mistake, it will be the last. You have one hell of a future ahead, plus you are one of my best cops. This is a good thing for both of us; so just don't blow it, Okay, son? Now, get out there and get to work."

With his head bowed in shame, Robert acknowledged the words of his commander. Special Agent Michaels was more than just a boss; he was a law enforcement icon combined with a fatherly figure; definitely a man with whom Robert did not want to suffer the loss of mutual confidence and respect. Despite the conquests in his career, Robert did not question the words of Agent Michaels, fearing the repercussions if this occurred. Robert stood up and started to leave the room.

"By the way, Rookie, even though it did not happen the way I wanted it to, I am glad to see Snakeskin Billy in jail—good work." Special Agent Michaels wanted his prized cop to know his good work was once again noted and the slight smile on Robert's face reflected that he understood.

Before hooking up with Investigator Ainsworth in his office, Robert raced to the phone and dialed Rusty Sims' pager number. Within seconds, the phone rang.

"Hey Rusty, I have a name to run by you. Does a guy named Blackie in Ft. Worth ring any bells?"

"Hell yea, Robert. Blackie is a big time crook but is definitely on my buddy list. Why, what do you need from him?"

"Just an introduction and a foot in the door."

"Ok, Mad Dog, but this is going to cost you a few bucks." Rusty's reply was no surprise to Robert. It had also been a while since anyone had called him by his nickname.

After a meeting place was established, Robert ended his conversation with the informant and hastily made his way to Adam Ainsworth's office.

"Grab your gear, Adam; we are headed to Ft. Worth. We need to meet with a CI on the Angela Tyler case. You may want to tone down the look some and put on some older clothes. We may be hanging out in the Stop-6 area of Ft. Worth tonight. You will get us mugged or shot going over to Dopperville dressed like that."

"Don't worry, Robbie, I can handle those folks. I can fit in anywhere, with anyone, anytime!" Adam replied in his typical cocky demeanor.

Robert tried to convey to his partner what a dangerous area Stop-6 was, due to the vast amount of illegal drug activity that occurred there constantly. Hardly a day would go by that the Stop-6 area did not make the news. Adam would not pay heed to these warnings, but seemed anxious to go, knowing this was a headliner case that could possibly lead to some good press time if they were able to solve it. With Robert being so motivated, Adam knew his effort could be minimal while his partner led the charge. Working with Detective James would have its advantages, such as a lot of action with little effort and paperwork on his part.

"Let's hit it, Robert, but this time we are taking separate vehicles. There is no way I am going to let you hijack my car again. And by the way, you actually did me a favor last night. After you STOLE MY CAR, I had several of the dancers at Fantasy Dreams offer to give me a ride home, and quite a ride it ended up being. Now, where are we meeting this confidential informant?"

"Just follow me toward Arlington," advised Robert. "If we get separated, just call me on the cell phone."

Both men then began their drive toward the mid cities, Robert in his truck and Adam driving the Porsche. The skyline of Dallas soon faded as both men rapidly approached Arlington. As they pulled into the parking lot of a small convenience store on Peach Street, Robert noticed his informant standing by the pay phones. This area was commonly referred to as the Peach Street Ghettos, riddled with a high crime rate and dope related offenses. This was not the typical up-scale neighborhood that most areas in Arlington reflected. Indeed, it was proof positive of how drugs could devour any neighborhood in any city. The Peach Street Ghettos were saturated with heroin and methamphetamine addicts, a perfect place for an informant such as Rusty Sims. The thoughts of this guy being little Paige's half-uncle were almost repulsive but most definitely a secret that would never be revealed to Rusty. This thought propelled Robert back in time for a few moments, causing him to think about, and miss, Lori Sims. The circumstances at hand caused his thoughts of Lori to soon be pushed aside.

Investigator Ainsworth then parked his Porsche in front of the store, which was well lit and filled with security cameras. After securing the car, Adam got into Robert's vehicle, which the informant had also just entered.

As with any investigation involving an informant, Robert and Adam spent ample time with Rusty, asking details about

Blackie and his operation. Rusty had been allowed in Blackie's home on several occasions, each involving the purchase of some methamphetamine. He went on to confirm that Blackie was indeed an ex-cop—a retiree from a neighboring state police organization. According to Rusty, Blackie's house was referred to as the "Junk Yard" on the streets, due to the potential to buy anything from dope to stolen guns and vehicles there.

"Can you get us in there, Rusty?"

"If the ol' wallet is singing a generous money tune, then sure can." Rusty then turned to Adam, examining him from head to toe.

"One thing though, Mad Dog, Joe Preppy here needs to ruff up his look some. If we go into the Junk Yard with Mr. GQ here, someone may just get shot. Either he changes or we don't go."

The informant's words seemed to aggravate Adam, but it was all Robert could do to maintain his composure. It pleased him to see a street junkie putting Adam in his place. A stop at a local Goodwill store was in order, so Adam could obtain a more fitting wardrobe. A few minutes in Goodwill both embarrassed and humbled Investigator Ainsworth, which brought great pleasure to his partner. The shopping trip did not take long before Adam exited with his purchase from someone's closet. Adam seemed disgusted as he entered Robert's truck, throwing the shopping bag containing his personal clothing in the back.

"Ok, the new threads look okay but you still look too preppy, dude. Robert, pop the hood and Adam, follow me."

Robert knew what Rusty was up to before the two even exited the truck. Rusty was going to show Adam how to look like a meth user. A common activity among the meth crowd was that most would work on cars while tripping on meth. Their sleepless days while on the drug made it necessary to find ways to pass time, so working on cars seemed to be a favorite among the meth community. The lack of engine grease on a man's hands would make meth users suspicious. Therefore, Rusty made Adam rub his hands on the motor so they would be stained with dirty oil and grease, a sign of the trade.

"You got to be kidding, Rusty!"

"No way, dude. Does your mother still dress you? I thought you were a dope cop." Rusty was definitely making fun of Investigator Ainsworth, and Robert was enjoying every minute of it.

"You girls get serious and get in here; we have business to take care of."

Robert had to put an end to their conversation before Rusty set his steroid junkie partner into a fit of rage. An episode such as this would most certainly end with Rusty getting hurt, therefore, putting an end to Rusty's assistance. Robert quickly remembered that it took some time before Rusty would work with Robert again after being punched out by the detective during a drug deal in Haltom City. Getting his ass kicked twice by dope cops would most certainly end Rusty's desire to be an informant, and Blackie at the Junkyard was too important for that to happen.

The men drove for several minutes and then reached an area that was comprised of decaying houses with doors and windows boarded up. These places reflected a recent endeavor by the city to have some type of impact on drug riddled neighborhoods. If a house was being used as a drug shooting gallery, or was the target of multiple search warrants or drug arrests, then the city would seize the house and destroy it. This theory worked similar to that of a person kicking an anthill to make the insects go away. This only caused the drug dealers and crack heads to move to the next block down the road, and the problems still existed.

"There it is, boys." Rusty then pointed toward a house and identified it as the Junkyard.

It was dark but streetlights circled all sides of Blackie's house. This was an endeavor by the owner, not the city. Streetlights in this part of town were not welcomed but some residents like Blackie, had a different motive for them. The owner intentionally placed lights around the Junkyard in order to light the perimeter of his home during the night hours. It was essential for the yard and house to always be lit up; thus, allowing the occupants to have a clear view of any cops approaching, or crooks wanting to rip them off. The neighbors would dare not complain about the florescent lights, nor try to shoot them out like they did to the ones the city owned. Any shots made towards the house or to damage Blackie's property would have devastating results for the perpetrator.

"Give me a few minutes in there and I will come back out and get you. Mad Dog, I need a few hundred bucks to get in the door."

Giving informants "buy" money was an accepted way of doing business. The CI's would take the money, enter the target location and then return back with the drug. This situation would be somewhat different. Robert wanted in the door, with an opportunity to meet the notorious Blackie. Giving Rusty a few hundred bucks was a mere price to pay for a chance to enter the Junkyard. Robert knew the money would be used to get in the door but only a small portion of the meth Rusty bought would make its way back to the detective. For the Angela Tyler case, a small return for his money was insignificant to him. At times, rewards for being a confidential informant went beyond receiving just money. Rusty eagerly anticipated the euphoria that awaited him. Blackie was known for being one of the best meth cooks in Texas, and Rusty knew this for a fact.

Robert then handed Rusty the money and explained the simple rules that most dope cops told their informants. "If" the CI tipped off the crook that he was with a cop, the CI would go to jail himself. If things went downhill and bullets began to fly, certainly one from the cop's weapon would find the informant. Confidentiality was a must in a scenario such as this.

As Robert pulled next to the house, several of the window blinds parted as someone looked out to see who the visitors were. The house was an old one, probably dating back to the mid 1940's as being its construction date. Numerous older cars, some junkers, were parked in the yard surrounding the home. Despite the late night hours, the Junkyard was apparently open for business. While Rusty was receiving his marching orders, several cars came to the house and then left a few minutes later. This was a tell tale sign of a place moving dope. Rusty then made his way to the house and disappeared through a back door.

While waiting for their CI, Robert and Adam began discussing scenarios about what they might encounter while inside the Junkyard. It was their primary objective to get in, meet this

Blackie guy and try to determine if he could be a suspect. The fact that Mr. Blackburn was possibly an ex-cop also intrigued Robert, but not his partner. A purchase of methamphetamine from Blackie would also be an objective of theirs. Even if he was not involved in the Tyler incident, at least they could put another meth dealer in jail and get his dope off the streets.

Most dopers have no concept of time and Rusty was no exception. A forty-five minute wait was beginning to try the patience of the awaiting cops. Finally, the door opened and Rusty exited the house.

"You're in guys, come on with me."

"Lock and load, Buddy." Robert instructed his partner.

"Who needs a gun, Robbie boy? You can hide behind that 40-caliber if you want but I have these nineteen inch arms to take care of myself."

Robert did not even bother to argue with his arrogant partner but instead, advised he would either take his gun or stay in the car. Reluctantly, Adam rammed the pistol into his waistband and exited the pickup. Rusty led the way, with Robert and Adam in close pursuit. A knock on the door was not necessary, due to a lookout observing every move they made after leaving the truck.

The back door of the house led into a small room where two men with pistols in hand sized up the guests. In the world of meth—paranoia is paramount, especially when dealing with new faces. No words were heard coming from the greeters, who signified their passage by a slight nod of the head. Rusty continued to lead the way into a well-lit kitchen area where several men were sitting at a table. One was in his mid-twenties and sat with a semi-automatic pistol in his lap. The other was an older man, possibly in his mid to early sixties, with a 45-caliber revolver lying on the table in front of him, and a cigarette dangling from his mouth. With a mere look from his elder, the younger man left the table carrying his pistol in hand but keeping the guests under constant eye contact.

Rusty then broke the silence.

"Blackie, this is the dude I was telling you about, Mad Dog. And hell, I can't remember his friend's name."

"You got a name?" The question seemed to take Adam by surprise.

"Robert, but I mostly go by Bob." These responses seemed to both surprise and aggravate Detective James.

I can't believe Adam is using my name. What an idiot!

"You guys cops?" asked Blackie.

This question was routine among the vice and drug world. These violators had some misconception that they could use entrapment as a defense to any criminal charge if the person were actually a cop and denied it. This was indeed a misconception. Rulings concerning such matters had made their way clear to Federal Appellant courts and been struck down. For a cops safety and welfare, they are allowed to deny their badge toting status, if asked. Robert waited for a reply from Adam but apparently he was not too spontaneous with such questions.

"Only if you have a ton of dope and a few million in cash lying around for me to grab!" A slight laugh accompanied Robert's reply.

"Well, Rusty tells me you want to score an eight-ball of meth. I trust this boy otherwise you would not have made it past my doors."

"An eight-ball will do; but, it would save me a trip back if I could score a little more, like half an ounce." replied Robert.

The request for such a large amount of meth for a first time visitor made Blackie uneasy. After advising his visitor he would have to think about the request, he grabbed the pistol and placed it in his lap. A push back from the table revealed he was crippled and confined to a wheel chair. Blackie immediately noticed the shocked looks coming from his guests.

"Believe it or not, I was a State Trooper in my younger days. A bullet to my spine ended my career when I was only forty-eight. No need for alarm guys, as you see I have changed course in my thoughts about life. An addiction to pain meds and women led me to where I am now. A poor pension did not support my lifestyle, or my addictions. Fortunately for me, the Junkyard takes care of all my needs. I will be right back with you."

Blackie then rolled his wheelchair into an adjoining room and disappeared. Two new gun-toting individuals then entered the room and watched Blackie's guests during his absence. Not wanting to draw suspicion on themselves initially, Robert and Adam did not have a chance to scope out Blackie's house but now the opportunity was theirs. In a hallway directly behind the kitchen table where they sat, was a bookshelf. Apparently, Blackie had been telling the truth about his prior life as a State Trooper. On one shelf stood a lone picture frame bearing the photo of a young trooper, who was dressed in his uniform and Sam Brown leather. The picture was taken outside, with the cop standing next to a state police car. Even though the photo was of a man in his thirties, undoubtedly this photo was of Blackie when he was a cop. Dopers seem to have a difficult time telling the truth, telling more lies than facts. Robert had hoped this would be the case of Blackie being an ex-law enforcement officer, but not so this time. The photo, along with the bullet to the back-story, was proof positive that Blackie had indeed been a State Trooper.

Further observation of the house revealed to the cops that it was larger than initially thought when looking at it from the outside. Numerous people in Blackie's house reflected the reason why so many cars were parked around it. This place was like a fortress, with armed men looking out of windows on each side of the house. Blackie had learned a lot during his days in law enforcement and apparently security was a primary concern. With this many hired guns in the house, Robert knew they had a big fish here.

Another sight took Robert back to the days he was initially training with Investigator Ronnie Bays, when they were in an informant's hotel room. Ronnie's informant was a man in his fifties, who was using a young fifteen year old teenager as sexual gratuity for his customers. Robert wanted to remove the girl from her filthy environment but was not able to. Investigator Bays explained to his rookie that they could not save the world, which consisted of millions of young girls just like this one.

As Robert looked around the house, he noticed several similar young female teenagers, who were scantily dressed and stoned out of their minds. Just as Ronnie Bays described, here were two more young victims that nature would just have to take its course with. The odds of these young girls kicking their drug habit and never returning to the streets were practically non-existent. Robert could only hope that once the police raids on Blackie's house commenced, at least one of these young victims would rehabilitate and find a better life. Yes, Robert could only hope.

A bit of time had passed before Blackie returned to the kitchen, holding a brown paper bag. For some reason Robert had won the confidence of the elderly drug pusher, and his request for one half an ounce of meth was about to be filled. As Blackie rolled his wheel chair back to the table, both the bag and revolver was placed on it.

"I hate to have to do business like this, boys, but this is your first time here. Like I said, if it weren't for Rusty, your little order here would not be filled, by me anyways. "IF" by some chance you are a cop, I am going to put a 45-slug between your eyes. I am too damn old to go to jail, so I would rather be dead. I guess you noticed a few of my own boys packing a little heat around the house, and then I have Big Bertha over there."

Blackie then pointed toward a closed door leading into an adjoining room. About five feet from the ground was a silver dollar sized hole, with a metal, round barrel pointing through it. Both men recognized that a twelve-gauge shotgun was trained on them. As Blackie slid the baggie toward Robert, he placed his right hand on the 45-pistol that was lying on the table. These cops knew Blackie would more than likely fulfill his death threat if their true identities were known.

Robert then took possession of the baggie and opened it up. Just as he had ordered, the bag contained approximately one half ounce of methamphetamine.

"That will be twelve-hundred big ones, Mr. Mad Dog. While you are digging into your wallet, tell me about how you came about that name."

As Robert was counting out the cash, there was a slight knock on the door they had entered through, and the guards let a visitor into the house. Robert had a full view of the hallway leading from the door, as did Blackie. Adam seemed to be affixed to the shotgun that was pointed at them. The steps were few before the visitor came into view and upon seeing Robert, stopped dead in his tracks. The visitor immediately went pale, as if he had just spotted a ghost. This did not go unnoticed by anyone in the room, especially Blackie.

The elderly drug pusher rapidly grabbed his pistol and pointed it point-blank at Robert, leaving only a few inches between him and the barrel. The visitor was one of Investigator Bay's informants, with a street name of Skitz Rick, whom Robert had to arrest one evening for Bays. The evening was about to go to hell. Trying to be inconspicuous, both Robert and Adam began reaching for their pistols. Both cops knew that if the lead started flying, they would probably die. Escaping this situation now inherently in the hands of Skitz Rick.

"How do you know these guys, Rick?" Blackie solemnly asked.

Skitz Rick got his nickname from his inability to shut up, and always running his mouth a million to nothing. Rick was always paranoid of everything, having such thoughts that cops would use satellite technology to spy on him. Both the paranoia and rapid speech was a sign of his addiction to methamphetamine. One evening Robert witnessed a biker threatening to cut Skitz Rick's tongue out because of his bizarre behavior.

As Blackie cocked the hammer back on his gun, Robert was doing the same with his pistol under the table. Once again, the drug dealer confronted Rick.

"Skitz, how do you know these guys?"

With probably just seconds left before the bullets began to fly, Rick's "caught in the headlights" look soon turned into a smile.

"Well, hell Blackie, this is the famous Mad Dog. This guy is one partying fool. He and I have done more meth together than you have ever sold. I have not seen Mad Dog in such a long time, I barely recognized him. If you are ever in the need of some heavy heat, this man can supply. Pistols, shotguns, assault rifles; Mad Dog has them all. Now, put that gun down and take care of this boy. Who knows, Blackie, that pistol there may have once belonged to the Mad one."

Obviously, Skitz Rick had remembered what Investigator Bays had told him about the first rule of a shootout; the CI catches the first bullet.

With caution, Blackie lowered his gun.

"Sorry, boys, but like I said, I ain't ever going to jail. And by the way, Rick, this was my duty pistol when I was a cop. If this gun could talk, I would probably be in prison awaiting the death chamber."

The pounding in Robert's throat from his heart's rapid heartbeat was beginning to subside. A glance at Adam revealed sweat dripping from his forehead. The intense situation must have also gotten to Blackie because he was also exhibiting the signs of profuse sweating, as was Adam. He then laid the pistol down and began rolling up his sleeves, which revealed two things. The first were tracks or scars, resulting from shooting meth into his veins. The other item was a tattoo. Just inches below his elbow was a devil's face that had been etched into Blackie's arm.

"Pretty cool tattoo there, Blackie. I bet there is a story behind that." Robert asked and then anxiously waited for his reply.

"A story but a pretty simple one. I am a Vietnam War veteran. Before heading overseas, the guys in my unit all got matching tattoos. We were the Fighting Red Devil's."

Robert was once again disappointed. Not only was Blackie a corrupt ex-cop, but also a Vietnam Vet gone bad. Even worse, he was a disabled man confined to a wheelchair, who just sported a tattoo from the war. This definitely was not one of Angela Tyler's assailants.

The detective then passed the payment for the meth on to Blackie and rose from the table. It was time for them to leave, while leaving was still possible. Robert could not help but feel dismay for the young teenage girls that were part of Blackie's harem, as he walked past them. Blackie could not help but notice Robert's stares.

"Hey Mad Dog, you like what you see? You can have a little piece of that action if you want to stick around."

His undercover skills were being tested. The thought of sexually being with a fourteen or fifteen year old girl was nauseating but he could not convey this to Blackie.

"Great offer but I will have to pass this time. I have some folks waiting for this stuff back in Dallas. I need to get there while the money is still good. See you soon, Blackie."

Adam, Robert and Rusty made their way out the door and started their short walk to the truck. Never before had Robert viewed his vehicle as a chariot to safety, but tonight it was. As they began walking toward the truck, each step they took seemed to force the second one to go faster. Not a word was said as they reached the vehicle and quickly entered, each knowing watchful eyes from within the house still had them under surveillance.

Robert then put the vehicle in motion. With the streetlights surrounding Blackie's house beginning to fade, Robert pushed the accelerator closer to the floor. For the first time since being assigned as partners, Adam Ainsworth sat in silence. Robert was expecting his partner to be bitching about him taking the Porsche the night before, or about almost getting him shot this evening, but nothing happened. Tonight Adam had left his cozy confines of a topless bar or that of a female stripper in a hotel room. He had just received a huge dose of real undercover police work, which had sucked the cocky behavior right out of him. Finally, Adam muttered a few words about how freaky that situation was and then returned to silence.

Rusty had nestled into a corner of the back seat, completely ignoring the two cops up front. Apparently, he had rigged up a shot of meth before leaving Blackie's house, so his trip to meth-heaven was awaiting him. What Rusty was doing was no secret to the cops in the front seat but his actions would be intentionally ignored. This was one of the rewards of being a snitch, in that he could have his little piece of the pie without having to pay for the dope, or be concerned about going to jail for using it.

"Rusty, I swear to God, if you begin rattling your hole after shooting that crap, I will beat your ass and toss you into a ditch". Robert wanted to make his CI know he was privy to his actions, and also was in no mood for the after affects the meth would have on Rusty.

"No prob, Mad Dog, I will keep it cool."

As the liquid began flowing through Rusty's veins, he took a deep breath and leaned his head back against the headrest. It was obvious the junkie had begun his short journey to Euphoriaville and his continuous ride to addiction hell.

Once again, silence filled the truck. At this moment in time, Robert truly understood Angela Tyler's experience with near death—he too felt lucky to be alive.

CHAPTER 18

Several weeks had now passed since the assault on Angela Tyler. About the only thing moving quickly on Angela's case was her recovery. It was a miracle she survived such an assault, and even more so that doctors were expecting a complete recovery. In many aspects this was a very unusual case. The fact that not one fingerprint, DNA sample or piece of evidence had been discovered was certainly an oddity. In addition, with Sam Tyler being so wealthy he was able to offer a reward, which was far beyond the abilities of the local Crime Stopper program. A five-hundred thousand dollar reward would sever any ties and loyalties to almost anyone who knew the perpetrators of this crime, or even had suspicions about a friend or family member being involved. Despite this huge reward for information leading to the arrest of his daughter's assailants, not one single bit of credible information had been received. About the only theory the investigators could formulate was this crime appeared to be a professional hit on Ms. Tyler.

Angela Tyler initially chose Detective James to be the lead investigator in her case and her decision stood firm. None of the other detectives involved in the investigation would have ever believed that a victim of such a crime would shun their help. In her case, this is exactly what Angela Tyler was doing. Not only had she chosen Detective James as her lead detective but now it was her choice for him to be the only law enforcement official she would discuss the case with.

Angela had recently been released from the hospital and was staying in an apartment complex in Ft. Worth that her father owned. Special Agent Michaels and her father had decided this was the best scenario for Angela's safety. Sam Tyler owned an array of apartment complexes. Each had numerous corporate apartments that were completely furnished. This would allow his daughter to be moved around continuously until these assailants were apprehended. With the exception of Sam Tyler, SA Michaels and Robert, Angela's temporary home was kept a secret. With the press all over her assault case, these animals would know by now that they did not successfully complete their mission; therefore, making the possibility of a second hit a reality.

On a daily basis, Ms. Tyler and Robert would meet at 3:00 PM sharp. Progress with Angela was going at a snail's pace. She would choose different locations throughout the metroplex to meet, each being a restaurant that was far beyond Robert's budget. This seemed to please her, giving Angela just a little control over her detective, since the bill would always be hers to pay. Robert was able to sense that Angela somewhat enjoyed this game of hers, but also noted a look and tone of fear when he questioned his victim about the assault. Information coming from the victim was very limited, as if she was holding back waiting for the right time to be forthcoming.

Doctors had informed Robert that post-traumatic stress would play a big role in Ms. Tyler's life for months, maybe even years, after she was released from the hospital. Being like her father, Angela was somewhat stubborn, which was noticeable when she refused any psychiatric follow-up treatment. Her detective had been following instructions by physicians to take things slow and easy with Ms. Tyler; in order to prevent a relapse in her recovery. Despite wanting to follow the doctor's orders, Robert had a high profile case to solve. On a daily basis he was required to give a progress report to Special Agent Michaels; each was short and non-eventful. At this point, Ms. Tyler was only giving descriptions of her assailants, and nothing else. Robert knew that his boss would only allow this lack of progress to continue for a short time before he would be replaced with another investigator from the unit. Investigator Ainsworth was assigned to help with this case, but Angela forbid him to attend her meetings with Robert. The last cop that Robert would ever wish on Angela Tyler would be Investigator Ainsworth.

It was once again 3:00 PM, as Robert was pulling into another posh and cozy restaurant in the Highland Park area. As usual, this was a place that would exceed his budget, therefore; causing Angela to pick up the bill. Her little mind control games were again in place but now it was time for Robert to take total control over his victim. It was time to get down to business with Ms. Tyler.

As Robert entered, he spotted his target sitting in the far corner of the restaurant. Angela had noted that Robert would always choose a remote location in a restaurant that gave him a visual advantage over most patrons that were already in or just entering the establishment. Upon questioning her detective about this habit, Robert explained how this was taught in the police academy to assure a vantage location for an officer's safety. As Robert neared the table, he could not help but notice the smile on Angela's face as he approached. More than once he thought about his victim beginning to show signs of a condition similar to the Stockholm Syndrome, but in this case the victim was becoming attached to the cop working her case. Despite Angela being a beautiful woman, he could not allow this to happen. Thoughts and fears of Special Agent Michaels discovering the fact that his child's mother was a prior informant, was always on Robert's mind. Starting a relationship with a victim would be almost as devastating to his career, especially since the victim's father was wealthy and politically powerful.

"Good afternoon, my dearest detective."

Robert returned Ms. Tyler's greeting and the two became involved in a few moments of small talk before the detective decided to roll the dice.

"Angela, I have been working on your case now for several weeks but with little progress. I am not trying to sound like I am being pushy but Angela, you have got to tell me more about the night you were hurt or my boss is going to take me off the case."

"He can't do that, Robert! My father requested you."

"Angela, your father and Special Agent Michaels are friends, so your dad requested federal intervention from our unit. Federal intervention does not mean specifically Detective Robert James intervention. Obviously, I am not doing my job well enough to aid in your memory of the incident. I do believe I am just days from being replaced."

Robert sat looking into the eyes of the beautiful blonde that now sat speechless. The high shirt collar hid the healing wound that still encompassed her throat. It would not be obvious to anyone that this woman barely escaped death a few weeks ago. She just sat and stared at Robert, trying to find the right words for the moment. Robert could tell the mind of this intelligent beauty was spinning a million miles an hour.

"Robert, I have to know that I can trust you. I mean, one hundred percent trust you."

"You know you can. I am all ears, Angela, so talk to me."

"Tonight, there is a party over in west Ft. Worth that I want to take you to. You will understand why once we get there, and afterwards I will tell you what you need to know. Can you be ready by about 7:30? There will be a few VIP's there, so dress to impress. Now, let's have some lunch before I have to let you go back to the hungry wolves out there. I need to take care of my man, you know!"

Angela Tyler's closing words were stuck in Robert's mind.

I have to take care of my man.

These words were reverberating through the detective's mind, sending several emotions through him. It was difficult sorting out which was the most prevalent—fear or flattery. Most men would feel more than fortunate to have the beautiful and wealthy Angela Tyler calling them "her man," but, the scenario was different with Robert. He was Ms. Tyler's lead detective, a public servant that needed to stay focused on the criminal investigation and not become entangled with personal feelings.

As the two finished their lunch, Robert stood and began bidding a short farewell to Ms. Tyler. Words were not completely suitable for Angela today, as she also arose from her seat and approached the detective. Robert knew what was coming, but for some reason he could not react before Angela wrapped her arms around him.

"Just a quick hug, Robert. I just wanted you to know how much I appreciate everything you have been doing for me."

Robert wanted to resist and push Angela away, but he couldn't. It had been months since he felt the warmth of a woman's body next to his. The last time was when he and Lori Sims embraced before the U.S. Marshals sped her away. Not wanting to resist, Robert slowly maneuvered his arms until they were also embracing Angela. Her body was warm, solid and fit, and very pleasurable to the touch.

"I need to run, Angela. I have some work to do before we meet tonight."

Angela did not respond as she continued standing by the table, watching every step her detective took as he walked out the front door. Robert's demeanor sent a message to Angela that he enjoyed their embrace as much as she did. This indeed, gratified Angela Tyler.

What the hell are you doing, Dude? The detective quietly questioned his behavior.

Robert tried to make sense of what had just happened inside the restaurant as he struggled between thoughts of business and personal pleasure. This mental diversion prevented the cop from noticing the male observer that was watching as he left the restaurant. Instead of the normal habit of being fully aware of his environment, Robert had let his guard down. This error allowed him to be on the receiving end of a telephoto camera-lens. The hunter was now being hunted . . . .

CHAPTER 19

The alert tone from his electronic pager snapped Robert back to reality after leaving Ms. Tyler at the restaurant.

"573-989-8899-1976". Robert could not help from smiling as the numbers of 1976 reflected the code that he and Chad Cooper used to signify themselves as the caller. This was primarily due to Chad having to change his contact number every few months. Being a CIA Agent, it was imperative that Chad was able to maintain his secrecy, which required him to deviate from any normal routine or behavior that most people practice and enjoy. Robert was not for sure if Chad changed his contact information a lot, or just made use of a multitude of electronic pagers and cell phones. Another theory and the most plausible was Chad was constantly changing numbers just to screw with people. Whichever the case, figuring out Chad was an impossible feat, so Robert did not question his methods of operation. Using the car cell phone was too expensive, so Robert guided his pickup to the nearest convenience store. These locations usually had an ample supply of pay phones, mostly due to the high volume of drug deals they were used for. Robert soon spotted a Quik Stop, when his pager once again went off, signifying some urgency on Chad's end.

Robert navigated his pickup into Quik Stop's parking lot and made his way to the pay phones. As expected, several individuals were hovering around them, obviously awaiting a return call that would give details of their drug drop. As Robert approached the first phone, a tall, slender man spotted him and pointed to the next phone.

"Use the next one, bud. I have a call coming in on this one."

Without a doubt, this man was a meth user and was looking for his next fix. Robert knew that if an attempt was made to use the forbidden phone, an altercation would occur. Nothing was going to stand between this meth addict and his next fix.

"No problem, it's all yours."

Robert then made his way to the neighboring phone and dialed the number that Chad had sent to his pager.

"What's up, Chad? Am I over due for praising you for the help with getting my truck back to Texas?"

"Robbie, ol' boy, you do owe me for that one, but that is not why I called. Listen, I just have a minute before I have to board a flight at JFK. Listen to this, my friend; guess who I am spying on right now?"

"Let me see, your next wife?"

"No, smart ass, a commercial airline pilot that both of us might just happen to know."

"My father?"

"Yep."

"Why the heck are you spying on him, Chad? Go up and say hello. Heck, I bet he will even lie and tell you how glad he is to see you again." Robert chuckled.

"It is too good to spoil the party. He is with some woman and they are right now standing face-to-face, just inches apart. Well, never mind that last statement, your ol' dad is either practicing CPR on the woman or is kissing her, and I will put my money on the second."

The airport's public address system could be heard in the background, calling for all passengers of Flight 3267 to board.

"Got to run, buddy. Just thought you would want to know. Now, figure this one out, Mr. Hotshot Detective and fill me in next time we talk.... Later!"

"CHAD!.... CHAD!...."

Screaming into the phone did not override the loud dial tone that he could now hear. The short conversation with Chad Cooper quickly ended, leaving Robert in awe. Today seemed to be filled with thoughts and emotions that weren't anything even close to police work. The lunch with Angela Tyler was a distraction; but, the news about his father kissing some woman now totally consumed Robert. When Paige was left in Missouri, his father did advise that he had been scheduled for a few flights due to the airline being short of pilots. There was no problem with this since Robert's sister would be watching Paige; but, he expected nothing like what Chad had just told him. In some ways Robert was happy for his father and that he was finally dating. On the other hand, his dad had not been seen with another woman since the passing of his wife nearly twenty-five years ago. Mixed emotions raced though Robert's mind as he returned to the truck.

During his moments of distraction, Robert failed to notice a verbal altercation between the meth addict who was still waiting for the return call on the first pay phone, and another individual that had just approached the phones. Apparently, a man had picked up the first telephone and slid some change in it, while Mr. Meth-Head turned his back to the phone to light up a cigarette. The newly arrived visitor was apparently injured, and had to support himself with a pair of crutches. This, however, did not excuse his intrusion on the meth addict's phone.

The loud voices soon caught the attention of Robert, despite the fact he was sitting inside his truck. Robert rolled down his window just in time to hear the intruder tell Mr. Meth that he had already placed his money in the phone and was not going to leave. Robert quickly recognized the wild look in the meth addict's eyes and feared the worse, but was surprised to see him walk away after a few seconds of giving the intruder a look from hell. The intruder's reprieve lasted only a few seconds before the meth addict returned, yielding a piece of 2x4 lumber in his hands.

Robert watched in amazement, knowing what was soon to follow. He wanted to warn the man who was now talking on the phone, but his movements to open the door were hindered by the unfolding of a violent assault that had now began to unfold before his eyes. Despite being six inches taller and at least forty pounds heavier than the injured man, the meth addict began swinging the board like a baseball bat, landing the first swing to the back of the intruder's head. The impact caused the crutches to go flying, after which the victim collapsed to the hard concrete underneath his feet. One could see that the first swing rendered the victim helpless and possibly unconscious. This, however, did not matter to the drug addict who continued to pound on him, seemingly in an attempt to kill his victim. Robert's police instincts kicked in as he quickly reached for an expandable police baton that was kept in his driver's door compartment, along with assuring himself the 40-caliber was still holstered in his belt.

"I'M A POLICE OFFICER. DROP YOUR WEAPON AND HIT THE GROUND!"

Robert shouted at the suspect as loud as possible. Both men's veins were now flowing with adrenalin and neither could guess the other's next move, except for the fact that no one would be backing down. Robert knew by looking at the suspect that he was strung out and tripping on his drug, which would result in a battle. In being a cop, Robert knew he had to protect the injured and bleeding victim, and take the assailant into custody. Despite his orders, the meth addict continued his aggressive stance, now directed towards Robert.

After seeing the massive injuries to the victim, Robert knew that deadly force would be justified against the man who was now walking toward him yielding the blood covered 2x4. In one swift movement, the cop's 40-caliber was drawn from its holster and was aimed mid-mass at the assailant.

"Mister, you are just seconds away from me blowing your ass away. One more time, drop the board or I pull the trigger, DO IT NOW!"

These words seemed to get through to the meth addict and put him in a temporary stupor, leading Robert to believe the suspect might be surrendering. He was wrong; the fight was far from over. The meth addict then lowered his weapon and revealed a sadistic smile to Robert, apparently knowing that if he was not using a weapon, the cop threatening to shoot him could no longer use his gun. The board then hit the ground and the suspect began his flight to possible freedom, away from Robert and the crime scene.

"STOP, YOU'RE UNDER ARREST!" Robert's words did not seem to faze the suspect as he continued to flee from the scene.

Without thinking about the injured man or waiting for backup, Robert began his foot pursuit of the suspect. Behind the Quik Stop was an apartment complex, which would supply many routes of escape. Robert's routine of jogging and working out at the gym was now paying off. Despite being hopped up on meth, after a few hundred yards the suspect was beginning to tire, as Robert was gaining on him. Seeing he could not out run the pursuing detective, the suspect stopped and turned on the cop, in a stance ready for a fight.

"You don't want this, Mister. Just get down on your stomach and place your hands behind your back and let me take you in before anything else bad happens."

"Screw you, Cop!" The suspect shouted as he lunged toward the detective.

As the suspect grabbed a hold of him, Robert was able to push away and ready his expandable baton. With a flip of the wrist, the short, metal baton soon expanded to four times its original length. Just as he was trained, Robert delivered a strong hit to the suspect's thigh, which caused his legs to fold, forcing the suspect to the ground. Despite the force of the strike, the man quickly regained his footing and began another attempt to assault Robert. This reinforced his theory that the suspect was on a meth trip, which would give him abnormal strength, along with alleviating his sensation of pain.

Once again, Robert delivered another blow with the baton to the suspect's mid-section, which only slowed him down for a few seconds before charging for a third time.

"I am going to kill you, ass-hole cop!"

Once again, the suspect lunged towards Robert, grabbing hold and striking the cop several times with his fists. Robert could also feel the suspect trying to find his weapon with one hand, while beating on him with the other. Just like the victim at the Quik Stop, the meth addict was again trying to kill but this time his target was a cop. The meth addict had extraordinary strength due to the amphetamines in his body, and was of the mind set to escape and kill the cop trying to arrest him. Robert knew he was now involved in a battle for his life but going out like this was not on his agenda. Many things were rapidly flashing through his mind, including his baby Paige, while the fight seemed to continue in slow motion. Mustering all his strength, the detective was able to throw the suspect to the ground, landing on top of him. Without having to think about his next move, Robert began pounding on the meth addict repeatedly with both fists. The strikes seemed to be effective, but were not incapacitating the suspect as with a sober person. Robert knew this would be his best and possibly last chance to overcome the suspect.

A simple prayer then went to the good Lord to give him the strength to overcome his violator. Then, precisely placed, Robert guided his fist into the temporal area of the suspect. As the punch found its target, Robert could hear the cracking of bones, and then the suspect went limp. The cop had just conquered his assailant but with the fear of cracking the suspect's skull, seriously injuring him. At this point Robert was not concerned about the injuries he had inflicted upon this felony suspect because tonight, he would go home.

"Officer, your hand!"

During his combat with the suspect, Detective James had failed to notice the crowd, which had gathered around to witness the event.

"I'm a nurse, Officer, look at your hand."

During the fight, the adrenaline rushing through Robert's body had the same effect as did the amphetamine flowing through the suspect's veins. The temporary metabolic changes in Robert's body clouded the fact that his hand was broken. No sooner than the nurse brought this to his attention, pain began to consume Robert's right hand. The nurse then gently took hold of it to contain the jerking motion the hand was engaged in, signifying broken bones and nerve damage. As Robert's mind began to clear, it became obvious the cracking of bones heard earlier were from his hand breaking, and not from the suspect's head. As his metabolism began to slow, so did Robert. The fight had drained his strength, so a good place to sit and rest became necessary.

Sirens were rapidly approaching the scene, as Robert sat on the concrete only feet away from his prisoner, where numerous men from the apartment complex were now standing guard. The arriving patrol officers had already been briefed of the situation, and knew Robert was a law enforcement officer. Upon seeing a female attending to Robert's hand and several men standing guard over the suspect, it was easy to differentiate who was the good and bad guy, here.

"You a cop?" asked a young, uniformed officer.

"Yes, I am a federal agent, Detective Robert James. Ma'am, can you reach my wallet in my back, right pocket? Officer, my badge and ID are in there, if the nurse here does not mind helping me. Also, I am armed with a pistol; at least I hope I still am."

"That we heard, Detective James. We have other units at the Quik Stop with the initial victim. That poor guy just had back surgery and now back to the hospital he goes. He has been beat pretty bad but he will survive. Now, let us mop up this hunk of trash for you."

The meth addict was now regaining consciousness as the officers placed on the handcuffs.

"What do we need to book him on, besides the aggravated assault on the convenience store victim?"

"Resisting Arrest and Aggravated Assault on a Police Officer. Please, get his ass out of here. I am sick of looking at that piece of trash!"

Robert's hand finally calmed down, after the tending nurse wrapped it with ice. A few broken bones were a minor price compared to what could have happened. This was a good ending for a bad situation. Robert refused to accept a ride to the hospital from a patrol sergeant, mostly because he did not want to leave his truck sitting in front of the Quik Stop for another doper to come by and take advantage.

The drive to the hospital was a short but painful one. Apparently, the patrol sergeant had alerted the emergency room that an injured officer was en route to their location. Upon pulling into the ER driveway, two county deputies working as security met Robert at his truck and escorted him past admissions and directly to a waiting room. Protocol dictated that there would be no waiting for an injured cop.

As usual, it was a busy evening in the hospital's ER. A police officer was a priority patient to the nurses and technicians, who rushed Robert through tests and X-rays. As expected, his hand was broken in a total of five different places. It was also suspected this cop had suffered nerve damage, but a doctor would have to deliver that diagnosis. Despite the VIP treatment so far, waiting for a doctor to pass along his diagnosis and treatment plan was not quite as swift. Robert had refused the doses of prescription pain medications offered by the nurse but instead settled for a few basic aspirins. Robert's ER room had become calm and quiet, as the staff left to attend to arriving patients. The quiet of the room, with the pain from his once throbbing hand beginning to subside, transformed this once violent day into a relaxing and tranquil one. Robert soon drifted into a slumber, causing his 7:30 appointment to pass un-noticed. Angela Tyler would surely be disappointed.

CHAPTER 20

Impatiently pacing the floors back and forth did not seem to bring the expected knock at the door that Angela Tyler had been waiting for. It was now 8:35 PM, and not a word from Robert. Her numerous pages to his pager went unanswered, which even aggravated her more. Angela's short temperament was not caused from being stood up for a date as much as it was for the fear that something may have happened to her personal detective. Angela was becoming emotionally attached to Robert, who was now more than just a cop to her. The man was single, attractive and caring, the ingredients for a perfect man. Not to mention being a responsible, single father of a young girl, which made the package even more attractive to this bachelorette.

In growing up, Angela was an only child. Despite the continuous begging to her parents for a sibling, this wish was never fulfilled. When Angela was a child, responses to this request and the ensuing questions were always vague. Not until she was in college did Angela discover the truth behind the denial of this one, continuous wish. Angela was then told that she was her parent's miracle child, in which modern science and research enabled her conception and birth. Her parents were advised this would be a one-time deal, and the possibility of another child for the Sam Tyler family would not be a possibility. Despite being sensible about dating, one of Angela Tyler's desires in life was to find a good man and have a family. Having two or three children was one of her desires from life, after a professional career had been established. Of course, finding that right, perfect man was a necessity before she would try to put this plan in motion. This thought had been tucked away in Angela's mind for several years now, knowing that it would take the right man to bring it back from her remote, mental closet. For some reason, Detective James seemed to have unlocked and opened the door to this long ago, dusty dream.

The detective was now one hour late and Angela could not wait any longer to leave. She had instructions from both her father and Detective James about not leaving the apartment without one of them present. Her father was a very protective man, who always carried a weapon on him. This was one of the luxuries of being a resident of the Lone Star State. Texas residents enjoy the right to carry a concealed weapon, once licensed to do so by the State. Despite her father's requests numerous times for her to obtain a permit to carry a pistol, this was not his daughter's wishes. Even after this horrific event, Sam attempted to persuade Angela into obtaining her permit to carry but the response was always the same; she did not want to. Angela had recently become a believer of God and destiny, and felt that each would take care of her. Sam tried to press the issue by using her assault to show the necessity for her to carry a pistol, but Angela's denial included the fact that God had saved her from death and protected her for a reason—certainly destiny at work.

The social gathering tonight was to include some of the wealthiest men in the Dallas-Ft. Worth metroplex, along with their wives, girlfriends or escorts. A phone call earlier that morning had made Angela privy to the party. As most social gatherings among the elite, they always offered an open door to Angela. Sam Tyler being her wealthy father, along with her added beauty, this gave Angela the key to most of the city's most prestigious gatherings. Tonight's social would be no exception.

Earlier this day Angela had received a telephone call from her friend, Senator Trey Buckley, advised her about the time and location of the party. Angela felt this was out of character for Trey, as he knew that she needed to stay in a protected status until her assailants were taken into custody. Plus, a few names on the party list for this evening's event concerned Angela, not because of personal safety issues, but due to Trey being a U.S. Senator with bigger political ambitions.

Included on the attendee's list was the owner of a local sports team, along with Donnie and Danny McBride. These brothers own a large car dealership chain, which included car lots in four adjoining states. These were men with too much money and at times, very little sense. Each had big money, fast boats and nice toys, accompanied by a lot of free time on their hands to play. At past social gatherings similar to this one, Angela witnessed the snorting of party favors by these players, namely cocaine.

One of the car brothers, Donnie McBride, owned several cigarette boats that were docked in Corpus Christi, along the Gulf of Mexico. Rumor has it that these boats are used for purposes other than just pleasure. The running of cocaine from the Mexico coasts to the shores of Texas was a real possibility for Donnie McBride. Despite being mutual partners and brothers, Donnie seemed to have more toys, bigger houses and more time to play than his brother, Danny. Even though siblings, Donnie and Danny are as opposite as two brothers could be. To Angela, this behavior difference was easily explained. At parties such as this one, Donnie was the sibling that was constantly engaging in the ritual of "powdering his nose," with his snow-white cocaine. Danny seemed to be his brother's party Nazi, cutting his brother off from the nose candy before he slipped away into oblivion. With the massive doses that Donnie would snort, a heart attack was always just one beat away.

Angela was violating the orders of both her father and guardian detective as she climbed into her awaiting taxi that was parked out front. She had waited long enough for Robert and needed to attend this party, for several reasons. It had been several weeks since her assault and being somewhat of a free bird, Angela felt the necessity to fly the coop and socialize. Plus, the oddity of Trey asking her to attend a social gathering with such a questionable guest list left her puzzled. Both were reasons that inspired her to attend, but she also felt the need to be accompanied by her guardian detective.

The ride to the remote mansion in west Ft. Worth took about twenty minutes, which gave Angela just enough time to put the finishing touches on her makeup, and straighten her wind blow hair. With Ft. Worth being the gateway to the flat plains of the west, the City's strong and gusty winds were no friend to a girl's appearance. The final brush strokes had just been completed when the taxi pulled up to the secured gates.

"Miss Tyler at the front gate. She is a guest of Senator Buckley." The cab driver announced into the speaker.

"She is clear, so please proceed on to the house," the voice from the speaker responded.

The trek to the house was a lengthy one, flowing down a perfectly paved and winding driveway for almost two miles past the entry gate. A turn past a few small hills left a clear and open view for miles, with the lights of a colorful dusk appearing as a gift from the heavens. Even though the house was still more than a mile away, the enormity of it left no doubt that this magnificent building was the home of a millionaire. The cars lining the driveway reflected the guest list was one restricted to the rich and prominent from this community. As the taxi pulled into the driveway, a valet attendant made his way quickly to the back passenger door and opened it for Ms. Tyler. The taxi's guest then exited and made her way to the mansion's front door.

A finely dressed hostess opened the door for Angela, and escorted her to a great-room located on the backside of the home. Their path through the home revealed paintings from famous, world-renowned artists, along with several who were Texas natives. Just the price tag alone for these pieces would equal a retirement check for most Americans.

As the two women entered the great-room, the greeter announced the presence of Angela Tyler. A visit from Angela after the horrific incident that she recently endured brought on a clapping of hands from those present. Most of the guests were surprised and ecstatic about her being alive and in their company. It was noticeable that her beauty and demeanor also mesmerized the males in the room. For whichever reason, Angela Tyler was a welcome addition to this social event.

"Angela!"

Her name being used in such an excited manner caught Ms. Tyler's attention. As she turned to locate the source of the voice,

Angela noticed her old friend, Trey Buckley, rapidly approaching. As the two met, they both embraced in a social manner.

"Great to see you here, Sweetie."

"You too, Trey. This is just what the doctor ordered. I was about to go stir-crazy being cooped up for several weeks. You know me, little Ms. Social Butterfly."

The reference of being Ms. Social Butterfly was a misrepresentation for Angela Tyler. She did possess a free will, but was somewhat introverted when it came down to social events. Being cultured and educated, Angela possessed all the skills necessary to blend into any group or event, and did so whenever needed. Her preferred forte' for a social gathering was a smaller group of friends getting together for a cocktail and just a "hanging out" session. She also did not mind hitting the town on her own. Self-entertainment was not a problem for Angela, such as her desire to take a solo venture to some local club for a night of dancing and relaxing. Despite her horrible fate at the August Moon Club, Angela was not going to let this event change old habits that she enjoyed so much.

A brief chat with Trey soon ended, as he soon broke away and began mingling with other attendees, including Donnie McBride. Angela hated to see this but figured Trey was a grown, responsible politician and could handle himself. Trey's rapid departure came as a surprise, especially since he was the one from whom she received the invitation. Things just seemed to be a little off key with her old friend today. She was being lead only by a hunch and gut feeling, but after their previous conversation on the phone and the short greeting tonight, this childhood friend was just not his old self.

Angela was first introduced to Trey when they were only three years old. As children, they were around each other constantly and thought of each other as brother and sister. One commonality they did not discuss with anyone was the strange tattoo both had emblazoned on the back of their necks. This was their life-long secret that they shared with no one.

As children, both Angela and Trey questioned their parents about the odd marking, but were always shunned and given elusive answers. Only after each matured did they learn the meaning of the strange symbol, and both were told at the same time. Trey and Angela had waited for years to hear the answer, which seemed too simple. Apparently, both sets of parents had fertility issues, which lead them to seek clinical assistance to conceive a child. The small tattoo was a necessary marking to identify them with a special fertility test project that few were privy to years ago. The parents also continued to explain this as being the reason why each was required to have a yearly doctor's checkup while younger, in which extensive lab work was conducted on them. Both accepted the answer but neither was too fond of the marking. Due to their embarrassment regarding the tattoo, along with the constant instructions from their parents to keep the marking concealed, Trey and Angela kept this image their little secret.

Angela mingled with several familiar faces and took a few solo strolls out back to admire the beautiful pool and waterfall in the courtyard. Sipping cocktails and casual conversation with many strangers was becoming boring to Angela. A look at her watch revealed that only one hour had passed but she was ready to move on. Trey had abandoned her after a short conversation and had not been seen since. Angela wanted to leave and had the perfect alibi to get her out the door. Recovering from a major injury was a valid excuse to be pardoned from her social captors and leave, and that time had arrived.

Angela could not go home without first bidding Trey a farewell. A search through the lower floor of the huge structure led Angela to a game room that she noticed several people entering throughout the evening. The voices inside were loud enough to hear through the solid wood doors that always remained closed. Without a doubt, the bar was in full swing in this room. As Angela entered, she was shocked by what she saw. This was no bar room, instead, in the middle of the room sat a polished, wooden table that contained several, large silver trays. On each were mounds of white powder, with rolled hundred dollar bills lying next to them. This crowd thought themselves too elite for the common practice of snorting cocaine through a measly, one-dollar bill. Other smaller tables encompassed the room, with several individuals inhabiting each. On small trays at each table were lines of the white powder in single file, and "blow monsters" holding their rolled hundred dollars bills extending down to the white lines of cocaine. With one single snort, the lines would disappear into the nostrils of their abusers.

What Angela saw next was even more troubling. Upon entering, she immediately recognized a small group of men hovering around one of the tables, and recognized Donnie McBride as one of them. Joining the men were two women, obviously strippers. This was no surprise but what she saw next stunned her. Close to Donnie stood the owner of a local sports team whose name was eluding Angela for the moment. It was clear that Joe Sportster had just snorted his line of cocaine, due to him wiping his nose and a small amount of powder still encrusted on the tip of it. A third individual with his back to Angela, was bent over the table and ridding it of several lines of the white powder. A closer examination of the man revealed the outline of a small tattoo on the base of his neck. Angela knew who this little coke-snorter was, and his actions prompted her to confront him.

As Angela approached, what she saw next stopped her in her tracks—the sight was both horrifying and confusing. As the individual stood, there was no doubt that her childhood friend and now U.S Senator was getting high on cocaine. The use of illegal drugs was something that Angela despised and a path she never ventured down, and always believed her friend, Trey, would avoid. Now, here he was snorting cocaine and without any concern for who was watching. Even among the elite, there would always be a whistle blower in the crowd.

"Well hello, little sister. Want to powder that beautiful little nose of yours?"

Angela could only nod her head signifying no. Being caught in the moment, she was speechless. The tattoo on the back of Trey's neck was not the one she had seen before. As children, she and Trey had always examined each other's tattoo and discussed the small pitchfork like symbol that had a bent rod protruding through it. On the back of her friend's neck she had just noticed two symbols, not one. At this time, Trey reached over and grabbed Angela's arm, pulling her toward the powder filled tray.

"I said, do a line, you little bitch!"

Despite being in her recovery mode, Angela was still physically fit and was able to muster the strength to pull away from Trey, slapping his face.

"Don't you ever talk to me like a dog, do you understand me, ass-hole!"

The confrontation brought the room to a silence. All eyes were on the Senator as Angela sped from the room.

"Just a little family quarrel, now hell, lets party on!" The Senator said in an arrogant and unremorseful voice.

Within seconds, the room returned to an atmosphere as if nothing had ever happened. The power of the cocaine was controlling all who welcomed it. The lines were being snorted as if tomorrow did not exist. This behavior prompted Angela to speed from the evil that was contained behind the heavy, wooden doors. As she made her way to the entrance, an open door to another room revealed an office. As Angela entered it, she became affixed to a telephone on the desk and soon began dialing numbers to a pager.

Come on Robert, call me back, PLEASE!

With a guarded hand, Angela sat hovering over the telephone. A short minute had passed before the phone rang, with Angela snatching it up before anyone else in the house could hear it.

"Robert?"

"Yes, Angela, it's me."

"Where the hell are you? I need to see you, ASAP!"

"Don't freak out, but I had to make a little detour to a local hospital. It's nothing major, just a broken hand. What's going on?"

"Oh God, Robert, when can I see you? It's time we talk. I am at a party in west Ft. Worth and just saw something that concerned me. I'm really worried. Robert, it's true. I never believed it before, but it's true!"

"Angela, what's true?"

"It's Senator Buckley, Robert. It's time to tell you!"

"What, Angela, is he using dope?"

"That would be the least of my worries right now. I just can't tell you over the phone. Robert, just come to my apartment when you get out of there. I have to go."

Angela hung up the phone and made her way to the front door. Upon being dropped off, she had given orders to her taxi driver to remain at the house until she was ready to leave. When she opened the front door, Angela saw that her orders had been obeyed.

"Where to, Ms. Tyler?" the driver inquired.

"Back to where you picked me up at, and get me there ASAP!"

"Yes, Ma'am, buckle up!"

The yellow sign on the taxi's roof was easy to identify as it sped down the private drive toward the entrance. Senator Buckley kept the car under surveillance until it disappeared around the small hills close to the main gate. The cocky smile soon evolved into a look of concern as he watched his childhood friend disappear.

"I never did like you, BITCH!"

Trey's words seemed to make him feel better about the situation but despite his cocaine-clouded mind, he knew a price would have to be paid for what he caused Angela to endure this evening. He knew his little friend would run to her daddy, or Detective James. Repercussions from Sam Tyler the Senator feared, but he was not frightened of the detective—Robert James could be handled. The Senator had just the man to deal with Detective James.

"Hey Adam, get your ass in here!"

CHAPTER 21

The news delivered to Robert by the ER doctor was not a surprise, five broken bones in his hand and a referral to an Orthopedic Specialist for possible surgery. The diagnosis had been delivered just minutes prior to the phone call he just received from Angela Tyler. Robert had broken bones on several occasions in the past, so he knew it would be a few days before his hand could be cast, due to swelling. The escape from the ER was simple this evening, just signing a few papers and he was off to a waiting, Angela Tyler.

    Robert's mind was analyzing many possible scenarios as he sped off towards Ms. Tyler's Ft. Worth apartment. Even though he had only known his victim for less than a month, this beautiful creature seemed to have an abundance of self-control. During their conversation Angela seemed scared, so whatever was bothering her this evening must be big. It appeared that mentioning his visit to the hospital with a broken hand did not faze her, or even register. Whichever the cause, this type of behavior was out of the ordinary for Angela Tyler.

    Trey Buckley was a close childhood friend of hers and a prominent U.S. Senator. During the few times Robert had spoken with him, the Senator seemed to be even more of a gentleman than what he reflected during his television appearances. He also appeared to be genuinely concerned about Angela's assault and wanted the perpetrators behind bars, at any expense. This was all now confusing to Robert, very confusing. Numerous situations were going through his mind, trying to find some reasonable explanation of what Angela was so fearful of. His detective side also generated thoughts about her possibly sampling some party favors in Ft. Worth, which had caused a short spell of paranoia. Maybe there was a part of Angela Tyler he had not yet seen, or been told of. These thoughts and more were now clouding his mind.

An unusual telephone ring seemed to bring Robert from his thoughts. Not often did he leave his car phone on, but apparently during all of the excitement he had forgotten to switch it off. It was the office calling, and Robert noticed the extension was Special Agent Michaels' phone. The call was short and the urgency in Agent Michaels' voice dictated to his detective there would be no negotiating with his orders. Reluctantly, Robert had to redirect his vehicle back toward Las Colinas, to comply with the orders just passed down by his boss.

The call to Angela Tyler was not what she was waiting for, or expecting. Upon ending her last conversation with Detective James, there was no doubt that he was en route to her location. Robert explained to Angela there was no negotiating with the boss when he makes a request from one of his troops. Robert had expected her to be upset, or maybe even irrational, due to the urgency in her voice during the last call. Angela seemed to understand and calmly directed him to call as soon as the meeting at the office had ended.

Thirty minutes after the call from his boss, Robert was in Las Colinas at the JDLST office, a place he had not seen much of lately. For the first time in weeks, every investigator from the unit was present.

"Ok, boys, listen up. Here is what we have. Investigator Mike Bales has information from a reliable source that there is a huge meth lab brewing a few miles east of Lubbock. Besides the reported enormity of the lab, this deal is pretty interesting. A man identified as David Smitz owns the lab. Besides being a dope cook, he is a self proclaimed minister who has a cult following. Mr. Smitz owns a small religious compound with about forty-five cult members living in it. Making dope to support a religious group is a little bit of a misnomer but nothing surprises me these days. Several weeks ago the Lubbock County Sheriff's

Department had some deputies engage in a pursuit with a vehicle, while sitting up on a possible meth lab. When a pickup truck left the property, the deputies tried to make a traffic stop to obtain some probable cause on the house for a warrant, and that's when the chase began. Soon into the chase, the suspects began firing on the squad cars with automatic weapons. I am not talking about 9mm pistols; I mean things like AK's and AR's, the real deal, assault rifles. Miraculously, only one deputy was injured but the good ol' sheriff lost two cars during the ordeal. Of course, the bad guys got away, but intelligence came in a few days later identifying one of the shooters as David Smitz. A license check on the truck came back to a Dewayne Ridder, who listed his home address as David Smitz's religious compound. In a nutshell, these guys appear to be very dangerous, so use your common sense and not your testosterone. Get into your teams and let's head to Lubbock and deprive some dope cook of his meth lab. And men, be careful!"

From the moment he entered the office until now, Robert concealed the wrapping that covered his broken hand, under the jacket he was wearing. If the bossman noticed the injury, Robert would be benched from action until it had completely healed. The detective had reversed his firearm's holster so the pistol could be easily removed with his left hand. That little problem was simply solved. Throughout his many hours of handgun training, Robert knew he was very proficient in shooting with his left hand, too. With so much going on, this would not be a good time to be taken out of the lineup, so for the time he would keep the injury to himself. Angela Tyler and his fellow investigators needed him right now, at least most of them.

Robert then noticed that Investigator Ainsworth was looking at him. A quick decipher of the investigator's facial expression made Robert feel as though Adam did not like this partner arrangement, but the feeling was mutual, neither did he.

"You ready Robbie boy? And by the way, we are taking my Porsche and I'm driving, THE ENTIRE TRIP!"

The two investigators loaded their gear into Adam's Porsche and headed off toward the staging location east of Lubbock, to meet up with the other team members. At this location, Special

Agent Michaels and Investigator Bales would brief the unit members of their assignments. Uniformed deputies from the Lubbock County Sheriff's Office would also be present to assist with the assignment.

It was apparent that Adam had not forgotten or forgiven the little episode at the Fantasy Dreams stripper bar, but Robert did not care. The assignment they were embarking on seemed to be a big deal and even more so, very dangerous. Investigator Bales was a seasoned cop and his gut instinct was alluding to this being a complicated and hazardous assignment. Being a narcotics officer put cops in harm's way on a daily basis and this was certainly no exception. When an undercover cop was in a dope infested housing project, or a biker bar buying drugs, danger always loomed but one knew what to look for. Working cult and supremacist group assignments were some of the least favorable for most cops. Numerous events over the past several years had shown the world these types of groups needed to be taken seriously. Most recently, cult and supremacist groups in West Texas and North Arkansas had made their way to front-page headlines.

Robert remembered speaking with a seasoned agent from the Bureau of Alcohol, Tobacco and Firearms (ATF), shortly after the North Arkansas episode. This agent was one of the "best of the best," and had earned the respect of the law enforcement community for some paramount and risky assignments he had been involved in. When conveying the North Arkansas story to Robert, he noticed the agent's wavering and slightly trembling voice as he told about their days and nights in the Ozark Hills. During this standoff, the ATF agents were being kept under surveillance by the supremacist cult members. This was not done by spotting scopes or binoculars, but within the cross-hairs of their rifle mounted scopes. The wrong move, or a slight flinch from a sneeze causing just one bullet to be shot, would have set off a massive shootout with numerous people from both sides being killed. After the standoff ended, the ATF seized several thousand guns from a mere eighty-five men. Once the standoff was over, the agents were relieved and amazed that a mass tragedy had been avoided.

Robert's eyes widened as another thought exploded in his mind. During the Arkansas standoff, a U.S. Senator, namely his new friend, Trey Buckley, helped negotiate possible resolutions and settlement terms with the supremacist. Senator Buckley was the Chairman of the Congressional Law Enforcement Ways and Means Committee, and worked closely with the U.S. Attorney General's office. During the Arkansas standoff, one cult leader wished to speak with a congress member about this country becoming one big Nazi Police State. At that time, Senator Buckley came to the aid of the attorney general's office, and after two days of negotiations was able to broker a peaceful settlement.

This senator is an outstanding individual, so what in heaven's name can Angela be so upset with him about?

This thought kept running through Robert's head as Investigator Ainsworth navigated his red rocket toward the staging location near Lubbock. It was apparent that both men were uncomfortable around each other, and a request for a new partner from each would soon be brought to SA Michaels' attention. Within minutes after leaving the office, Robert advised Adam that he was tired, so a little shut-eye would be taken advantage of during the ride. This allowed him some time to figure out Angela Tyler's call about Senator Buckley, along with psyching himself up for a possibly dangerous confrontation with the David Smitz's group. It was obvious that Adam did not take his job seriously and used it for his own personal pleasures and advantages. The night at the Junkyard revealed to Robert that his muscle-bound partner did not have the fortitude for real undercover work. Now Robert was beginning to understand the boss's concern about Adam Ainsworth.

Investigator Ainsworth's driving practices were comparable to his personal life, operating at a fast pace and basically out of control. Despite being the last team member to leave the parking lot, Adam passed three of his colleagues during the two-hundred mile trip, and only slowed down because he knew the boss's vehicle would be next. The speeding car made Robert uncomfortable but not as much as Adam himself; so, he continued playing opossum to avoid a conversation.

The staging point had been reached, which was a remote insurance office agency near the lab location and the agent himself was a reserve deputy. Almost twenty marked and unmarked cop cars, along with two black SWAT team vans, filled the parking lot. As expected, Adam slid his Porsche into a Handicapped parking spot near the front door.

"Too far to walk from way out there, Robbie Boy. Besides, there won't be any crippled folks here tonight, will there?"

Robert resented Adam's demeanor and disrespect for all others but it was not worth a confrontation at this point. Some serious police work lie ahead for them and the clock was ticking. Many meth cooks followed the practice of setting up a lab at a location just once, reducing the chances of detection. Investigator Bales had no idea how long this lab would be cooking, so time was always of the essence in these situations.

Special Agent Michaels and Investigator Bales led the briefing, with a few county deputies breaking in to give local intelligence and land schematics. Before the search warrant could be signed, one last piece of probable cause evidence had to be obtained, and Investigator Bales was in the process of gathering it. Apparently, an informant who had reported the lab initially agreed to enter the lab location to do a controlled buy. This CI was a female that was an occasional sex toy for the meth cook, and felt she could enter the lab and come out with some of the dope, or at least a sample of the precursor chemicals used to make the evil potion.

These snitches always have a motive for turning someone in to the law, and as the old saying goes, "nothing is mightier than a scorned woman's wrath." In this case, the female informant was somewhat dating the meth cook to the point she expected his loyalty, but earlier this morning discovered this was not the case—he was a cheater. In order to seek revenge, she would aid the cops in bringing the cook's lab down and put him in jail.

As a solo set of headlights approached the staging location, Investigator Bales made his way out to meet it. The informant had arrived but Bales would make sure she did not come in. This was to assure the secret identity of the undercover investigators inside, and could possibly protect the CI's identity from a cop that might unintentionally expose her at a later time.

Only a few minutes had passed before this unidentified visitor was driving away, then Investigator Bales returned to the room. The glowing look on his face announced what the baggie in his hand revealed. Mike Bales had his evidence, one quarter of a pound of methamphetamine; the last piece of probable cause needed for a search warrant. A short drive into Lubbock would be required for a judge's signature.

"I will be back in about thirty minutes and I need everyone ready when I get here. According to our CI, there is a massive cook going on inside the target location and this is their second batch this week. She estimates there are seventy to eighty pounds of finished product in there, with about double that amount brewing away right now. The only drawback is the CI says this place is heavily guarded with a bunch of rednecks with rifles. Game time boys; let's get ready to rock and roll."

As Investigator Bales sped off toward Lubbock, Special Agent Michaels began giving assignments to all involved. While Bales was seeking the warrant, surveillance teams had to be assigned to make sure the suspects did not leave the site. If any car was seen exiting the location, a surveillance detective would radio a patrol car, which in turn would stop the vehicle and secure the occupants. Then, once Investigator Bales returned with the signed warrant, the SWAT team would make entry to secure the building before the JDLST investigators began securing the lab. With a high-risk warrant such as this one, four SWAT tactical teams were gathered for the task. The target location was an old three story farmhouse; which meant there would be a lot of ground to cover once the entry had been made. As the informant advised, the house was filled with "red necks" with rifles, so this would indeed be a dangerous search warrant. This risk included the possibility of frequent booby-traps, and the inherent dangers of the meth lab itself, which are highly volatile.

Upon concluding the briefing, Special Agent Michaels directed all surveillance and patrol units to immediately man their assigned surveillance positions. Robert had seen his partner leaving the building a few minutes prior and found Adam in his Porsche making a call on his cell phone. As he approached, Adam immediately exited the car.

"Hey Robbie Boy, give me just a few minutes alone. I have some hot chick on the phone and I'm trying to set up a date. This will only take a second."

Robert was furious...

"A second is all you have." Robert replied. "Actually, sixty seconds and then I am in there. We have work to do, Joe Playboy."

"10-4, Dude."

I would like to show you a thing or two, DUDE! The thought of pounding the life out of Adam was a pleasurable one for the moment.

Less than thirty seconds later, Robert saw his partner hanging up the phone and then he joined Adam in the car.

"Is it OK if we get to work now? I mean, I know your personal business is probably more important than our little dope lab here, but just humor all of us, okay Adam?" Robert was filled with ire.

Not a word was said between the two men as they began their three-mile trek toward their surveillance location. After barely leaving the driveway, the traffic approaching seemed rather heavy for such as small county road. Robert then broke the silence.

"Five, six, seven vehicles. What the heck do you think is going on, Adam? These aren't kids out road-drinking; they look like a bunch of scum bags."

Investigator Ainsworth's car was one of the close-quarter vehicles, which was assigned to set up surveillance in close proximity to the lab itself. It soon dawned on Robert what was happening.

"Federal Unit 664 to any Lubbock County deputy on special assignment." Robert bellowed into his radio, but it remained silent.

"Federal Unit 664 to any Lubbock County deputy on assignment, please respond—urgent traffic here!"

There was nothing, as Robert's outcry went unanswered.

It did not take long for the detective to figure out what the vehicle caravan was all about. If his hunch was correct, the meth lab had been tipped off and the suspects were all leaving the lab location.

"Must be a dead battery, Robbie."

"No way, Adam. I just took this thing out of the charger before we left."

"Stuff happens, Rob." Investigator Ainsworth replied in a non-chalant manner.

"Do you have the sheriff's office dispatch number? We can call them."

"Nope, Robbie, sure don't."

"Then follow them but keep your distance and cut your lights."

Adam quickly turned his Porsche around and began following the vehicles, at a distance in which they would not be detected. The meth lab site was at a location where three county roads joined in close proximity, so investigators and patrol cars went in many difference directions after the briefing. At this point, they were without any backup and the attempted apprehension of anyone would be dangerous, along with compromising their identities.

"Let's just see where they are going, Adam, and then we can run a warrant on them after we take down the original lab."

Investigator Ainsworth carefully followed the caravan for several miles as it made its way down numerous small and unmarked county roads. Then break lights could be seen from all vehicles as they slowed to turn into a private driveway. Adam tried to maneuver his vehicle closer but time proved this would be a futile task. The moon lit night prevented the cops from moving closer and remaining undetected.

What Robert and his partner saw next was not expected. The caravan of vehicles had disappeared behind a large gate and fence that surrounded some type of compound. Without a doubt, this was the home of the David Smitz cult.

"Come one, Adam; let's get back to the original lab site."

Both men possessed keen navigation skills, so despite the winding trail they were led down, Adam was able to guide his car back to the lab. Upon arriving, an initial drive-by of the house was conducted, which was very disappointing. There was not a car in the yard, or a light on inside the house. Most likely, Robert and Adam had just witnessed a caravan that transported the meth lab to the David Smitz cult compound. Team member Mike Bales would soon be disappointed.

Investigator Ainsworth and Robert then took their assigned post just west of the lab, while waiting for the warrant to be signed. The SWAT vans soon came into sight, and hell in black was about to be unleashed on anyone who might still be inside. Robert then recognized the two cars following the SWAT vans; it was Investigator Bales and Special Agent Michaels. With them passing, all other units were to fall into place.

After the crashing of doors by the ninja-caped tactical officers, a search of the house for suspects was conducted. As usual, the wait for the investigators posted outside the house seemed to take hours, but actually only ten minutes had elapsed before the SWAT team leader gave the "all's clear" command.

The ensuing evidence search for Investigator Bales was a disappointing one. The sour odor of the liquid raw meth product, P2P, and the piercing fumes from the drying agent, Ether, were extremely strong, indicating a working meth lab had once inhabited this structure. Some lab glassware and a few chemicals had been left behind, along with small amounts of liquid P2P and powdered meth. For some cops this would still be a righteous bust but not the case tonight, knowing that over five million dollars of dope had just walked away, which would have a possible street value of double or triple that.

When initially clearing the building, the tactical officers did make several interesting discoveries. First, one man was found hiding in the kitchen ceiling, which turned out to be the owner of the house. The individual had inherited the home a few years ago from his grandparents, and had since converted it into a drug house. Another find of interest was a hidden, safe room on the first floor. No evidence was discovered inside, and upon interviewing the ceiling dweller, he did not even know the room existed. Apparently, it had been built by his grandparents, who kept it a secret from all friends and family members.

The last discovery was the most troubling. The third floor of the home contained about one-third of the square footage of the lower two. Each side had a dormer with a window extending over the roof. On the inside of each, sections of wood and sheet metal bolted together provided a protective wall for anyone standing behind it. In each section were numerous holes that were large enough for gun barrels to extend through with some flexibility. Resting on the backside of these barriers were several high-powered rifles, with numerous cases of ammunition. The bad part was many of these boxes of ammo did not have a weapon to match. These boxes contained 223 and 308 bullets—those of modern assault rifles.

A short interrogation of the man left behind soon left the detectives knowing what they had missed. First, a high yielding methamphetamine lab had left the location a short time before the cops arrived. Second, this was a lucky day for many of the cops because they had just avoided a sure death trap. The third floor had been occupied by four men armed to the hilt, who would have been heavily rewarded for shooting anyone trying to trespass—especially a law enforcement official.

The lone suspect was removed from the location by Investigator Bales and taken to his car where the interrogation continued. It did not take long to have the name of the meth cook, along with his accomplices. Apparently, the homeowner belonged to a local religious cult and gave the name of David Smitz as his spiritual leader. Pastor Smitz, as he was referred to, had convinced this man that his god would allow the making of meth to support and broaden his ministries. For some reason, this fool bought into the scam and joined the cult, which gave Mr. Smitz and his cronies' access to his home. Tonight, this homeowner would only have access to the county jail.

Robert was able to give Investigator Bales the remaining pieces of the puzzle, telling about how they followed the caravan of vehicles to a compound several miles from the lab. This information, along with what the homeowner had just told, gave Bales all of the probable cause needed to take down David Smitz.

The only piece of the puzzle that was missing was who tipped of the crooks about the soon to executed police raid of their house. It would not be unusual to find out that the female who snitched the lab off, also snitched to the meth cook that she saw cops staging up the road. This was in chapter one of the, "How to work a snitch" manual. For Investigator Bales, this was the one and only theory about who snitched off the raid but to Robert, another possibility existed.

Investigator Bales would find the informant in a few days and question her; but tomorrow, David Smitz would have to pay for his sins!

CHAPTER 22

Collecting all of the evidence at the lab sight was a time consuming effort that took the entire night to complete. Due to the men being tired, along with the logistical planning needed for a law enforcement raid on David Smitz's compound, Special Agents Michaels ordered all investigators home to get a day of rest before the search warrant would be executed. These instructions were music to Robert's ears and not because of his desire to sleep. This would give him the time needed to make contact with Angela Tyler, so her story could be heard.

"Hey, Adam, I have some business I need to finish in Ft. Worth, instead of going back to the office. Can you drop me off downtown?"

"Be glad to, Robbie ol' Boy, be glad to." Unlike about half of the words that came out of his partner's mouth, Robert knew these words from Adam were sincere.

As with the trip to Lubbock, the return journey passed as quickly, with Adam putting the hammer down on his Porsche. Despite the brief encounter they had with Texas State Trooper working radar, they made it back to the Ft. Worth area in record time.

"Where do I need to drop you off, Rob?"

"Give me just a second. I need to call someone and see if they are at home. I need to borrow your car phone real quick, Adam, it's company business."

Robert then reached behind his seat and fished around for a second before finding Adam's cell phone. Being in a Porsche with little room but a lot of police raid gear, made looking for a phone a tricky feat. Anxiously, Robert dialed Angela Tyler's telephone number, which he now had memorized. It did not take but a few rings for the call to be answered. Only a few words were exchanged before he had confirmed Angela was at her apartment and was ready to see him. She had actually made a trip to the first floor lobby to get some vending machine snacks, so told her detective that she would meet him there.

Robert could not recall the exact address but guided Adam to the Tyler's apartment complex on Commerce Street.

"This is it, pull on over, Adam."

"Who lives here, Rob?"

Robert did not want to tell Adam about this being a safe house for Angela Tyler. During their partnership, Investigator Ainsworth had been losing the confidence and trust of his partner; so, giving away the home of this protected witness would not happen. Robert eluded a truthful answer by advising Adam this was the home of a young lady he had met a few days prior. As he coasted the Porsche into the loading zone in front of the building, Adam was too busy taking the phone from Robert, so he could make a personal call himself. On this evening it would have been worth Adam's time to have been more observant; so he could have possibly noticed the set of eyes watching him from the building's front lobby.

On one occasion, Robert was driving the Porsche when he met Angela. This lady was privy to many of the finer things in life, including automobiles. The Porsche immediately caught her eye, as did the identity of the passenger in the vehicle; it was her personal detective. The sight of Robert brought a smile to Ms. Tyler's face but this look of joy quickly diminished when she observed the driver. Upon seeing Adam, she quickly hid from view to await Robert's entry. If the driver would also approach, she had made up her mind to elude them both by sneaking out the back door. Angela was relieved to see the Porsche speed away after Robert made his exit. She was very cautious to stay hidden until the car was out of sight. As the front doors opened, Angela ran up to Robert and before a word could be spoken, latched onto him as if he was her life preserver in a sinking ship.

"Hey, hey, hey . . . what's up Sweetie?" Robert asked in a sincere manner.

"Just hold me for a minute. My world has gone to hell and back tonight, and it just now got worse!"

"What do you mean, Angela? Relax for a second. Let's go on up to your apartment and talk this thing through."

As Robert pulled away from Angela's grasp, he quickly noticed the tears streaming down her face. Not once since this investigation began had Robert seen his victim so upset, including when she discussed the details of her assault. Leading the way in silence, she took hold of her detective's hand and led him to the elevator. Robert did not resist and returned it with a reassuring grip, letting Angela know that he was her protector and cared—maybe even more than he should. The elevator sped its way to the top floor where they both exited and went into Angela's apartment.

Once they entered, Angela directed Robert to the sofa and made her way to the refrigerator where several bottles of wine were chilling. Both of them shared a commonality with their taste for wine. Neither cared much for red wine, with a Chardonnay or White Merlot being a favorite, and chilled, of course. Ignoring the fact that her detective might still be on the clock, Angela filled two large wine glasses to the brim of the slightly red, fruit of the vine.

Robert remained quiet; waiting for Angela to describe whatever it was putting her in overload mode. She then took a seat on the sofa next to her detective.

"Who was driving the Porsche, Robert?"

"That was my work partner, Investigator Adam Ainsworth—why?"

"Well, your partner is a real piece of work there buddy. How much do you trust him?"

"Let me put it this way. Having him as my partner was not my choice and it still is not. The bossman partnered us up, hoping that I could motivate Adam into getting his heart into the job. Ok, Angela, let's stop the question and answer game and get to the point. What's going on with you and what are the Adam Ainsworth questions all about?"

"The party that you missed in Ft. Worth, well, guess who was on the guest list? Robert began to respond to her questions, but was cut off before he could mutter a word. Angela then sprung up from her seat and began pacing the floor.

"Let me answer that for you, it was Investigator Ainsworth. And what the hell do you think he was doing? I will answer that for you, too. I walked into a room and saw your buddy nose deep in a mound of blow, as in COCAINE BLOW!

Robert was shocked but was able to sneak in a few words before Angela's next line.

"Maybe he was there in an undercover capacity and was simulating using the dope?"

"Wake up, Robert! I guess you still believe that Santa Claus is true, too. HELL NO, your boy was sucking up that crap like there was no tomorrow, along with a couple nude-dancing whores he brought along as party favors. Robert, your partner is dirty!"

Once again, tears were flowing from Angela's eyes. Robert could do nothing but listen, both out of respect and embarrassment.

"He is no better than the people he is putting in jail, Robert. Lucky for Adam, he carries a badge in his back pocket for protection, and snorts cocaine in the name of the law!"

There was nothing Robert could say to convince Angela or himself that Adam Ainsworth was anything but the obvious—he was a dirty cop with a cocaine problem. It was all making sense now. The stripper in the hotel room, the constant topless bar endeavors, along with his lack of productivity, all substantiated Angela's conclusion. The JDLST team had a druggie in their own unit. A sudden thought snapped Robert from his mood of disappointment.

"Ok, but you just figured out Adam's identity when we pulled up in front of the building. You were already upset when you called. There was something else, so talk to me, Angela."

Angela again sat down next to her detective, chugged her wine until the glass was empty. She then tilted her head back and began taking a few deep breaths, holding each for a few moments and then exhaling. Ms. Tyler had now totally captivated her observer. The sofa they were sitting on was located next to a large, glass window with a captivating view of the Sundance Square in downtown Ft. Worth. The combination of lights against the dark night sky silhouetted Angela's perfect profile like an artist's painting. She was indeed a breathtaking creature. Her beauty was once again noted by the detective, which captivated his attention about as much as this headline story she was about to tell.

Angela was starting to relax, and she began to feel her heartbeat finally slowing. She knew that Robert would be taken back by the story she was about to convey to him. Many questions were rushing through her mind as she began scrambling for words to begin the story, or at least part of it. The time had arrived to talk to her trusted detective. Angela moved closer to Robert, with him accepting the violation of his personal space. The closeness and warmth of her body was pleasing to him, and it took all of his effort to ignore his feelings and listen to the victim he was there to protect.

"What you are about to hear, Robert, may sound unbelievable but it is 100% the truth. After my parents were married, for years they tried to conceive a child but their efforts were in vain. After about ten years of trying, they almost gave up. My mother tried to talk dad into adopting but he would not, somewhat of a pride deal for him. Mr. Sam Tyler was too proud for this method of having children because in his mind this would show he was weak or not the total "he man" that he constantly conveyed. My dad is an ex-war veteran, and a high profile, wealthy and influential Texan, so adopting was completely out of the picture for him."

"After the thought of having a child had almost been completely dismissed by my parents, dad was told of a new fertilization program the Federal Government was testing in a remote area in Missouri. It was referred to as "The Devil's Elbow Project," named after a small town along a river in the Ozark hills. This was listed as a top secret project, due to Hitler and WWII still being not that far in our rearview mirrors. One thing the U.S. did not want was to let the public know they were experimenting with reproductive methods, which were only being offered to political figures or the country's wealthy families. A public perception that a nation was attempting to create another supreme race would not be accepted. So, Mom and Dad had to sign their lives away to become part of this program and if they leaked out any information about it, they would lose their fortune and probably be incarcerated and prosecuted as an Enemy of the State. And the proof is standing in front of you that the program was a success."

Robert sat watching intently as his storyteller conveyed her tale. The Devil's Elbow part was making some sense now, but there were still many questions to be answered. Angela sat in silence for a few seconds, letting her audience digest what had just been told.

"Ok, Angela, I understand so far but I can tell there is much more to the story, especially the part about someone trying to kill you. After you collapsed on the hotel floor, you kept repeating the words, "the Devil's Elbow." What the heck was that all about, and the tattoo?"

"Ok, here we go . . . . I know that you have noticed my eyes; one is blue and the other brown, along with a deviation in the pupil's shape. Back then, reproduction science was just being researched and developed, with many hurdles to jump. There were imperfections, and my eyes are an example. How I was conceived was by taking sperm cells from my father and combining them with those from a male donor. This would allow weak sperm to attach to strong ones; therefore, increasing the probability of fertilizing the egg. At the same time reproductive eggs were extracted from my mother and later combined with the sperm from dad and the donor. After a short incubation period, the fertilized eggs were implanted into my mother's womb, allowing her to carry and give birth to a child, namely, Angela Tyler. Now you know why I am referred to as the miracle baby. When it came time to give birth, my mother had no choice but to return back to The Devil's Elbow lab for delivery. This would allow the doctors and scientists to examine their final product and run intensive tests. Each baby born at the lab was marked with the special tattoo on the base of their neck, such as I have."

"As I just said, things go wrong with these types of experiments. My parents first learned about The Devil's Elbow project from Governor Kenneth Buckley, Trey's father. The Governor and his wife had the same issues as my parents did in wanting a child but not being able to get pregnant. The Buckley's and my parents entered the project at the same time, which is why Trey and I are so close in age. With me, the only abnormalities they could find were my eyes, but the Buckley's were not as lucky. For some reason after the egg was fertilized and implanted in Mrs. Buckley, it split and produced twins. The Buckley twins were the first ever born into the Devil's Elbow Project. One day when Trey and I came home from college during Spring break we got really drunk and Trey began telling me about his identical twin brother. He briefly explained that his brother has some horrific mental problems and had been institutionalized his entire life. The Buckley's did not even get a chance to name the child; instead he was assigned a name by a psychologist in the lab. The twin brother's name is Levi, short for Leviathan, the Biblical surname for Lucifer the Monster. Trey rarely mentioned Levi, just using the old cliché of his brother being the "evil twin." I was sworn to secrecy and to this day, you are the first person I have ever spoken to about this."

Robert continued listening intently.

"Is this making sense, Robert? If this were a game show, would you have solved the puzzle yet?"

"No, Angela, help me out here."

"The party I was at in Ft. Worth where your little cop pal was snorting cocaine, guess who was standing next to him and doing the same? Initially, I thought it was Trey but what I saw next convinced me it was not?"

"What the hell do you mean, Angela? You know Trey like a brother."

"When the man I thought was Trey was bending down to snort the coke, I saw the back of his neck. Robert, what I saw were two tattoos similar to mine. I know for a fact that Trey just has one, which is identical to the one I have. Throughout his life, Trey had only seen his brother a few times, due to his violent and uncontrollable nature. He also told me that Levi has two of the devil markings on his neck, not just one. While at the party, the man I thought was Trey slapped me and began getting rough before I could break loose. During this ordeal, he was also cursing me. Robert, this was not Trey, I know it was Levi who was impersonating his brother."

"After I was drugged at the August Moon Bar and taken up to the hotel room, it was like I was fully aware of everything going on around me but I could not move or respond. After one of the men cut my throat, he told me that I should have come home to The Devil's Elbow and this was my punishment for not listening to daddy. Just before that dreadful night, I received a telephone call from someone advising he was one of the doctors from The Devil's Elbow lab, and I needed to return for some testing. When I refused, the voice told me this was an order from the lab director, who everyone referred to as the father of The Devil's Elbow Project. The caller became furious with my continued refusals and told me I would have to pay for my insubordination, and then slammed the phone down. Robert, I know it was Trey's twin. The beast is loose, Robert, and Trey might be dead!"

As Angela ended her story, she broke down and collapsed onto the chest of her detective. Robert held her close, letting his shirt become wet from the tears of this woman. This was the first time since meeting Angela that had he seen her totally break down. Robert knew this moment was coming, and it finally arrived. He sat holding her close, letting the wounded woman know he was her comforter and protector on this evening. A combination of emotional exhaustion, aided by the wine, caused Angela to soon fall asleep in the arms of her detective.

A fascinating story he had just been told and despite the concerns of Angela, Robert believed every word of what she said. Tonight, he was finally one step closer to solving the riddle of Angela Tyler's heinous assault. The mystery of the Devil's Elbow had been revealed, and he had been given some answers to why the place was so well protected. If what Angela had told him about The Devil's Elbow Project was released to the public, political heads would roll. Someone from the lab had ordered a hit on this beautiful and intelligent woman that had been basically created there; and Robert was going to find out who, and why.

Angela's theory about Trey's brother was the most plausible one they had, which would complicate this investigation even more. An insane man pretending to be a U.S. Senator, with the true Senator possibly injured or dead, was nothing less than a prime-time movie leaving Detective Robert James having to write the ending to the script. And at the mad-man's side was a corrupt, drug addicted federal agent. Robert's world had just become enormously heavy....

CHAPTER 23

The silence that consumed Ms. Tyler's apartment allowed Robert's mind to finally relax, at which time a forgotten little problem began to creep back to him. A throbbing from his right arm reminded the detective of the fractures he had forgotten about, due to the intensity of the evening. His wine glass was empty and there was nothing close to wash down a prescription painkiller the hospital had issued. Robert was in need of relief but moving from the sofa would certainly awake his beauty that was calmly sleeping on his chest. A decision was made to stay put and let this woman have her peace.

As he sat holding Angela close, Robert was once again affixed to her beauty and the fit body that was now completely pressed against him. The lights from the city had dimmed, allowing Mother Nature to let her moonlight enter the apartment and illuminate Angela Tyler's perfect form. Robert was unable to take his eyes from her and just sat watching as she slept like a graceful angel. He took the time to examine every inch of Angela's features, head to toe and not missing a spot. The serenity at hand was now overcoming the rest of the world. Robert's body was also relaxing, and began a slow slide downward until the pillows from the sofa and Ms. Tyler's body caught his fall. The two had molded into each other and became one. Robert had entered that mental place where his mind had surrendered to the urge for sleep and he was fading fast.

The beginning stages of Robert's slumber were soon interrupted by the touch of a soft hand to his face. At first he thought the sensation was unreal, but this passionate touching continued until he was able to slightly force open his eyes. Like a dream, a pair of unique but beautiful eyes were staring at him as if trying to pierce his soul. Her minor deformity had just become another attribute to Angela Tyler's beauty. The detective was mesmerized by the woman before him. Her body then became slightly more rigid as she pulled her second hand up and placed it on Robert's other cheek. In slow motion, Angela pulled her man's face slightly closer to her lips. Robert wanted to resist but he could not, like being entangle in a web with no way out, but a web of pleasure was now at hand. It had been months since Robert had been with a woman, which contributed to his desire to let Angela continue. A passionate kiss was then planted on Robert's lips, like none he had ever experienced. Angela Tyler now owned her detective. Mother Nature had just taken over, allowing destiny to run its course. For this moment, the mental and physical pains of life had just dissolved and the world was once again a perfect place for them both . . . .

CHAPTER 24

The rays from the morning sun seemed to creep in through Angela Tyler's living room window much sooner than the couch dwellers expected. The full moon from the night before was still visible but was beginning to fade due to its brighter companion that was rising in the east. Robert was not a morning person but on this day, this type of awakening was welcomed. Angela was still asleep on the sofa, wrapped in a thin sheet she must have pulled from the closet after he had fallen asleep. She still possessed her angelic appearance while sleeping in the cotton-cocoon. This woman did not need a morning dose of makeup and hair styling to enhance her looks—Angela Tyler was a natural beauty.

Robert was careful not to wake her as he moved from the couch and began searching for clothes that had been carelessly tossed to locations throughout the living room. Today would be a busy one for the detective and the two hours of sleep he was just awakened from was typically not enough, but for Robert, today he would be operating on a mental high from what he had just experienced. Thoughts of the guilt and apprehensions he felt after his night with informant Lori Sims were just the opposite of the emotions he was experiencing right now. Except for the gift of little Paige resulting from that night, Robert wished he could turn back time and take a different path than he did with Lori. With Angela Tyler, the thoughts and feelings were just the opposite. This morning did not make him feel like he was walking away from a one-night stand or a remorseful evening with a confidential informant—today all was good. The only thing Robert was dreading was having to leave his little angel without telling her goodbye, or his reason for sneaking away during the early morning hours. A short note left on the table containing a brief explanation would have to suffice. Angela would surely understand.

Hailing a morning cab was an easy task on a Saturday morning in downtown Ft. Worth. About the only signs of life at this hour were the city workers who were removing the reminders of the partygoers from the night before. Just one block down from the apartment complex was the Cowtown Plaza Hotel, which had numerous cabs sitting in the driveway.

"Sneaking away from some coyote-bait, my friend? The morning sun sometimes reveals our mistakes from the night before!" The cabbie seemed to enjoy sharing his wisdom with his new passenger.

"Nope, it's just the opposite. Leaving the beauty that I was with was hard but there is work to be done. Guide this thing toward Las Colinas, please, Sir."

It was not often that Robert saw the DFW area at this time of day. These massive freeways and interstate highways were almost barren and would leave a visitor with confused thoughts about why they were needed. One trip during the morning or evening rush hours on these roads would make most think just the opposite, and wish for more dirt to be moved and concrete poured. The sparse traffic allowed the cab to snake through the concrete jungle in record time. The twenty-five dollar fare was a mere price to pay for such a trip on a day where every minute would be essential.

As with most commercial buildings this morning, the parking lot of the complex where the JDLST Unit was housed contained only a few vehicles. Some belonged to mid level, corporate executives that were in the endless pursuit for a larger pay check or a more distinguished title on their desk-top name plate. In another area sat Robert's truck, surround by several typical detective cars, which were rarely used by members of the unit, with the exception of Special Agent Michaels. Vehicles with lights and sirens were not needed much when one is an undercover narcotics investigator.

The Devil's Elbow Project

Robert knew he had little time to prepare before the bossman would be arriving to begin preparing for the execution of a search warrant on the David Smitz's compound in Lubbock. Upon entering the office, Robert quickly proceeded to the vending machine for his routine diet cola and chocolate chip cookie. With his culinary pleasures in hand, Robert made his way toward his office. With pen in hand, he began to quickly scribble out a rough plan for what needed to be done. The first item came easy—Adam Ainsworth would have to be dealt with. A dirty cop had no place in the unit but Robert wanted to meet with his soon to be ex-partner before taking the problem to the bossman. Adam was apparently close to Senator Buckley, or his twin brother-imposter, and could be a valuable source of information. Once Special Agent Michaels was privy to the newly found information about Investigator Ainsworth, he would immediately fire Adam and the chances of obtaining information from him would be gone. This morning would be the perfect time to confront Adam Ainsworth.

The telephone keypad was probably warm from the friction of Robert quickly punching in the numbers to several of his trusted, fellow investigator's pagers. Adam Ainsworth was cocky and arrogant, and often thought of himself as being untouchable and bulletproof. Today he would have to be taken down a notch and there was no better way to do it than to be confronted by several of his peers. In Robert's opinion, the JDLST team contained some of the best cops in the business, and they could certainly handle one of their own.

Reponses to Robert's page were almost immediate. The team members knew each other like brothers, and seeing an early morning page coming from Detective James was a rarity to his fellow team members. Within minutes, Investigators Ronnie Bays, Blake Waterman and Mike Bales were en route. If this team could not get the truth out of Adam, then there was none that could.

Once the fellow investigators arrived, Robert began to give details of his investigation involving Angela Tyler, and the cocaine cowboy cop that was a part of their unit. While the saga was being conveyed, there were no comment being made, they were all ears. With a seasoned group of cops like this, someone in the crowd usually had a smart-ass comments to make, but, today there were none. When a law enforcement group discovered that a crooked cop was among their ranks, usually rage and anger were their responses. In this instance, things were different. All seemed to share the thoughts of Robert; they had a huge problem on their hands. Despite what a person might read and hear, it was a rarity that a law enforcement agency gets involved with the investigation of a dirty cop and politician at the same time. In addition, The Devil's Elbow Project and twin brother theory were huge topics to digest, and even larger to devise a plan to tackle. Plus, this was all transpiring on the dawn of dealing with the David Smitz cult.

"This is your ballgame, Robert, and it sounds like we are in the ninth inning with bases loaded. We are here to help, but you need to make the calls. And you know how the bossman is; he will be expecting you to have some ideas to convey as soon as you brief him about the case. Time is critical right now, especially with the Lubbock situation hanging in the balance."

"You're absolutely correct, Mike, and here is what I would like to do. First of all, we need to confront Adam and see if he will give us any information." Robert responded.

"Adam will either talk to us or Uncle Bays here will have a little prayer meeting with the boy, and his entire body will look like that arm of yours. By the way, Robert, what the hell happened to you? Did you go and piss off another of your one-night stands?"

"Actually, my southern Cajun friend, I got that kicking your sister's ass last night."

"That's not true, Rookie, that woman can handle both of us!"

A brief moment of typical cop ribbing was just what the doctor ordered to ease tensions of the forthcoming battle this band of brothers would soon be encountering. Even though this case was a huge burden to carry, Robert felt a lot more comfortable knowing he had the best cops, and loyal friends, that one would want when engaging in this type of situation.

"Let's rock and get this show on the road." Investigator Waterman was not one to stand around and waste time when so little of it existed for all that needed done.

Despite Adam being a team member, no one in the unit had ever been invited to Investigator Ainsworth's home, so his address was unknown to all. Robert knew that Special Agent Michaels kept a personnel file for each investigator in his office, but retrieving this information would require trespassing onto sacred terrain. The bossman's office was off limits to all, when he was not there. A quick vote among the men found Robert to be the chosen one to invade the boss's territory. It was no secret where the files were kept, which would make this chore a quick one. As bad luck would have it, the moment Robert pulled out Adam's file, the front door opened and in came Special Agent Michaels. He was met by the other three investigators but their physical barrier between the boss and his office was not sufficient enough to shield the view of Robert walking out of it.

"Ok, you four stooges, would anyone mind telling me what the heck is going on here? We weren't supposed to gather for the Lubbock raid until eleven. I usually can't get any of you in here before noon and here it is 8:45 on a Saturday morning and I have almost a full house. Detective James, I know you must be sleep walking because I can swear that I just saw you leaving my office. And why is your arm all wrapped up like that? Should I sit down first, because I know that a bunch of B.S. is about to come my way?"

"I called this party, Bossman, and I do think that maybe you should sit down for this one."

The briefing with Special Agent Michaels went as expected. It was definitely an overload of information that was given to him and the response was just as Investigator Mike Bales had predicted. The bossman agreed that Adam needed to be dealt with immediately, and reluctantly gave consent for his team to confront the wayward investigator. Usually a supervisor dealt with personnel matters such as this but in this instance, Adam Ainsworth possessed crucial information. Robert also had to explain the injury to his hand, resulting in only a shaking of his boss's head as the response. After their mission had been blessed, Robert jumped from his seat and began walking toward his work brothers, who were waiting near the front door.

Before they could escape, Special Agent Michaels exited his office for some final words with his boys.

"I will head on to Lubbock and wait for you all there. At noon today, we have a group of sixty SWAT members that will go knocking down the doors of the David Smitz compound. Once they are in, we are anticipating taking several hours for SWAT to secure the scene and check it for weapons and booby traps. I want you guys down there no later than 2:00 PM to begin your search. Ronnie Bays, I need you to advise Adam that he is not invited to this party and to meet me at the office at 8 AM sharp on Monday morning. You all got that?"

Numerous "yes sirs" were the responses from his team.

"By the way, Robert, from this point on you are on light duty until that hand heals up. We will talk details on Monday morning."

This was an expected move by the boss but one that Robert had thought he temporarily escaped.

"Yes, Sir, I understand."

As he watched his men leave the office, Special Agent Michaels doubted the fact that his young detective really did understand.

It was no surprise to see that Investigator Ainsworth lived way beyond his means; his comrades discovered as they rolled into the plush city of Plano. There was no doubting the city's reputation of being one of the wealthiest in Texas, and probably the nation, just by looking at the real estate and commercial zoning requirements. Adam's house was no exception and there was no wonder that the boys in his unit never received an invitation to come visit. Compared to other homes in Plano, Adam's was not a standout but it did not take long for his fellow investigators to estimate that he was living in a home valued at probably three-quarters of a million dollars.

Like a hungry pack of wolves, the four approached Adam's house. The doorbell was seen but intentionally overlooked as Investigator Bays pounded on the door. The thought of a dirty cop infuriated all members of the unit, but for some reason it seemed to affect Bays the most, which was demonstrated as he pounded one more time.

"Hey Bays, we needed Adam alive so we can talk to him first, so just chill a little, okay?" Robert's intervention was noted as Investigator Bays took a few steps back.

Footsteps were then heard walking toward the door.

"Who are you and what do you want?"

This was not the voice of the Investigator Ainsworth but instead, that of a female. Robert then approached one of the glass panels on the door's side so that he could possibly get a look at the female. A side profile of the woman could be seen but it was all that was needed for Robert to recognize she was the stripper he met at the Grand Park Hotel with Adam a few weeks prior. Robert knew the woman would be protective of Adam and would possibly not let them in.

"This is Adam's friend, Robert. We met a few weeks ago at the Grand Park Hotel in Arlington. I have Adam's paycheck, so can I just hand it to you?"

Robert's little lie worked, knowing that in addition to her drugs, money was one of this woman's golden idols. As she cracked the door, Investigator Bays shoved Robert aside and led the charge inside. Robert was able to reach out and grab his jacket, slowing Bays down. This was a signal to remind him that they needed information out of Adam. Despite the fact their fellow investigator was dirty; the rest of them had to remain the professional cops they were. This would be exceptionally hard, especially after seeing a tray of white powdery cocaine sitting on a small table in the living room.

Apparently, Adam heard the commotion and came from a back room. Most people would have welcomed a visit from friends and fellow employees but when he saw the four investigators standing in the foyer, his face turned flush. Despite Adam's normal demeanor of arrogance and feeling like he was untouchable, Adam could tell by the looks on his fellow cop's faces that he was their target. When one sins they know that someday they will have to pay, and Adam instantly knew this would be his day of reckoning.

In most situations where a cop was going to interview a suspect, a quiet, bare room was used for the interview or interrogation. The cop would usually begin a small conversation before discussing the incident, where he would note and gauge the responses to the questions so a base line could be set to aid in interpreting the suspect's responses. However, this type of ploy would not be used on Adam. Getting him to own up would take more than this routine method that he himself had used so many times. Today, direct and aggressive questions with the added presence of four cops was the only way Adam would talk. The female could be seen moving toward her man's side but Adam quickly motioned her to a back room and she reluctantly complied.

Tactics for numerous scenarios had been discussed while the investigators were en route to Adam's house. One scenario was that if Adam was stoned on cocaine, he might try to find a weapon and engage in a suicide shootout with his fellow cops. It was apparent by the fact Adam was only wearing his briefs that he was not armed, but a quick dash to his room could have rapidly changed that. So, it was a relief to see Adam walking toward his sofa and having a seat amid his peers, who all remained standing. This was his first sign of submission to the group. Adam's words soon cut through the stares of daggers aimed his way.

"So, to what do I owe the honor of this visit?"

The rest of the group remained standing, as Robert took a seat next to Adam. He was plain spoken to his ex-partner, eluding the games that were normally played at this point in an interrogation.

"Adam, we know about your cocaine problem, and Senator Buckley. We need to know details—all of them!"

The ease of Adam's admission to his cocaine problem stunned all.

"In short story form, Robert, I blame body building and the use of steroids as being the major contributor to my little issue. Throughout my life, I have been very athletic and excelled in sports to the point I was able to obtain my Bachelor's degree on a four year, free-ride football scholarship. During a game in my sophomore year, I tore a calf muscle and a part of the rehabilitation included a prescription steroid that would expedite my return to the game. During this rehab process, I was in the gym working out more than ever, and noticed the rapid muscle growth throughout my body, giving me a physique most women could not resist. When the rehab was over, so was the access to my prescription steroids. I loved the results achieved from that drug, and I knew that just south of the Texas border in Mexico were drug stores that allowed a person to purchase all of the roids they wanted, and without a prescription. I soon became a frequent customer, and a supplier of the drug to numerous muscle-heads at my local gym. Since the possession of steroids initially was not illegal, I justified my actions and enjoyed the financial perks associated with it."

"The cocaine, Adam, what about the cocaine?"

"Well, Robert, I just kept making more and more trips to Mexico and my bank account began to swell. Then, I know this will be easy for you to believe, I was at an after-hours party at a local stripper's house and was offered a snort of cocaine. I had been drinking and was surrounded by hot, half naked women, so I figured what the heck, one line won't hurt. From that first line of snow, I knew I was a goner and it did not take long for the drug to own me. It was just like all of those training manuals informed us, but even more powerful. During one of my journeys south of the border, I met a runner for the Cartel. He was looking for someone to help funnel some cocaine into the U.S, and I immediately told him I was a cop. I thought this would scare him off but instead, it had just the opposite effect. He loved the idea, knowing I could badge my way across the border and most likely, elude all drug check-points that were set up near the border in Texas. The money he offered was mind-boggling, so I was in. Before I knew it, I was making more money in one month than I could in ten years as a cop. I party and spend money like there is no tomorrow, and am still able to live like a king."

"Many kings are dethroned, Adam, and today is that day for you. Now, I want to know about Senator Buckley, you know, the man you were snorting cocaine with in Ft. Worth a few days ago."

Adam hesitated at Robert's next question, reflecting a worried but cunning look in his eyes.

"If I answer that question depends on you, Robbie boy."

After being so submissive, Adam's sudden change to arrogance was a surprise, forcing Ronnie Bays to jump in.

"Let me take it from here, Robert. I will give this arrogant bastard a sample of my negotiating skills!"

Adam did not reply or even look at his pissed off, co-worker.

"Ok, Robert, you want to hear the rest?"

Robert looked at Investigator Bays, signaling him to back off. Bays then confirmed to Robert he would be willing to hear Adam's terms before pounding on the punk.

"I want immunity, complete immunity, along with being assigned to the Federal Witness Protection Program. With this guy, I dare not proceed unless I have your word; otherwise, I will end up a dead man."

"You have my word, Adam. I will get you in but you know the rules; you have to produce and help us bring him down."

"That I will do, Robert; I am in."

Adam then continued with his fascinating but disappointing story.

"Robert, about six month ago I was at the same house in Ft. Worth that I was this week when your little snitch saw me. At that time, Senator Buckley snuck up on me while I was taking a little toot of coke. When I turned around and saw who it was, I thought I was a goner. Instead, the senator buckled up next to me and before I knew it, we had totally inhaled the entire pile of cocaine that was on the tray. Buckley then started talking all of his smack about how he wanted to be a major controller of both cocaine and meth in this state, and then expand to be a national drug king. The senator told me about being the chairman of some national law enforcement committee, which would give him an inside to law enforcement intelligence, including that from the DEA. At first I thought he was full of crap, but the more we partied together, the more I believed him. Before I knew it, I was working with this guy and he was lining my pockets with more money than I had ever thought possible. I was rich, Robert, rich!"

"Go on."

"This is where things are a little strange. I was never allowed to initiate contact or call the senator. It was always his call and under his terms when we spoke or met. I knew we had to be careful but who would really suspect a U.S. Senator and a Federal agent being involved with improprieties? On a few occasions I tried calling the Senator but was forced to leave messages. There was one time I did get through to him in Washington, but Buckley acted as if we had never met, and invited me to come and visit his office in D.C. with my family. The Senator concluded by telling me how much he appreciated the efforts of the JDLST team and enjoyed the fact we were putting the bad guys behind bars. I just don't get it, Robert. I know that cocaine had its affects on people but this guy is Dr. Jeckel and Mr. Hyde."

"You know that you have to help us bring this guy down, Adam, or I will personally toss your ass in the can and throw away the key." Robert reinforced his point by pointing toward the tray of cocaine sitting just a few feet from Adam.

Despite being in an "under the bus" situation, Adam's attention was turned to a television that had been on, but in a muted state. A special news bulletin had caught his attention. Adam then reached for the remote control and cranked up the volume.

> "This is just in from Lubbock, Texas. Federal officials are running a search warrant on the David Smitz cult compound, which is located just outside of the Lubbock city limits. The only information we have at this time is the federal agents will be searching for illegal drugs and weapons at the compound. We have reporters en route to the location, so we will keep you apprised of the situation."

"That's one of his, Robert, that's one of his!"
"Who, Adam, and what?"
"Senator Trey Buckley . . . David Smitz is one of his biggest suppliers of methamphetamine in the state."
"How long have you known this, Adam?"
"Months, Robert, probably three to four months."
This statement enraged Robert.

"So, you're the one! You snitched us off last night before the raid. You made the call and I sat there and watched you! YOU BASTARD!

Adam's silence signified his guilt to all. It rapidly became a struggle for Robert to maintain self-control. His first instincts were to pull Adam from his seat and pound the living hell out of him, but with a broken hand he let self-control prevail. Instead, Robert stood and tore a page from a magazine on the coffee table. While all watched, he proceeded to the small table where the cocaine was located and dumped the white powder on the paper in hand. Carefully, Robert folded all corners so not one grain of the coke would escape. He then looked toward Investigator Bay and gave a slight nod of the head.

"I want your shield and gun, Adam, and now!"

Adam did not dare to question or challenge Investigator Bay's request. His fellow investigators watched as Adam lead Ronnie Bays to a back room. They all knew what would happen next. After a shout of a few demeaning expletives, a short, physical altercation ensued. Adam Ainsworth was experiencing some good old Texas justice from this short tempered, Cajun cop—Ronnie Bays had just kicked his ass. As Mr. Bays re-entered the living room, in one hand he held Adam's badge and ID, and in the other, the ex-cops gun. Investigator Bays soon noticed Robert's stares.

"What? He resisted arrest. What can I say, Robert?"

"He wasn't under arrest, Ronnie."

"Oh, well, he just resisted then. Tried to shoot me, or something like that."

No one further questioned, or cared about what had just happened to Adam Ainsworth. No longer was he a cop; now Adam was just a civilian criminal, a scumbag like the rest who peddle their drug of poison to societies' consumers. Today was a sad day in the history of the JDLST team. A crooked cop had lived among them, and used his badge to promote illegal drugs throughout their state and nation. Indeed, this was a dark moment for law enforcement.

CHAPTER 25

Investigator Bays pulled his vehicle to the front of their office building to let Robert out. The order from the bossman had been given, which put Detective James on light duty. This in turn meant he would not be traveling to Lubbock with the other three investigators. The raid on the David Smitz compound would mean a lot of hard labor collecting evidence at such an immense crime scene. Therefore, Robert was left behind, to book the evidence seized at Adam Ainsworth's home, and to complete the paper work regarding the incident. This all had to be done before Monday, so Special Agent Michaels could meet with Adam to discuss his future as an informant, not a cop. Robert knew he had plenty of work to do at the office; but, a quick feeling of jealously flowed through his body as he watched his fellow investigators speed toward Highway 121, with lights and sirens blazing away.

The office was quiet, which meant the best atmosphere for typing reports and developing a confidential informant plan for his ex-partner, Adam Ainsworth. This was painful for Robert and the others because Adam had taken advantage of them and violated his oath. All knew that Adam needed a nice, cold jail cell but fortunately for him he held a valuable card, which could be played in this game called freedom. As Robert sat at his desk he noticed the message light flashing on his phone. Being a non-work day, he almost ignored it, figuring whoever was calling could be helped when he came in on Monday. Everyone of importance in his life knew the number for the pager he constantly carried, so most chose contact in that manner.

As Robert fired up his computer, curiosity was killing him, so he reached down and dialed the code to retrieve his phone messages. He then sat in horror as he listened to the message on the phone:

> "Robert, this in Angela. I am sorry I have to do it this way but I am going to The Devil's Elbow in Missouri. I did not contact you because I needed a day or two head start, so I could get some answers before we meet again. I know this may sound dangerous but I am not worried about myself anymore. After last night, I have a desire to clear up any obstacles in my life; so I can maybe, possibly, have a chance of spending some more time with this wonderful man that spent the night at my apartment last night. I know that as long as this case in hanging in the balance, I am just your victim and there should be nothing more. If the case were over, then we could possibly have a shot at a normal, dating relationship. I may be presumptuous here, Robert, but I think you feel the same for me, as I do for you. Plus, I truly believe that my friend, the real Trey Buckley, may be in grave danger. Please understand and don't do anything until you hear back from me. Until then, please keep our moonlit night at the front of your thoughts! See you soon, my Dearest."

The detective could not believe what he had just heard. These people had just about killed Angela Tyler a few weeks ago and if a second chance arose to finish the job, they would surely do exactly that. Angela would be a sitting duck, totally defenseless against the trained professionals who guarded the sacred Devil's Elbow lab. Plus, if the mentally deranged Buckley twin was at the helm of her assassination attempt, he would show no mercy to

The Devil's Elbow Project

this defenseless woman. Robert knew he had to get to Missouri, and fast.

A private jet usually sat at Dallas-Love Field, ready to go at a moment's notice for any federal agency that needed it. This would be his ticket, a quick ride into Fort Pulaski and then on to his destination a short distance away. After his trip to Florida on the Gene King case, Robert and Captain Mullens, the pilot of Federal Air Unit 30, had befriended each other, staying in touch and being Happy Hour buddies on occasion. In turn, special favors were available if needed. Robert had both the office phone at the hangar, along with the Captain's beeper. In hopes of finding his pilot friend at the hangar and ready to fly, Robert decided to try that number first. An unfamiliar male voice then answered the phone, but he could tell it was not the Captain.

"Is Captain Mullens in?"

"No sir, he is not. The Captain had a few days off and is on reserve duty at the Naval Air Station in Ft. Worth. Can I ask who is calling?"

"Sorry, this is Detective Robert James, with the federal JDLST team. Next question then, is the jet available for use? I have an urgent case in Missouri and I need to get there ASAP."

"I hate to tell you this, but our air unit has four jets assigned to the state and at this time, all are tied up in the raid in Lubbock. I hear that things are getting pretty intense down there, so all of our pilots have been told to remain there."

This was not what Robert wanted to hear. Despite his personal fear of flying, he knew that time was of the essence and driving to Missouri could result in the demise of Angela Tyler. This was not acceptable. Robert recalled that Captain Mullens and a buddy of his co-owed a twin engine private plane; and the offer had been there for its use in the past. Robert scrambled for the Captain's pager number and quickly punched the numbers in. The few minutes it took for Captain Mullens to return the call seemed to take hours. Patience was not one of Robert James' best virtues, especially when such a dangerous situation was at hand. Finally, the phone rang and as hoped, it was the Captain.

Robert then spent several minutes explaining the situation to the Captain, stressing the urgency to get to Missouri but needing to leave out the intricate details. Giving all of the facts would mean a long explanation and there was no time for that.

"Right now, Robert, I am on active reserve duty out at the Naval Air Station. I am a reserve jet pilot and am currently at the pump refueling this F-14 bird that I need to log some hours in. Plus, from what I hear all of the company jets are tied up in Lubbock right now."

"Do you have to be there 24-7? And what about that private plane you own?"

"I have two more days at the base before I can leave. Everything I do has to be business in this bird of mine. My private plane is in Montana right now and won't be back for a week. I want to help but I am out of ideas right now."

"I understand but this is also a matter of national security involving a United States Senator. Captain, numerous lives are hanging in the balance here—I hope you understand. If I don't get to Missouri ASAP, there is a bad guy out there who will start dropping the hammer, and numerous people could die. I am open for suggestions, I need your help!"

A short pause ensued before the Captain responded.

"Robert, here is what I want you to do. Get to the Naval Air Station as soon as possible. I will call the front gate and get your clearance to enter, just make sure you bring along that badge and federal ID of yours. Ask the guards where Building 14 is and I will be waiting. Kick it son, and get your hind-end over here, ASAP. And Robert, I would suggest that you show up with an empty stomach." A slight chuckle from the Captain ended the conversation."

In a matter of a minute, Robert had dropped the cocaine from Adam's house into their evidence safe and shut down his computer. A dash to the key cabinet revealed that another Mercury detective car was still available in the parking garage. A vehicle with lights and siren would be needed for the twenty-five mile trip to the Naval Air Base in Ft. Worth. There was no time for a call to the bossman, plus with all that was going on in Lubbock; the probability of his call being answered would be remote. Robert then left a brief note on the desk advising Special

Agent Michaels that Angela Tyler had gone to The Devil's Elbow and he was in route to Missouri to stop her.

As Robert steered the car onto Highway 121, he was flooring the gas pedal, causing the engine's roar to blend with the sound of his siren. The adrenaline was already rushing from the urgency of the situation, and the speed, lights and siren just added to Robert's self induced chemical high. At this moment, nothing would stop him—Robert felt invincible. The weaving through cars and the cursing of stupid drivers was typical for a Code-3 run for him. Some things never change, which was obvious with his high-speed journey to the military base.

The front gate was now in sight. Robert shut down the siren but kept the emergency lights flashing, signifying to the guards that he needed immediate clearance through the gate. Numerous cars were in line in front of Robert, but the gate guard signaled for him to enter through the exit lane, which was void of any traffic. Stopping just for directions to Building 14, once again Robert floored the car in route to his destination. Upon pulling up to the building, Robert saw the familiar face of his buddy, who was dressed in full flight gear. He then motioned the detective to a side parking area where he could leave the car.

"Are you ready for this, Robert?"

"I think so Captain, but if you are going to do what I think you are, how the heck do you expect to pull it off?"

"The F-14 is a two-seater, one for the pilot and the other for the navigator. Today, my friend, you will be my navigator. I have some flight gear for you in the locker room. Get changed as soon as possible. Once you are in a suit, no one will be able to recognize you and won't be asking any questions. Robert, can you handle this?"

"I am not sure but I have to. I can pass out after this is all over. Just be gentle and none of that fancy stuff, okay? Just speed, Captain, just speed."

Feelings of fear and anxiety consumed Robert, but on this day his fear of flying came in second to the possible losses at the hand of the Senator's emotionally deranged bother. One last call was made before leaving the building. Transportation had to be arranged from Fort Pulaski to a car rental center, so Robert was going to ask another favor from a new friend, Chief Tom Dennis, from Robertsville PD. The chief told Robert in the hospital that if he ever needed anything, to just pick up the phone and give him a call. Today, he would call in the favor from the Chief. Plus, this would give Robert the opportunity to inquire about the explosion at the truck stop, which sent him to the hospital. He was in luck; the Chief was at the station and agreed to be his personal taxi service to the rental agency.

The walk down the concrete to the awaiting F-14 was cumbersome, due to the heavy flight gear that Robert had never dreamed he would be wearing. Captain Mullen's aircraft bore his name near the cockpit, along with a symbol representing his unit. The jet appeared to be a lot larger than expected and was a magnificent example of American superiority and muscle. The F-14 was indeed a beast, and Robert was about to have a rare chance to hitch a ride in it.

Captain Mullens guided Robert into his seat and helped secure him in place. Once he was in, the Captain took his position in the pilot's seat. After a few short seconds, the engines began to rev up and the canopy was lowered to its closed position. Robert knew he was about to experience the ride of his life.

"Federal Unit 30 to NAS Tower, requesting clearance for a Signal 200 takeoff."

These orders given by Captain Mullens signified to the control tower that he had just been activated to conduct an urgent assignment, which would allow him to forgo the filing of a flight or assignment plan. Using his call sign of Federal Unit 30 also indicated this would be a government or law enforcement mission and not one of routine military training. This type of flight was rare but could be used in certain situation by pilots with full time, federal law enforcement jobs.

"NAS Tower to Federal 30, your Signal 200 flight has been approved. Proceed to Runway 4 and you are clear for immediate takeoff."

"Okay, Robert, take a deep breath and let it out slowly and try to relax. Just for your information, we will be traveling at approximately 1400 miles per hour, and should be landing at Fort Pulaski in about twenty minutes. Will that work for you?"

Robert could barely whisper an "Okay", since he was totally absorbed by what was about to happen.

The jet quickly made its way to the given runway, hesitated for a few seconds and then began emitting a roar of thunder that was almost deafening, even with ear protection. The lunge forward propelled Robert back against the seat, where he remained for several minutes after takeoff. Captain Mullens was easy on his first time navigator; climbing gradually and not making use of a near vertical assent the jet was capable of. This trip was unlike his first flight aboard the private, multi-passenger company jet. When in the F-14, the mach speeds could be felt throughout every inch of Robert's body. This machine was nothing less than a cockpit attached to a rocket.

Once the jet leveled off, Captain Mullens felt he should see how his passenger was doing. He found that his federal agent buddy was in awe over the magnificent scenery he was taking in. Robert's first flight was at night and he was too apprehensive to look out the window. Things were different on this trip; there was no place to hide. There were no shades to pull over the windows, or naps to be taken. If one's eyes were open, they were forced to notice they were thousands of feet above mother earth.

"How is my navigator doing there, Detective James?"

"A lot better than I thought I would be. I can definitely see why you are still a reserve. If I ever had a chance to pilot one of these babies, it would be hard to permanently walk away. Not to get religious on you here, but one cannot doubt there is a God when you are up here touching the heavens. You have the best of both worlds, my friend."

"I can't argue that point. Hey, did you hear the latest about the raid in Lubbock? It appears that David Smitz's group opened fire on the federal SWAT teams during their entry and now there is a massive standoff. The news is indicating there are several causalities from both sides and the feds have backed out to avoid any further deaths. Hostage negotiating teams are in route but it sounds like a bad deal. Glad you are up here instead of Lubbock right now."

This was not what Robert wanted to hear but the thoughts of Angela Tyler and the Senator were overshadowing all others right now. Robert could not help but think that if Adam Ainsworth would not have snitched off their previous raid, the Lubbock standoff would not be happening right now. But then, would the lookout men in the loft of the meth lab had shot them if the search warrant went off as planned? Maybe Adam Ainsworth unknowingly did them a favor.

"Robert, look down to your right, about one o'clock. Any idea what that is?"

"Can't say I do. Clue me in."

"That is Fort Pulaski. Yes, we are already there."

Once again, Robert sat in awe. As the jet descended, he knew an unpredictable mission lie ahead. There was no plan and no backup for this one, he was on his own. If Angela Tyler was being held at The Devil's Elbow lab, the odds of him being able to rescue her were practically non-existent. Robert then closed his eyes, knowing the need for a prayer had arrived.

CHAPTER 26

As Captain Mullens taxied the F-14 off the runway, Robert could see an awaiting marked police cruiser sitting next to a small hangar. Just as promised, Chief Tom Dennis was there to pick up his federal friend. The Chief seemed to be a little shocked when he recognized that Detective James was one of the individuals who was approaching his car, and still wearing his flight suit.

"You feds never cease to amaze me, Detective James. Now, get out of that monkey suit and jump in here. I don't want to rush you but we have a lot going on right now."

Robert then bid Captain Mullens a farewell, along with many words of appreciation.

"No problem, Robert. Glad to be of help. Plus, you now owe me one. The best of luck, my friend."

The F-14 pilot immediately returned to his ship and soared back into the heavens, destination Ft. Worth. With a short, forty-minute flight, none of his flight team would have probably even noticed his absence.

The rental car agency was only a short distance from the main gate, so there was little time for each man to ask questions. As expected, Chief Tom Dennis was curious why the detective arrived in Missouri aboard a F-14 jet, and alone. Being a retired military police supervisor, Tom knew that such an expensive mode of transportation meant that Detective James was on an important mission. Robert's response was that he was just taking advantage of a once in a lifetime opportunity from an old friend.

Over the last couple of weeks Robert had been too busy with the Angela Tyler case, to inquire about the incident at the truck stop which landed him in the hospital. When asked about the progress of his personal case, Chief Dennis explained that no arrests had yet been made but a possible suspect was under their scope.

"Detective, it appears that this had nothing at all to do with you. There is a strong-arm for one of our local mobsters, and his name is Stephen Friedman. This man is nothing less than one of Satan's sons and has been a person of interest in numerous homicides around here. Apparently, there is a local private investigator that was hired by Stephen's wife, of all people, because she thought he was cheating on her. Actually, there is no "thinking" about it because his boss runs several of the local whorehouses and Stephen does their pre-employment interviews, if you know what I mean. You just happen to resemble the private investigator in appearance, and drive a pickup almost identical to his. Stephan is very street savvy and noticed the private investigator following him around on several occasions. He warned his wife to call her dog off, which she did, knowing that Stephen would kill the man if he caught the guy following him one more time. Unfortunately for you, Stephen thought you were the private investigator, so it was game on. He wanted to teach you a lesson not knowing you were a cop. When we put the word out on the street who the actual victim was, Stephen's wife spoke with us after being promised total immunity, in case we felt she was associated with some of her husband's illegal endeavors. She then explained how Stephen confessed to her and was mortified after hearing that his victim was a federal agent. Her motive, of course, was in hopes that her husband would be sent to prison. We brought Stephen in for an interview, but that guy is just too seasoned to rat on himself. So, right now we have no concrete evidence on him but we are still working on it."

Robert expressed his appreciation to the Chief as he exited the patrol car.

"Robert, are you sure there is nothing else I can do for you? I will be done with my meeting shortly, and have no plans for the remainder of the day."

"Thanks, Chief, but not at the moment."

Thomas Dennis was a seasoned cop with over thirty years of law enforcement work under his belt. He could tell there was a lot more to Robert's visit than what he was telling. Also, the demeanor and look on the young detective's face reflected a troubled person. Tom had seen this look before, and had been in the same place as his federal friend many times. There were times in a cop's career that he had to venture down a dark road, alone, in order to find a clue to what he was searching for. Detective Robert James appeared to be making that trek right now.

"Detective, don't forget that I am just a phone call away."

In a goodwill gesture, Chief Thomas flipped the parting detective a quarter.

"I am just a phone call away. Take care, my friend."

As Robert walked from the car, he knew the Chief could sense that trouble lie ahead for him.

Of all vehicles, the rental agency could only offer Robert a plain white colored Ford Taurus, which took on the appearance of a police detective car. Robert had no choice in the matter. Besides, there would be no sneaking up on The Devil's Elbow lab, with the tight security they had.

During his drive to the lab site, Robert's mind raced as he thought of numerous scenarios for entering the lab, but not one of his plans could promise safety. Surveillance on the facility would be futile and would be detected in minutes. Trying to sneak into a facility where no intelligence existed, was just as ridiculous, and would most likely be a suicide mission. There was only one way to find out for sure though, and the time was now at hand.

Robert parked his Ford in front of The Devil's Grill, and exited the car. One more quick check assured Robert that his forty-caliber pistol and two clips were secure under his jacket. His federal badge and ID were draped around his belt, just to the inside of his gun. Therefore, a person would see he was a cop before the gun was noticed.

Detective James did not hesitate as he made his way to the basement entrance in the back of the building. This was the only way he had a chance to find Angela Tyler, even though this was a high-risk plan. The Devil's Elbow Project was a top-secret operation, and anyone poking around would not be welcomed. And, if Senator Buckley had met with foul play from his twin, the situation would become even more risky. Whatever the situation was, Robert had to take a chance. He had not heard from Angela Tyler for twenty-four hours, which was not a good sign.

As he stood preparing to knock, the door opened and two security officers armed with automatic weapons appeared. Not a word was spoken as they patted down their guest and removed the pistol and clips from Robert's possession. The men left the badge and ID on Robert's belt as if there was no need to identify him, almost as if his arrival had been expected. The escorts did not say a word as they led Robert into the bowels of the facility. As the men walked further into the dark lab, Robert could smell and feel that cool and damp air was beginning to surround him, signifying they had entered the cave. The hallways were barely illuminated, which prevented Robert from seeing much of the building he was walking through. In here, there was no escaping except though the door he had just entered, unless one was privy to the built in escape tunnels that were constructed prior to the lab being occupied. Robert knew he was now at the mercy of the unknown person that awaited him.

As they proceeded, an eerie feeling came upon the detective. He realized he was walking through the halls that his mother once roamed nearly thirty years ago. A mother he barely knew was once a vitally important figure at this facility, and then her cancer deprived both family and government of her presence. Robert could not help but wonder if something from the lab caused the cancer that consumed his mother. The walls that she helped build were now imprisoning her son, what a contrast this was. For some reason the thought of his mother once walking in his exact footsteps was somewhat of a comfort.

The walk had taken them nearly a quarter of a mile into the cave. Being an avid runner, Robert could calculate distances almost to the exact foot. A hand then reached up and grabbed Robert's shoulder in an effort to stop him. Still, his escorts were saying not a word, but the pressure of a gun barrel in his back guided him down a secondary hallway. A dim lit wall-lamp reflected this would be a short walk, since the hall was coming to an end just a few feet ahead. After one of the guards knocked, a faint command allowed them to enter. A shove from the other armed escort caused Robert to stumble into the office. A quick survey of the room revealed the rich, elegant décor and furnishings that it possessed. This had to have been the room of someone important, possibly even the former director of the facility.

The smell of cigar smoke and a slight flame caught Robert's attention. Standing in the corner of the room in the shadows was a man that was the keeper of a rolled tobacco log. As the figure emerged, Robert recognized a familiar face—it was Senator Trey Buckley.

"Detective Robert Lee James, welcome to my one and only home. I have been waiting for the opportunity to have a little chat with you, so here we are, at Hotel Hell."

Robert did not respond and waited for the Senator to continue.

"Cat got your tongue, Detective?"

"Beg my forgiveness for the correction, but we have actually met and spoken on several occasions. It was I who was assigned as the lead investigator in Angela Tyler's case and we spoke several times at the hospital."

"That was not me, you fool, it was my twin brother! You and I have met, though, but just for a brief time. Last month there just happened to be a little accident on Interstate 44 down the road from here. I was in a black SUV that had crashed, damn those deer. I remember you getting out of a pickup truck and approaching us right before the troopers rushed me to another car. I have a photographic memory and never forget a face or name, unlike that self-righteous brother of mine."

"Then it is true, you are not the senator, but instead his twin brother Levi, just as Angela Tyler told me."

"To hell with that bitch and my brother! For years I was kept locked up in this dungeon while they were out enjoying their youth and freedom. After being trapped in here for that long and being stuck with needles and probes like a guinea pig, I started to look for ways to escape this hell-hole. Even after the government officially closed this joint, they kept it alive to service their creations. This place is one of those secret projects that Congress funds but has no idea that it even exists. I have lived here all of my life and hate this place. Do you know how many times I escaped this top-secret and well-guarded facility, Robert? Well let me tell you, twelve times, twelve times! You know what, Robert? My brother and that know-it-all little blonde can't even figure out how to escape one time. Yes, detective, both are now my houseguests and they are never going to leave this place. I am the smart one, detective, and because of that I am now the Senator, not my brother."

"Can you believe that when I was born those doctors named me after the devil, the damn devil, Robert? Why couldn't I have been a Bob, Jim or TREY, anything instead of Leviathan? In the grand scheme of things it really doesn't matter anymore because I am the new and honorable, Senator Trey Buckley. I have to admit, I do find it rather amusing that tonight, Leviathan the Monster, will be sending you to heaven while you sit next to Angela, whose name is a derivative of God's angels. Actually, instead I hope you both go STRAIGHT TO HELL!"

What was before Robert was indeed a mad-man, just as Angela Tyler had described. Levi was a mentally deranged person with a lust for drugs, power and money—an extremely volatile combination. There was no doubt Robert knew that he, the Senator and Angela were in grave danger of losing their lives. The Devil's Elbow was definitely an appropriate name for Levi's home, and here Robert stood at the mercy of this mad-man. He had no gun, no way to communicate and was trapped a quarter of a mile underground. Robert knew that his death would be imminent if he did not get through to this possessed individual.

"Can I ask you a question, Levi?"

"Correction, Levi no longer exists; I am the new Senator Trey Buckley! If I ever hear you refer to me as Levi again, I will put a bullet between your eyes, UNDERSTAND ROBERT! Now, ask me your question, you simpleton!"

"These guards know who you are. There are people out there who have seen you snorting cocaine. How do you expect to keep this all a secret?"

"It's money, Detective, it's all about money. I pay these guards well to protect me and do as I say. For instance, over the past week three of my treating physicians just happened to go away, like forever! I now own this place, Robert. On the outside I have made new friends who actually like the "revised edition" of Senator Buckley. Besides the cocaine, do you have any idea how much cash I have collected from private interest groups lately? This is the life my friend, and you are missing the boat. Do you actually think that an insignificant little group like the JDLST team can stop a genius like me? You make me laugh, you little insect. Now have a seat, it's show-and-tell time."

The guards forced Robert into a chair and turned it toward a television screen.

"Look at this Robert!" His attention was now focused on the news brief that was coming to them live from Texas.

"See that compound, Robert? The news is referring to it as the David Smitz compound, but they are wrong. I own David Smitz, so that place is technically mine. That idiot runs some of my top producing drug labs, but I do have one little problem with him. There is a big standoff at his compound, with the Department of Justice trying to negotiate a peaceful surrender. I can't let that happen because I can't totally trust David Smitz. I am sure that David would not mind snitching me off in order to save his own hide. Giving up a U.S. Senator is big news and a powerful negotiating tool. David would give me up and then enjoy a nice life-long vacation in the Witness Protection Program. I have been in prison all of my life, Robert, and I like my newly found freedom way too much to be locked up any longer."

Robert could do nothing but listen to this mad-man ramble. He knew the more Levi told him, the less chance he had to escape alive. Surely there would be just one second that this man and his guards would slip up, leaving him an opportunity to capitalize on their mistake. First, he needed to find out where Angela and the Senator were being held. For the time, he would have to humor Trey's brother and see what he was alluding to regarding the David Smitz situation in Lubbock.

"Want to know how the Lubbock deal is going to end, Robert? Well, let me look into the future and tell you. I guess you are aware that my brother is the Chairman of the Law Enforcement Ways and Means Committee. This means that he is that he is the most powerful person in Congress when it comes to you cops. Just prior to your arrival, and I should say your easily predicted arrival, I made a little call to the Director of the FBI. In our brief conversation, I advised him that David Smitz is making a fool of our federal law enforcement officers and that he needed to end the situation, immediately. I gave the director a 5:00 PM deadline, which was a safe number knowing it would take David Smitz weeks to consider surrendering. So, in two minutes we will hit that golden hour. Let's tune in to see how well the Director obeys his new master. David Smitz needs to die, Robert. He can't be around to spoil my party."

The first story on the five o'clock news was about the Smitz compound in Lubbock. The update was showing a massive second run on the cult compound but this time federal agents were making use of light military armor. It was apparent the negotiations were now over and this standoff was about to come to an end. Neither Robert nor his captor were saying a word as they watched this grim story unfold in front of their eyes. Gunfire and the churning of tank-tracks could be heard as the blasts were intensifying. Smoke and gunpowder filled the air, with loud bursts from small artillery overwhelming the small weapons returning fire from inside the compound. Tanks and armored vehicles were smashing through walls, making gaping holes to expose the enemy within. Within minutes, the compound was on fire as reporters and bystanders gazed on in horror. This type of assault would most likely result in the deaths of all occupants in the compound. Unlike other similar situations, the David Smitz cult was composed entirely of adults; as children were strictly forbidden. Therefore, all of the adult members had made a choice to be there and for some reason, also elected not to surrender to authorities.

For those millions who were watching the standoff coming to an end on national television, they were probably thinking that federal agents had learned their lesson from similar situations, where days or weeks of negotiations were usually futile. Despite the tragedy, most would believe this was the cult's decision and this grim ending was their choice. Little would anyone believe that the violence before them was the result of a mad-man, who was impersonating a United States Senator.

As the two men watched the saga unfold before them, the Senator's brother could barely hold the cigar in his mouth due to the huge grin that was stretching across his face.

"See my Boy, what money and power can do? I, not my brother, just destroyed a cult compound and all of those within by using the mere weapon of a telephone, along with the status of my name. Welcome to the world of the new, United States Senator Trey Buckley!" Robert then watched as Levi bent over and sucked a long line of cocaine into his nostrils.

"Care for some, Mr. Dope Cop?"

Robert refused to give the imposter the satisfaction of acknowledging his madness.

"I will deal with you along with the others, and that time will be very soon, Robert my boy. You three are the only obstacles now in my path to power and success, and I just can't tolerate the possibility of anything going wrong. Enjoy the last few hours of your life, Mr. James," said Levi as he turned his back to the detective, signifying their conversation was over.

"Now toss this guy in with the other two." The two guards were ordered by their deranged boss.

As the two security guards pulled Robert from the room, the detective knew he was being taken to where Angela Tyler and Senator Buckley were being held. The fear of his impending death was not his priority, instead, for some reason the thought of just seeing Angela Tyler again was calming, and for the moment, strangely exciting.

Being a hostage was a situation that Robert had received little training for, but as a cop you were always taught never to go out without a fight. Robert concluded that he would save this effort for after he made contact with Ms. Tyler and the Senator. Since both of them had been in this facility numerous times in their past, it was Robert's hope that each could contribute information about the layout of the lab, along with some possible escape routes. Also, Senator Buckley appeared to be a man who was in good physical condition and could possibly handle himself, if needed. Three minds would be more resourceful than one, so hopefully a plan of escape could be improvised.

The trek down a long hallway revealed numerous rooms that needed little explanation. A sign plate, or for some a nameplate, was affixed to each door, signifying the identity of its occupant. The numbers kept getting bigger and Robert soon knew where his stopping point would be. Room #46 was approaching and when the men were only a few feet away, Robert slowed and stopped. For some reason, Angela was able to recall the room number that Levi had lived in and conveyed that to her detective in a previous conversation.

"This must be it, gentlemen."

Robert was in the beginning stage of some psychological warfare with his escorts. Any time that he could find a trump card to play against these guys, Robert would do just that. For the first time, one of the guards spoke.

"Get in there and join your friends, Mr. Dead Detective." The guard's words ended with the shoving of Robert through the door.

The furniture and décor in this room were dull and minimal, unlike the extravagant furnishings of the office he just left. Each wall was gray in color and the room was illuminated with a solo light fixture. The bed was nothing more than a mattress, and a small toilet and sink occupied one corner of the room. This room was nothing more than a jail cell and especially not something for a child, no matter what kind of disabilities they possessed. For a few short seconds, the detective felt sympathy for his captor. If a person was not crazy when he got here, spending years in this room would certainly push him over the edge.

The detective's only reward for being a captive was sitting on the bed next to Angela. As the door closed and locked behind Robert, Angela Tyler jumped up and latched onto her man. She was overwhelmed to the point of being speechless. Angela would not let loose, as if clinging to a lifejacket after being thrown overboard from a ship. The Senator then stood to greet the new guest.

"I hate to say this because you are now part of this horrible situation, but we certainly are glad to see you, Robert. I know my brother very well and he is a severe mental patient, and all of the drugs he is doing are just making matters worse. Robert, Levi confessed to sending the two assassins to kill Angela, this was after he tried to coerce her into coming back to the lab through several phone calls where he was posing as one of the facility physicians. The taking of Angela's blood was so it could be tested to verify her death, and as a trophy signifying his kill. Levi is so sick, Robert, that he keeps one of the vials of blood on a shelf in the office. Also, the standoff in Lubbock with the David Smitz' cult; I personally overheard a conversation between my brother and the FBI Director, where he was impersonating me. During the call, he threatened political and financial repercussions if the FBI did not attack the compound and immediately take possession of it, even if this meant sacrificing all cult members within. Levi told the FBI Director that his organization was embarrassing the nation, and the Director bought into his B.S. Robert, if we don't think of something soon, we are all going to die at the hands of my deranged brother."

"Senator, I hate to be the barer of even more bad news, but the David Smitz' compound in Lubbock is now a huge pile of burning lumber and dead bodies. An all-out assault on the compound took place about an hour ago and everyone that was inside is believed to be dead."

"Oh, God, oh God; my brother is indeed Satan's child . . . ."

CHAPTER 27

Thomas Dennis did not earn his chief status just because of his joking demeanor because he's a nice guy. He was a seasoned law enforcement veteran, who had grown to rely heavily on his gut instinct when someone or thing did not look or feel right. When a young federal detective arrived in town and his mode of transportation was a F-14 fighter jet, this was unheard of. Being a cop for thirty plus years also gave the chief the ability to tell when someone was not telling the truth, or was in some sort of trouble. With Detective James, this internal warning bell was off the chart. Something was just not right and the chief had a hunch where the trouble might be. After Detective James was injured at the truck stop diner, Robert conveyed to him and Sergeant Parks that he had just left The Devil's Grill before making a stop at the truck port. During his tenure in the military and at the police department, Tom was able to recall the numerous rumors about a top-secret government project being operated out of The Devil's Elbow area. This hunch was too strong to ignore.

The next stop for Chief Dennis would be The Devil's Grill. It was time to see if this internal clue was correct. Bingo—as he drove past the business Tom was able to identify the car he had seen Detective James renting. For the next two hours, numerous drives past the bar reflected that Robert's car had not moved. This began to concern the Chief, so it was time for a bar check.

"100 to Dispatch. Show me out on a business check at 1204 River Valley Road."

"10-4, Car 100. Do you want a unit to assist?

Even though his own policy dictated that bar checks required two uniformed officers, today the Chief could be violating it. Tom did not want to share any details about his hunches, and if Robert was in the bar, he would not have to share his identity to any of the other officers. When one is a cop and wearing a uniform, trouble can come from any direction, but due to the small crowd at The Devil's Grill, this was not expected. Plus, at this location backup was always close by, since the bar's owner was a retired law enforcement officer.

A quick walk through the place did not turn up either trouble or the elusive Detective James. For most people, a vacant car in the parking lot of a bar usually meant just a cab ride home, or a friend preventing a drunk driver from operating a vehicle. For several hours Robert's car sat vacant in the parking lot, and later a bar check did not reveal him either. Things just were not right and Chief Dennis felt the need to roll the dice on this one and call Robert's boss in Dallas. If this turned out to be a wild goose chase, then no harm was done. On the other hand, if the young cop was in trouble, help needed to be called in. Chief Dennis was aware that the owner of the bar and grill had recently installed a video surveillance system.

"Hey Travis, does your surveillance system cover any of the parking lot of that little business next to your bar?"

"Sure does, Chief, both front and back."

"I am looking for something in particular and would like to borrow your video-tape recording for today. I should have it back to you by this time tomorrow."

It took less than a minute for the bar owner to return, holding the tape.

"All yours Tom, and take your time with it. There is nothing on there I need."

With video in hand, Chief Dennis returned to his police cruiser and left the scene.

Five hundred miles away the members of the JDLST were all staging at their office, awaiting their clearance to be in route to the David Smitz compound in Lubbock. After watching the devastating situation unfold before their eyes on public TV, Special Agent Michaels was not surprised when their mission was cancelled by top ranking officials from the Department of Justice. The David Smitz compound was in smoldering ruins and due to the fire and explosion hazards still at risk, special teams from the Bureau of Alcohol, Tobacco and Firearms would be taking over the scene and moping things up. Helping the ATF would be specialized FBI units, who would be indentifying the mass of dead bodies the raid left behind. The role of the JDLST team would be only minor now, which would include detailing reports about the pre-incident events, along with their probable cause for the search warrant. Never in his career had Special Agent Michaels encountered such an event with any of his investigations. No matter what the reason, mass casualties were a hard fact to accept, especially when he was the supervisor who started the ball rolling.

A call to Special Agent Michaels was a welcomed interruption but he was taken by surprise when a police chief from central Missouri was on the line inquiring about one of his JDLST detectives.

"Are you sure about this, Chief? He was in my office earlier this morning and there is no way Detective James could be in Missouri and missing for the past two hours."

"Agent Michaels, I hope you are sitting down because I have a story to tell you. Yes, your detective is in my city right now and wait until you hear how he got here . . . ."

"WHAT, you have got to be kidding me! Hell, he does not even like to fly!"

"No, Sir, I'm not –saw it with my own two eyes. Your boy gets an A in my book for resourcefulness."

The next few minutes involved a briefing from the Chief, along with the exchange of ideas about what Detective James was actually doing in Missouri. One name that kept coming up was The Devil's Elbow. Both men were convinced that Robert was onto something but the brainstorm of ideas still could not produce the answers they needed. One thing they both agreed on was that if this riddle was not solved soon, tragedy could lie ahead for the young detective.

"I do have a little something that might give us a little clue, Agent Michaels. Give me about fifteen minutes and I will call you back." Chief Dennis knew a valuable clue might be contained on the video-tape he had obtained earlier from The Devil's Grill.

"Ronnie, Mike, Blake; in my office, now!"

All work in the adjoining offices came to a stand-still as the team members immediately responded to the boss's orders.

"I need to know everything that each of you know about what Robert has been working on lately. I just received a phone call from a police chief in Missouri, telling me that Robert flew into town today on an F-14 fighter jet, yes, I said a F-14 fighter jet. I need to know what could have been so urgent that Robert ignored his fear of flying and climbed into a super-sonic jet. Help me boys, we need answers, and fast! Your fellow detective may just be up to his ass in alligators in Missouri. Myself and Chief Dennis both believe Robert needs our help."

Throughout their session of putting together facts and clues, the Angela Tyler case, Adam Ainsworth's involvement with Senator Buckley and The Devil's Elbow, all seemed to be common denominators.

"You guys pack your stuff because we are leaving here in fifteen minutes for a road trip to Missouri. We are taking the detective cars—this will be a Code-3 run. Now, get with it!"

After adjourning the quick briefing, Special Agent Michaels struggled with the fact there was one telephone call he needed to make. Sam Tyler had left numerous messages on his answering machine, requesting immediate contact. With the Lubbock situation going on, hopefully he would understand the delay in returning the call. Even though time was a key factor right now, Michaels felt compelled to return Sam's call. Once they spoke, he was glad the call was made.

Sam Tyler conveyed to his friend that he was concerned about his daughter because it had been two days since he had seen or heard from Angela. This was very unusual, especially due to her recent assault. Even prior to the incident at the Grand Park Hotel, Angela always returned her parent's calls. This indeed signified trouble.

"One of my own is missing too and I think we have an idea where the detective might be. Sam, we need to talk and I need the honest-to-God truth from you. This may be painful and possibly even violating a prior contract you made with Uncle Sam, but I need to know everything you can tell me about The Devil's Elbow in Missouri. In the process, I also need all the information you can give me about Senator Trey Buckley. Yes, I know all about the cloning, after being told about it by Detective James' father. I know this is a wild coincidence but Robert's mother was a doctor and scientist for The Devil's Elbow Project. This is a small world, Sam, and I think that place holds the key to our missing kids."

Special Agent Michaels could tell that Sam Tyler was apprehensive to convey with this sensitive information, but there was nothing in this world that Sam loved more than his daughter, Angela. A lawsuit or criminal prosecution was nothing compared to the thoughts of losing her. What Agent Michaels heard next was more than he ever expected. The main headlines included the human reproduction projects from which Angela and Trey Buckley were conceived and the tragedy of Trey's mentally deranged twin brother, Levi, who was never released from the confines of the lab. An occasional escape was the only time Levi ever saw the outside world. A danger to family and society was one of Levi's final diagnoses. Special Agent Michaels concluded the conversation by promising this secret would be kept just between the two of them, and that all efforts would be made to locate his daughter.

Unit investigators were waiting outside their boss's door as he finished up his call to Sam Tyler, which took much longer than expected. Almost as soon as Special Agent Michaels' hung up, his phone rang again. The caller was Chief Tom Dennis. The information he delivered to Michaels was the most crucial piece of this puzzle. Captured on video was Detective Robert James being forced into the back door of the neighboring business of The Devil's Grill, by two men with automatic weapons. Both cops now knew exactly where the Devil's Elbow Project lab was located, and they no longer doubted that Detective James' life was in danger. Chief Dennis would have marked units waiting for the JDLST unit at the Fort Pulaski Airport, and his SWAT team would be ready to deploy.

"We have a change of plan, boys. I want your assault rifles and sub-machines guns going with us on this trip, along with your raid equipment. I just made arrangements for a jet, so let's get up to our hangar at Love Field. Robert James' ass is on the line right now, and I have good reason to believe that Angela Tyler and Senator Trey Buckley are with Robert and in the same boat. We have got to haul!"

Military double-time had nothing on the JDLST unit at this moment. Carrying the extra weight brought on by their weapons and equipment did not slow down the run to the parked Mercury sedans. The lights illuminated the darkness of the parking garage, and the sirens echoed and thundered through the stormy skies. In an attempt to maintain their secrecy, never would the JDSLT cops leave their parking garage in such a manner, but tonight things were different. If it took blowing the cover of each investigator in the unit to rescue their fellow officer, then so be it. The order to leave the parking lot running Code-3 was a direct order from the boss because he knew that his investigators would be testing the full potential of their cop cars. The usual keen awareness to their surrounding traffic on this evening would be at a low, with an expedited drive to their waiting jet at the airport being their only focus. The procession of four black detective cars running with lights and sirens down the interstate even caught the attention of several Dallas radar cars working traffic on the highway. Special Agent Michaels could hear one of the traffic units on their Mutual Aid channel, trying to make contact with the screaming, unmarked units. Tonight, the inquisitive officer would have to remain baffled to the purpose of this Code-3 run.

Captain Mullens was tipped off to the approaching JDLST members, due to the wailing of their sirens. It made the Captain chuckle when a German shepherd that usually roamed the hangars began to return a loud, wolf-like howl in unison to the approaching cop-cars.

It did not take long for these emergency vehicles to come screeching to a stop next to the jet hangar. The soft humming of the aircraft's engines indicated this bird was ready for flight. The JDLST investigators quickly boarded, lugging their heavy equipment with them. Once they were all aboard, Captain Mullens sealed the door and pressed the throttle-arm forward.

"Federal 30 to Dallas-Love Field, requesting immediate clearance for a Code 200."

"Dallas-Love tower to Federal 30, proceed to Runway 12. You are then clear for a Code 200 launch."

"10-4, Love tower, proceeding to Runway 12 for takeoff."

"Where to, Special Agent Michaels?"

"It's good to see you, Captain. I was trying to reserve one of these birds yesterday and was told you were on military reserve duty, and all jets were being used for the Lubbock situation."

"Well, I was called back to work under a military provision allowing pilots like myself to be released for national affairs involving critical incidents. Due to the Smitz' standoff, someone in Washington allocated a few additional jets to keep on reserve in Dallas, so here we are. Where to, Michaels?"

"Ever been to a military base in central Missouri called Fort Pulaski?"

Captain Mullens exploded into a smile so large he was unable to immediately reply.

"So, Captain, why the 'cat who ate the canary' look?"

The Captain still could not speak . . . .

"Wait a minute, here . . . . You just came back from reserve military duty. And let me guess, Captain, you are a reserve pilot, more specifically an F-14 pilot! You certainly do know where Fort Pulaski is, because you just came back from there earlier today after giving Detective James a ride!"

"You should have been a detective, Michaels!" Both men were consumed with a brief moment of laughter.

"Did he tell you anything during the trip?"

"Not much, Michaels, except that it was a critical, life-and-death situation, and possibly involved a national politician. You know my policy, I try to know as little as possible about your assignments. Besides, the flight from Ft. Worth to Fort Pulaski is a very short one while riding in an F-14 Supersonic jet."

"I'll bet it is. Now, Captain, can we put the hammer down on this bird?"

Based on the sound of the engines being maxed out during the trip, Captain Mullens was complying with Special Agent Michaels' request. In less than an hour, Federal 30 was putting his bird down on Fort Pulaski's tarmac. As promised, Chief Thomas Dennis was waiting with a fleet of officers and his SWAT van, when the jet landed. Despite the fact they had never met, both leaders walked directly toward each other for a quick introduction.

"Agent Michaels, to save time I thought we would just brief right here. I just happen to know a retired Army Colonel, who was fortunate enough to have done a security detail at The Devil's Elbow lab years ago. It took some talking, along with a smooth bottle of Bourbon, to make him spill the beans. I have mapped out a plan for us to hit the place through one of the escape tunnels located inside a cave in the hillside. This should give us the element of surprise. Also, I printed off a few photos from the neighboring bar's surveillance video, which captured some good shots of the two goons working security there."

"Sounds like a plan to me. Chief, you have no idea how much help you have been. Now, let's ride!"

CHAPTER 28

Room 46 was cold and damp, which only intensified the nervous shaking that Angela Tyler was now displaying. This room only consisted of bare necessities and a warm blanket was not on the list. During the hours of waiting for their execution, Robert and Senator Buckley decided their only hope for escape would be an attempt to overpower the guards when they opened the door. Both of them were in good physical shape, but overpowering these muscle-bound guerillas would be a chore. Plus, more than likely each possessed a usable knowledge of self-defensive tactics. This was Robert's first day of imprisonment and two meals had preceded him to this point. The senator and Angela Tyler were not as fortunate—both were weak due to the lack of any food for more than twenty-four hours. Hand-to-hand combat with the guards would be an up-hill battle, especially since Robert's arm was broken. But what other choice did they have?

Their opportunity was now or never, as footsteps could be heard approaching the room. The plan of attack was to pounce on the guards once they were inside the room and just within arm's reach. They could now hear the door being unlocked and the same two guards entered.

Unfortunately for Robert and Senator Buckley, they did not have a chance to implement their plan. Trey's twin must have anticipated a rebellion, so the guards were armed with stun-guns. Before the guards were even close to the men, their electrified weapons were aimed at their prey and discharged. Both Robert and Trey were immediately incapacitated by the electric current, rendering them helpless—their plan had failed.

Upon seeing both of her men curled up on the floor, Angela immediately surrendered to the guards, thinking that an ensuing bullet would be less painful than those electric guns. Once the guards secured both Robert and Trey with handcuffs, Leviathan the Monster entered the room. The white residue which still remained on Levi's nose indicated that once again he had been snorting his nose candy.

"Now, come to Daddy, my Dear. And I promise, this will be the last time you ever hear these words from me, you little witch!"

With their massive strength, the guards were able to carry both Robert and Trey over their shoulders, while following Levi as he led his blonde captive down death row. This journey was a short one, ending up in a chamber of the cave that had a dirt floor and a small stream of water flowing through it. A perfect place for a murder, they had just arrived at their final destination.

The guards sat Robert and Trey against a rock wall, while the twin brother pulled Angela toward the men.

"Now, go sit next to your lover, Blondie. Yes, I know all about you two. It is nice having a cop on the payroll with the ability and knowledge to conduct a productive surveillance. I have videos of your rendezvous at the restaurant and your apartment, Angela."

Angela had accepted the fact that today she would not be as lucky as the night she survived her attack at the Grand Park Hotel in Arlington. On that dreadful evening, she began a journey toward a bright, warm light but for some reason was given a second chance at life. Even though she lived through her brutal attack, Angela had a near death experience and found it to be calming and very spiritual, thus alleviating any fears of the hereafter. She did not question why she was allowed to live from her stabbing, just so she could be executed in a remote cave a month later. At least fate was allowing her to die with the man she was falling in love with.

The silence of the cave immediately turned into a war zone.

"Federal agents, drop your weapons and hit the ground, NOW!"

The cavern was now lined with a small army of law enforcement officers. These words were music to the ears of the captives, but immediately sent the Senator's cocaine induced twin into a frenzy.

"This is all your fault, Detective James! If you had not started snooping in my business, I would be the King! Now, look what you have done!"

Robert sat helplessly against the cave's wall, as he tried to focus on the scenario unfolding in front of his very eyes. This was almost surreal, like a television movie where the good guys were rescued from the bad ones, and just in the nick of time. Despite the Calvary arriving, this would not be Robert's lucky night.

The deranged Levi had managed to pull a pistol and aim it at Robert, in what seemed to be a fraction of a second. Robert did not hear the blast before he felt the intense heat and pressure as a bullet penetrated his chest. The small piece of lead felt like a bowling ball that was on fire. Breathing immediately became difficult, and he felt the strength rapidly being drained from his body. Robert's torso began to slowly slide down to the cave's dirt floor. His eyes were the only part of his body that were still functional.

A volley of gunfire erupted, making Robert's shooter their main target. In an instant, Levi Buckley lay within five-feet of the wounded detective, both men face-to-face. The cocaine freak was dead before he hit the ground and Robert's life was slipping away, too. The screaming Angela Tyler tried to make her way to Robert but was held back by Agent Michaels, who was trying to protect her from the inevitable.

"Oh, Lord, please don't let me die lying next to this devil!"

Robert was barely able to mumble these words before his world faded to black....

CHAPTER 29

The steady tones from the monitor seemed to echo throughout the room, breaking the calm silence that surrounded the patient. The aching and burning sensation that had once totally consumed his chest was now gone. The air no longer reflected a musty smell and was now thin and warm in texture, making it easy to breathe. The sun's ray that had awakened him were bright and almost blinding to the eyes. His entire body was warm, comfortable and totally relaxed; completely opposite from the last moments he remembered.

Am I alive?

His first attempt to move reminded Robert that he was indeed still alive, as pains radiated throughout his torso. A bullet to his chest was not just a bad dream. The tremendous aching on his left side would be there for some time to remind Robert of his fate. At this moment Robert felt like the ultimate optimist, since he was given a second chance at life—Lady Luck had been standing by his side. His decision to remain still and calm would be the wisest one for the time being.

Besides the fact he was in a hospital room, Robert had no idea where he was. He lay in the bed, motionless, but visually scanning the room; Robert discovered he was not alone. Maybe he was dead and had gone to heaven because sitting across the room were two of the loveliest angels he had ever seen. A beautiful blonde, securely holding a young baby in her arms and both were napping. The sun's beams seemed to highlight them even more, adding to the possibility that both had been sent from the heavens. Robert was not for sure how long he had been unconscious, and at this moment he did not care. The sight of Angela Tyler holding his little Paige was the most wonderful one he could have ever imagined.

Ten, or maybe twenty minutes had passed, with Robert doing nothing but visually absorbing Angela and his child. A little stream of saliva from the baby awakened Angela from her slumber. She carefully reached for a towel from the baby-bag sitting next to her chair. At the same time, Ms. Tyler seemed to be rummaging for something else—ah, a small pack of chocolate chip cookies. She was definitely a woman after his own heart. Robert observed as she gently cleaned the child's face, being careful not to wake her. Trying to be quiet but obviously anxious for her culinary delight, Angela began to tear into her pack of cookies.

"Do you always tease men like this? You know I am a chocolate-chip cookie junkie, don't you?"

The sound of Robert's voice stunned Angela, almost causing her to drop the baby. She then stood, and slowly made her way to Robert's bedside. With her free hand, Angela reached out and placed it to one side of her detective's face.

"We both missed our favorite man—we are so glad that you came back to us."

"There is no way I could leave my two favorite girls. How long have I been out?"

"Four days, Robert—four, long, days."

Robert was able to maneuver his left arm to touch the soft hand of the woman standing next to him. Words were not necessary at this moment, as their hands firmly embraced each other. He then became affixed to the child that was still sleeping in Angela's arms.

"Can you lay Paige on the bed here next to me?"

"Robert, I don't know . . ."

"Just for a second, Angela. She can't hurt her dad."

Angela complied with Robert's request, gently guiding the infant to a spot next to his side. Baby Paige was not wakened and lay contently next to her wounded father.

"I will be right back, Robert. There are a few people in the waiting room wanting to see you."

Within minutes, Angela returned with Robert's father, who entered the room holding hands with an unfamiliar female. Mr. James slowly approached his son, with the woman following close behind.

"Robert, can you not find a better way to take a few days off from work?" As usual, his father was again attempting to master the art of dry-humor. Or more likely, contriving a way to hold back his tears.

"You scared the hell out of us, Son. Welcome back, we all missed you!"

Mr. James then extended his arm in a jester for his female guest to join him. As she came closer, Robert began to experience an uneasy feeling, not in a threatening manner but a feeling of anxiety. Before a word was said, his father's guest bypassed an introduction and leaned over Robert, placing a kiss on his forehead.

The two became affixed on each other. Her eyes, the kiss to the forehead, and that voice; Robert knew this woman, and almost immediately she was able to sense that her identity had been detected.

"It is great seeing you again, Robert. I have missed you."

"It has been a long time, Mom. Welcome home." . . . .

About the Author

Author Ronald Long was born and raised in the Ozark Hills of Southern Missouri. After graduating from high school, Ronald attended college at Central Missouri State University, where he obtained a B.S. Degree in Criminal Justice and later entered the CMSU Master's program.

In his second year of college, Ronald diverted his long-time goal of attending law school, to that of a law enforcement career. After graduating, Ronald accepted a full-time position with the St. Robert, Missouri Police Department, where the author's rewarding and exhilarating career began. Two years later Ronald moved to Texas, where he spent twenty-six years of combined service with the Arlington Police Department, the Tarrant County Sheriff's Office (Ft. Worth), and the Travis County Sheriff's Office (Austin). While in Texas, Ronald was also very active in the insurance fraud arena and served as a senior investigator with Texas Farm Bureau. The author is still active in the investigative field and is the owner of Ronald J. Long, LLC, and Central States Investigations, LLC.